PRAISE FOR STEPHEN LAWS!

"Laws is a master craftsman."

—*Shivers*

"Stephen Laws presents a fresh, chilling voice among the multitude of authors feverishly clawing to imitate Stephen King or Peter Straub. Laws is no imitator!"

—*Seattle Post Intelligencer*

"Laws's work typifies a new generation of horror writing: [It] inhabits the world as we know it, and is all the scarier for it."

—*Maxim*

FEAR ME
Named Best Novel of the Year
by the Dracula Society

"First-rate horror. Gripping to the last page."

—*Locus*

"A sleek and sexy book, laced with horror and triumph. No other author today is writing horror as effective and as powerful as Laws."

—*Starburst*

"A big, ambitious book, eloquently written, inventively plotted, perfectly paced. Great stuff."

—*Interzone*

"Laws updates the vampire story, weaving a compelling tale that is all the more effective for ditching the standard stake-and-garlic trappings. Very well done."

—*The Times* (London)

THE BEAST AND ITS PREY

It crouches, watches, and waits.

The scent of its prey is strong for one so small. And although it has already eaten and has none of the hunger pain, that musk and the promise of living food so near makes its stomach churn and its jaws slaver. Belly low to the ground, it shifts and flexes its muscles. It will be easy to take this little one; easy to seize and rend and devour, to take the life and add to its own life.

It feels the breeze through the long grass in its face. It lies instinctively downwind, and the prey is coming through the long grass straight toward it, unaware that it patiently waits. It shuffles again, its sleek black body pressed down hard to the earth.

It can hear the prey coming now, through the long grass—making its way straight toward it, unknowing. It tenses, ready to make its killing run if the prey should suddenly scent it, or veer away. There is movement ahead now, the grass stalks moving as the prey comes on and...

Other *Leisure* books by Stephen Laws:

FEAR ME
THE WYRM
DARKFALL

FEROCITY

STEPHEN LAWS

LEISURE BOOKS NEW YORK CITY

This one's for my blood brother,
Steve Gallagher.

A LEISURE BOOK®

January 2007

Published by

Dorchester Publishing Co., Inc.
200 Madison Avenue
New York, NY 10016

Copyright © 2007 by Stephen Laws

ISBN 0-8439-5695-X

Printed in the United States of America.

Visit us on the web at www.dorchesterpub.com.

ACKNOWLEDGMENTS

I could fill several pages with thanks to the people who have helped me during the writing of *Ferocity*, but there are a few people who I need to thank this time for very specific support, assistance and inspiration for the novel you now have in your hands— and they are—

Don D'Auria—for his continued faith.

Mike Thomas of Newquay Zoo.

Sergeant Eddie Bell.

Keith Durham—whose cup (or mug) of friendship came at a vital time, and will always "runneth over."

Will Haughan—who knows all about the Fingers of One Hand.

Paul Simms—inventor of Domestovision and Iron-O-Rama (and who deserves a knighthood for same).

David Williams of Sedalia—a place at the end of the trail that is also close to my heart.

The Wednesday Boys (sometimes Tuesday).

TGW of the Bent Ear.

JB—for "Sit Him High."
EM—for "La Cosa Buffa."
EB—for "Rampage."

And for Mel, Eve, Jon, Alan, Pam, Alison, Andrew, Rachel, Peter, Andrea, Rick, Ray, Jane, Charlie— whose presence has enriched my life.

FEROCITY

ONE

"Give me the money," said the man in the woolen hat, and suddenly there was a knife in his hand.

Cath looked at David, then back at the man who had stepped out of the doorway onto the rain-washed street before them. He was wearing a long, dirty coat with no shirt underneath, bare-chested even in this dank and freezing New York weather. Cath looked back at David, and their eyes met—what else was there to do?

They both burst into laughter.

It was a good joke.

The man threw the knife from hand to hand, the way a seasoned knife fighter might do. But he fumbled the catch and when the knife skittered to the wet sidewalk, David guffawed, his breath rising in a cloud around his head. The man cursed, stooped and grabbed the knife back up as if his dignity in this enterprise was at stake. Wiping his nose with the coat sleeve of his other arm, he drew a deep breath and shook his head as if he was angry that he'd gotten off to such a bad start and wanted to begin all over again.

"I said give me the fucking money."

"No, you didn't," Cath said.

"What?"

"You didn't say 'Give me the fucking money.' You said, "Give me the money."

"What?"

"There wasn't a 'fucking' in the first thing you said."

Cath looked back at the reception doors behind them. Beyond them lay the offices of her American publisher. Her agent was still in there, talking with Cath's editor about 'other business.' Over coffee, they had spent the morning discussing minor changes to Cath's latest manuscript—laughing at some of the English phrases that required amendment for an American readership. Words like 'line,' instead of 'queue.' From there, the conversation had somehow moved to bad lines of dialogue from corny books and movies. Now here was this guy, just outside Cath's publisher's office, asking for their money and dropping his knife. Was Cath's agent standing just inside the doors, laughing at the joke he'd arranged?

He must have moved quickly to arrange something like that.

It *was* a joke, wasn't it?

There was a scuffle of movement and Cath looked back to see that the man was running away, ragged coat flapping, breath streaming around his head. His foot twisted in a gutter; he staggered, cursed and ran flapping into a side alley. David was watching the man go, his back to her. Cath laughed, uncertain now—and moved to touch his arm. Before her fingers made contact, David suddenly sank to his knees on the sidewalk.

And Cath knew then that it wasn't a joke at all.

Because David was kneeling on that sidewalk, getting the knees of his expensive suit trousers soaked. He was clutching his stomach, his head bowed, and the steam of his breath was coming in short, frozen bursts around his head as he fought for that breath.

This had gone too far. It was time to stop.

"Stop . . ."

Her voice was real, the rain was wet and cold, and the sidewalk was hard and shining. The sky was heavy and solid; piles of dirty snow in the gutters looked carved from dirty stone. And where David was kneeling on the sidewalk, the rain was turning dark and red. He was trying to look up, trying to speak to her—but could not find his voice. Cath could see the dreadful terror on that strong and handsome face; a terror that if he moved, if he took his hands away, something awful—something horribly awful—would happen. Taking away his hands would mean that they wouldn't be able to rewind this nonsense and go back to the start again. Cath was moving to him, but oh God why was she moving so slowly? David was gingerly taking one hand away from himself, and Cath could see his wedding ring shining somehow luminously bright against the thick warm blood that covered his fingers.

"Cath?"

There was blood on his lips when he was finally able to speak, and his voice was thick with fear and horror. Now she knew that the breath-steam coming from his mouth was David's life, evaporating up and out of him into the harsh, cold New York air. There was no one here to help, and she couldn't move, couldn't even reach out to touch him. She wanted to touch his face, grab for his outstretched hand. She had to hold him, wrap herself around him and keep him warm. Stop the life from escaping and bring it back. It would be all right. He'd be all right. Someone would help. Someone would come and . . .

"CATH!" David screamed. Suddenly there was blood everywhere on that rain-washed sidewalk where he knelt, as if something inside him had ruptured. The horror instantly broke Cath from her immobility. In the next moment, she grabbed his ice-cold hands in her own pulling them to her own chest, and all she could moan was:

"*Noooo . . .*"

Because in the moment their eyes met, they both knew—and in that horrifying instant, they saw their daughter: Rynne.

David wasn't ready, and she wasn't ready.

Cath tried to pull him close, and David sprawled against her. There was no warmth in him now. His flesh was as cold and as hard as the wet slab of sidewalk on which they were kneeling. Was that it? Was he turning into some terrible, frozen travesty of himself—turning into dead stone?

"DAVID!"

And Cath was sitting up in bed, weeping, and enveloped in that same deep grief that was such a fundamental part of her life now. She'd been weeping as she slept, she realized. Her face and pillow were damp. The bedroom window curtains were open—she always slept with them open now, terrified of the claustrophobia that crowded in during the night. Rain was runneling down the windowpane, filling the room with a swirling kaleidoscope of blue and black streamers. And that terrible New York morning was five years away on the other side of the ocean.

Had she cried out in her sleep? What if she'd frightened Rynne?

Quickly, Cath slipped from the bed—no blurriness as she flung back the coverlet. Instant wakefulness, like every other night these nights; as if her subconscious mind was always alert and waiting for some terrible alarm call to come. Perhaps in some way she might be transported magically and instantly back to that cold, wet New York street—maybe she'd have a chance to do things differently. Maybe wait for five minutes inside those reception doors until the man in the woolen cap and long coat had found someone else to accost. Was she still, after all this time, waiting for David's dying voice to summon her? Whatever— she was up and out of bed and standing in the doorway, hands braced against each side of the doorframe. Ready and waiting for the next signal, the next sound.

It was only then that her waking mind caught up with her.

Only then that Cath's conscious mind arrived, taking over from that dull-witted and slumbering twin. She paused to listen in the darkness, looking across the landing to her daughter's bedroom. The door was ajar, and there were no sounds. She must still be asleep. Somewhere, distant thunder grumbled in the valley. Cath remained braced in the doorway, taking deep breaths to clear the terrible, recurring nightmare. This was so much more than a bad dream. It was a vivid replay of what had happened years ago, so long that Rynne had no real memory of her father. It was a real-time replay of the actual event with all of its grotesque absurdity, its horror, its fear and terrible loss. So very real every time it played.

There was no sound from Rynne. Cath hoped she was still asleep.

Wiping the moisture from her face, Cath moved quietly to Rynne's door and looked carefully inside. The only sound from within was the faint hiss and bubble of the aquifer on the small goldfish tank standing in the corner. Rynne's three goldfish cruised silently around their underwater castle. Did fish ever sleep? Did they dream?

Cath moved inside.

Rynne was lying facedown, quilt pulled back. Her mouth was open, long blond hair tousled around her head. Books scattered on the floor, toys heaped in the far corner—despite early evening pleas for the room to be tidied before bed; and of course, she looked so much like her father—even down to the way he'd looked when he slept. Cath moved to the bed, began to reach out to stroke the hair away from her daughter's forehead—and then she felt it again; rising from deep down, rising from the place where she kept it guarded under lock and key in her heart. The thing her counselor had called submerged, unresolved grief—but what she called The Beast. She'd been told that if she didn't let nature take its course, if she didn't allow that grieving process to take place, then she could never be healed. But no matter what the textbooks said, Cath knew that if she allowed The Beast out of its cage, it would overwhelm her. It would drag her down and destroy her—and hadn't there been times when she'd wished that it would? Only one thing had prevented her from giving in to it on those bad, dark days. And that one thing was a person—her seven-year-old daughter, now lying blissfully unaware in a safe place of her own. Cath looked down at Rynne and felt The Beast rising from the darkness. It was coming, and it would overwhelm her if she let it.

No, I can't.

She'd spent so long not giving in to that grief, had spent so much time fighting it. For the sake of Rynne, yes. But for her own sake, too. If she allowed it to drag her down into despair, she feared that she'd never emerge from it again.

I won't give in to it. Not now.

Cath withdrew her hand and stood back from the bed. Rynne mumbled in her sleep, moved her lips and turned over.

Carefully, step-by-step, Cath backed out of the room onto the landing. When the thunder grumbled again, it was like the sound of a caged animal. Now, she had the crazy feeling that she was on some kind of video rewind, backing out of the room in the hope that the feelings inside her could be rewound, too. Perhaps she could go back to bed and pretend that she'd never have the dream again, that she hadn't come into Rynne's room and found the aching darkness and despair waiting for her—a darkness not healed, no matter how much she pretended, always waiting for her.

Cath stood at the top of the stairs, staring down into the darkness. So dark that she could see the same phantom movements that lived behind her eyelids when she lay in bed at night. They were the same movements that could swirl and twist and form into faces and places and wild, unbidden configurations. As a child, she had often been frightened by them at night—had been so relieved when her father had told her that everyone saw the same things; that they were corpuscles, magnified against the dark backdrop of her eyelids and that the mind took them and made shapes from them, reflecting every thought she'd ever had, every sight she'd ever seen as her mind and body 'wound down' for the night—like a cinema screen. As an adult, Cath had come to believe that the phantom light show was some huge, complicated trailer for the dream world. Perhaps the place her stories came from—the same fantasy world that she had loved so much it had led to her brief flirtation with acting in her early years (in two "dire movies" as she often referred to them).

But tonight, she felt like a little girl again; and her father's reassurances were the words of a ghost-person who had become part of that dream place. Those dark and swirling shapes that filled the staircase were real. They were beckoning to her now, swarming and rising toward where she stood. Her childhood terrors were tangible, real, soul-sucking. She could see no details of the staircase, the walls or the floor or the ceiling. She felt, rather than willed, her hand rising to the light switch. But if she switched on the light and dispelled the phantoms, wasn't that giving in to the childhood fears? She was a grown woman, with a child of her own.

Giving in now would be like lying to Rynne.

What would David say?

David, his breath rising from his mouth, like his spirit escaping into the frozen air . . .

Cath withdrew her hand, started down the staircase into the darkness.

Soft carpeting under her feet. The handrail at her left.

The darkness undulated around her. She felt like a blind person headed straight for a brick wall. Didn't they say sometimes that blind people could sense a solid obstruction ahead, like some kind of extra, unknown sense? She could feel it now but kept descending, waiting for the moment when her face would press up horribly close to some ghastly, contorted face in the darkness—or until something slammed hard into her with agonizing pain.

But now she could see a faint slab of gray below. The window in the front door. There was the lounge door on her right, more gray rectangles against the deep black.

Cath wasn't a fearful little girl. She was a thirty-seven-year-old woman whose husband had been murdered on the streets of New York. She was a writer, with seven novels and two movies to her credit—one of the latter being half-decently good. And this house was the "house in the country" that she and David had talked about long before Rynne was born. Once, it had been a fantasy-dream place. Now it was a retreat—because she couldn't bear to live under the same roof in the city where David and she had shared so much love, so much of their lives. Everything about that house reminded her of him. The bed, of course. The wardrobes, even the bathrooms and—God help her— the cutlery drawer in the kitchen. Not only the tender and meaningful moments but also—perhaps even more keenly distressing—the everyday, ordinary things, like preparing an evening meal together. Sometimes those memories were almost too terrible to bear. And whereas most people assumed that the move from the city to the country represented some kind of reflection of her growing status as a writer (especially the monetary side of things)—in truth, she had been trying to escape that ongoing cancer called grief.

Had it been a successful move? Only time would tell.

But she couldn't ignore that old but profound cliché.

You can't escape what's inside you.

9

Bleak and hollow, Cath returned to bed. She was cold, felt she would never sleep again that night.

But she did. As she always did—and on the following morning, there would be the guilt that she was able to sleep at all.

She felt that there should be dreams.

But there were none.

There was just a low, barely discernable rumbling—perhaps faraway thunder—like some beast pacing its den, wanting out.

TWO

Drew Hall cursed as the Land Rover pitched in a rut at the side of the road. He steadied the wheel, and shifted down a gear as he continued on through the night. He'd thought about cutting across country over the Fell. It would take less than half the time than using the village road, but he'd busted the exhaust last time he'd tried that at night—an expense he could ill afford. Now it looked like he'd bust it again or maybe blow a tire on this badly maintained stretch. There were no lights on this route beyond the village leading to his farm, and no moon. The Land Rover's headlights cut a swathe through utter darkness.

"Need cat's eyes in the road," he said aloud, and allowed himself a grimace. It had been yet another unsuccessful night hunt, and not for the first time he wondered why he was doing this at all.

The road took a sharp swerve to the right, and he could see the distant lights of the writer's house. When he drove past it, he'd be only a mile from home. The road acted as a boundary to his farmland, and although he'd seen her distant figure from the hillsides above, they'd never been introduced, had never spoken. She had a daughter living with her, perhaps seven or eight years old. Faye Roche—once the village school-teacher, now long retired—was working for them part time as housekeeper. But he'd not seen Faye to speak to since the writer had bought the place and moved in, more than a year ago.

The lights of the writer's house were larger and nearer. He wondered if she was burning the midnight oil. Not long now.

Even above the sound of his own vehicle, Drew heard the roar of a high-powered car up ahead. Head-lights swept in an arc in his direction. The car was heading down the road toward him, and it was travel-ing fast. He slowed, eased the car closer to his side of the road. The headlights swerved again, now full beam and directly in his eyes.

The farmhouse was less than fifty yards away.

"Too fast!" hissed Drew. "You're coming too fast!"

The road was just wide enough for two cars to pass, but even though he was fully caught in the oncoming headlights, it seemed as if the other driver just didn't know that he was there. Tires screeched, the headlights veered to the sky—then came straight back full beam. The other driver was making no attempt to slow down, still had his or her foot hard to the floor—and was right in the middle of the road, coming straight at him.

Drew slammed his hand hard on the horn—once. In the next moment, he wrenched the wheel over. The Land Rover slewed up onto the grass verge with a jud-dering screech and spray of soil, twisted up onto two wheels and jounced back on its suspension. Drew's head whacked against the side window.

The oncoming car was gone, still traveling at the same speed in the direction of the village. Rock music pounding from its open windows faded into the night.

Cat's eyes.

He saw them again in his daze, as he'd seen them on that day two years ago. Opal green and deep. Cold and still and holding a secret. A mysterious and terribly dangerous secret.

"I saw them . . ."

Someone or something was pulling at him. He tried to pull away, but he was in a dream and there was no strength in his limbs. Cold air enveloped him, and now that dream-mistiness was leaving him as he came back into focus.

"I saw them . . ."

"Drew, are you all right?" It was a woman's voice, somehow familiar.

"I did see them."

"I'm sure you did, honey. But they either didn't see you—or didn't care to see you. Come on now. You're hurt."

The Land Rover door was open and a woman was holding on to his arm, trying to ease him out of the car. He knew her, but couldn't yet put a name to her.

"They forced you off the road! I saw it from the kitchen window." The sound of outrage in her voice was very familiar.

Drew! Pay attention—your mind's wandering again. You're here to learn, not to dream.

"Miss Roche . . ."

"Miss Roche? Goodness, it's a long time since you called me that. Come on now. You're head's bleeding—we'll get you inside."

Someone else was running up to them now. A woman, with a young girl close behind.

"Is he all right?" Not a Northumberland accent. Southern maybe. Perhaps London.

"I think he's concussed. Help me get him inside, Cath."

The cold air was reviving Drew quickly, but when he tried to take his arm away from Faye's shoulder, she hauled it back.

"I'm okay, Faye. Really . . ." When he touched his forehead, there was blood on his fingertips.

"Best come inside," said the woman with the southern accent.

The young girl joined her mother. In the Land Rover's headlights, they were mirror images. The same shape of face, the same color hair. The woman called Cath leaned quickly into the Land Rover and switched off the headlights. When she moved to help him, this time he did not pull away.

THREE

Drew winced as Faye dabbed disinfectant on his cut temple, noting how the little girl—dutifully holding a strip of Elastoplast at the ready—winced too. The soft, warm lights in the cottage kitchen seemed to give her blond hair a golden halo. Her big eyes studied him, as if he were some strange and new roadside find that the adults had brought in for examination. He couldn't help noting how the décor, the furniture and the easy decoration compared to his own kitchen back at the farm. This was clearly a home, whereas his own place was . . . well, not a home.

"What happened?" The woman called Cath moved into his sight as Faye continued to dab, studying the cut. He could smell her perfume.

"Ran him off the road," murmured Faye, concentrating on her task. "I saw it from the window.

"Best get this seen to properly, Drew. At the infirmary. The cut's not much, but you might have a concussion. Do you feel dizzy, or sick, or . . ."

15

"I'm fine Miss . . . I'm fine, Faye. Wouldn't be the first time you've patched me up."

"You know each other then?" Cath asked.

"I was his teacher once. More years ago than I care to remember. Oh, I'm sorry—this is Drew Hall. . . . Rynne, let me have that Elastoplast, honey."

Drew winced again as Faye smoothed the tape into place. "I own the farm on the other side of the road. A mile or so up. I guess you can just see it from here."

"The one with the crackly walls?" asked the little girl.

"Rynne," admonished Faye, giving her a "look."

"Well, it *has!*"

"That's the one." Drew smiled.

"I'm Cath Lane, and this is my daughter Rynne."

"You're the writer?"

"Yes," Cath replied, moving to the kitchen bench and lifting the kettle. Why did it still make her feel uncomfortable answering that question after all these years? "Who's going to have some tea?"

"Great," Drew replied. "I'd ask for something stronger if I didn't have the Land Rover."

"You can leave it here," Faye said. "I'll drive you up to the farm."

"No, no—I'm okay. Really."

Faye transferred her "look" to Drew.

"Really, Faye! I'm fine. It just shook me up, is all. And tea would be great, thanks."

Cath smiled—but there was something fractured about her smile that made him wonder for a moment before she turned her back to fill the kettle.

"Haven't read any of your books, I'm afraid," he said, wanting to say something—and now worrying if that had come out wrong.

"I haven't read any of yours either." Cath turned to

smile at him, and this time there was no shadow in it, just good humor.

Everyone laughed.

As Faye sat back to admire her handiwork, Drew said: "You patched up the other side of my head when I was a kid, remember? Football in the schoolyard? I took a heavy tackle and ran head-first into a wall."

Faye raised a finger and looked at Rynne, as if some great dawning memory was coming. Then—emphatically—she said: "No."

Rynne hooted with laughter, wrapping an arm around Faye's neck.

"Then there was the time you broke up a fight between me and Billy Hunnam? One kid in each hand—lifted us apart. Very impressive."

"You sure you've got the right teacher?"

"Was she scary then?" Rynne asked.

"Scary? No, not scary. But she had a way of making sure that you didn't step out of line."

"Like when she makes that face? Like she did just now?"

"Rynne!" Cath admonished from her tea preparation.

Faye stuck out her tongue and moved to help Cath.

"I'm going to report this," Cath continued. "That other car, I mean. You could have been killed."

"Don't think that'll do much good," Faye said.

"Why not?"

"Because I recognized the car right off, even in the dark."

"Who was it, Faye?" Rynne sat opposite Drew, where Faye had been, now staring intently at the Elastoplast, perhaps to see if it moved.

"It belongs to Kapler Dietersen."

"Who the hell is Kapler . . . ?" began Drew.

"Kapler Dietersen." The note of derision in Faye's voice was unmistakable. "He bought Oakley Estate up past the Fell."

"Right . . . I thought I saw removal vans and stuff up there."

"Hold on," Cath said, pouring tea. "You're all leaving me behind here."

"Sorry, honey. Oakley Estate is fifteen miles on the other side of the Fell. Big country house and gardens. We drove past it a few weeks back."

"Right. Got you."

Drew watched Cath raise her eyebrows in inquiry about how he wanted his tea. He suddenly realized that she was a very beautiful woman. "Milk, no sugar please."

"The Oakleys were gentry," Faye continued. "But they were broke. Couldn't maintain the property, and no one was interested in paying a tenner a ticket to walk around the place. They moved out about a year ago. And now Kapler Dietersen, millionaire businessman, has moved in."

"Okay, so why don't you like Mr. Dietersen?" Cath handed cups around. "Quite apart from the fact that he just ran our neighbor off the road."

"It's your face again," Rynne said. "Keeps giving you away."

"You are a cheeky madam—but you're right. I don't like him."

"It's not like you to be so judgmental," Cath said.

"Let's put it this way—I have friends who have met him and had dealings with him. He seems to think that money will buy him anything and everyone. And no one seems to know where he gets his money *from*."

"The man who owns everything also seems to think he owns the road," said Cath.

Drew finished his tea and stood.

"Look, you've all been very kind. But I need to get back. There are things I have to . . . be doing."

"What about the police?" Faye asked. "Are you going to report him?"

"I'll get back to the Land Rover. If it's damaged, I'll take it further. If not—well, I'm inclined to let it drop."

"But he shouldn't be allowed to speed down country roads like that. You could have been killed."

"Like I say, if there's damage—I might ask you to back up any claim I make."

"You can count on it, Drew. But I still think that you should maybe have an x-ray or something. You can't be too careful."

"I'm fine. Really."

FOUR

The two women and the girl watched from the kitchen window as the Land Rover's headlights passed the cottage. Faye waved, and Drew tooted the horn as the vehicle was swallowed by the darkness.

"He's a strange one," she said after a while.

"Strange? How?"

"He's . . . well, he's very . . ."

"You should be a novelist, Faye. You know how to draw out the tension."

"Sorry. He's changed so much from the time I knew him. His wife died tragically, and he was never the same afterwards . . ." As the words came out of her mouth, Faye caught the expression on Cath's face. It was only a fleeting and passing shade, but it was still there. Instantly realizing the territory she had unwittingly entered, her next words poured out as if to anxiously heal over any wound she might have opened. "He keeps himself to himself. Doesn't want to get involved with anyone or anything—other than those Big Cats."

"Big Cats, Faye?" asked Rynne. "What Big Cats?"

Faye grabbed for the girl, pulled her close and tickled her—glad for the interruption. "The Big Cats that aren't there."

"What?" laughed Rynne.

"Nothing, nothing, nothing!"

She kept Rynne close, still hugging and tickling—trying not to notice the way Cath was standing still and silent, arms tightly folded as if holding herself in, looking out of the kitchen window into the darkness.

FIVE

Cath bundled the bag into the back of Faye's hatchback car.

"Mum!" Outraged, Rynne pushed past her and stroked the bag. "Don't be rough with my stuff."

"What?" laughed Cath. "I'm not being rough."

"You'll break something."

"How can you break a towel, a fresh top, a pair of trousers and three cuddly toys?"

Faye emerged from the cottage.

"Your mum can't help being rough. She writes rough, tough novels remember?"

"With a soft sentimental center, remember?"

"If there wasn't a child listening—eager to get to her play group—I'd make a rude reference to spherical objects."

Cath scooped up Rynne, hugging her close. Rynne pretended to struggle, kicking her legs and flopping her arms.

"Did you say the play group was finishing early this afternoon?"

"Only half an hour early. Mrs. Guernin's got some-one coming in to fix some slates on the school roof. She doesn't want kids around while they're working up there."

"Okay . . ."

"But look—I thought I'd just stay in the village with Rynne. Maybe take her for ice cream or something. Bring her back the usual time?"

Letting Rynne slide carefully to the ground, keeping one arm around her, Cath pulled Faye close with the other arm and kissed her on the cheek.

"Writer's cliché Number Seventy-three. I don't know what I'd do without you."

Faye made a dismissive, half-embarrassed sound, pulling away to the car.

"Just make sure you get the two thousand words done. No slacking."

"Yes, miss. No replacement activity. No unnecessary tea making, walking around the house or staring out of the window. Just fingers to keyboard, pen to paper." Rynne also pulled away, running to the passenger door and clambering inside.

"I'll be checking your work when I get back."

"Ooh-err. Will you be using the red pen on me?"

"Go on—get back in the cottage and get on with it."

"Do lots of work, Mum!" Rynne called, struggling with her seatbelt.

"Did he really call you miss?"

"What?"

"You know—Drew Hall. When the Land Rover went off the road last Tuesday."

"Yes—yes, he did. That's what made me worry about concussion. I think . . ." Chewing her bottom lip, click-ing Rynne's seatbelt in and then adjusting her own,

23

Faye paused and looked straight ahead as Cath leaned in at the driver's window. "I think I might check on him. He won't have gone to the doctor, you know. Stubborn. Always was. Not stupid stubborn. Just very, you know—mind made up, do it my way. And he's up there on his own—no one to look out for him."

"What happened? To his wife, I mean."

Faye turned to look directly into Cath's eyes, remembering the way she had frozen and looked out the window when she had first mentioned it. Cath realized what was happening.

"It's all right, Faye. Honestly. I'm not . . . this stuff doesn't bother me. I'm okay."

"No, you're not always okay, Cath. And you know it. There are times. I've been there, I've seen it."

"I make a living out of death, doom and disaster. Don't you know that?"

"I know more about what goes on inside you than you think, madam."

"You're school-marming me again. Come on, what happened?"

"It was an accident. Farm equipment."

Cath waited for more. Faye switched on the car engine in exasperation.

"Come on, Faye!" Rynne called. "We'll be late."

Cath stood back as Faye began to reverse.

Without making eye contact, Faye said: "A harvester. She got caught in a harvester. Killed her instantly—and completely wrecked Drew's life. There, now you know."

"Bye, Mum!"

"Bye, love. Be careful."

The car slid backwards into the lane. Cath walked slowly with it, arms folded.

When Faye turned the car and slipped into first gear, she looked back.

"You *are* all right, aren't you?"

"Yes, of course."

"I didn't want to tell you. But you know—there are other people out there hurting as well, aren't there?"

"Yes, there are, Faye. And I'm okay, honestly."

Faye looked at her steadily for what seemed a long time.

"Faye!" Rynne called again. "Come on!"

"Okay. We'll be back usual time."

Cath watched them go. Just before the car rounded the bed, she heard Faye call:

"Two thousand words!"

SIX

Back in the cottage, Cath strode into the living room, switched on the television, then switched it off again. She looked at the CDs piled by the player, rattled through them and when one case slid to the floor, she let it lie there and moved into the kitchen.

Nothing on the radio was what she wanted, despite quickly moving the tuner right across the wave band.

Standing at the window, arms folded again, she realized that she was behaving in the same way that Faye had warned her against.

"Damn it! I hate it when she's right all the time."

Upstairs, in the study, Cath rearranged the papers, switched on the computer and reread the material she'd written the day before; trying to convince herself that it was usable. Back downstairs again, she made coffee that she didn't want, drank it, paced and said: "Damn it!" again.

The work hadn't dried. The words were still coming out. But there was something wrong with the novel she was working on. It wasn't coming . . .

"Alive!" she said aloud, banging the coffee cup down on the bench. "Writer's cliché Fifty-six: The book isn't coming alive." The novel was something that she had originally been working on when the Bad Thing had happened in New York. The new novel had been delivered to her New York publisher and her—their—visit that day had been their way of showing how much faith they had in a project they believed would be the new big best seller. The fact that they had been right—that the book had gone on to become a runaway success, and subsequently an award-winning movie, had brought with it financial security beyond her dreams. The cottage she'd bought outright, the money still coming in. It wasn't as if she were dependent on the next book becoming a success to maintain that security, even five years later.

But on that day, on that cold New York street, her life had been ripped apart. None of the success or the financial security meant anything to her—other than the safety and security of her daughter. No, her writing since then had been blocked because of something else. She wanted the new project to mean something, she wanted it to . . . to . . .

"Come alive," she said aloud again.

But David is dead.

"I know. I know that, damn it!"

She needed this book—the first after her life was torn apart—to . . .

"Come together. I just need it to come together."

So that she could move on.

And leave David behind? Leave the memory of him behind?

"No!"

This was the internal, irrational argument that had blocked her.

The novel she was working on wasn't about her and David, it wasn't about their life together, wasn't anything to do with how she'd struggled to cope after his murder. She needed to complete this independent entity with its own heartbeat, its own rhythm, its own form and being to prove that she could still create, that she could still be what she'd always wanted to be: a writer. But she continued to struggle, had given up on the project several times—but she always returned to it because it was something she *needed* to do. If she could only . . .

"Break through. If I could only—break through!"

Then she could finish it, and become—

"Whole again."

Angry with herself, Cath returned to the study—opened Word and threw herself at the keyboard. Half an hour later, and four hundred useless words later, she saved and exited the document—refusing to delete the unsatisfactory work she had done. At least she'd have something to delete when she came back to it.

Outside, the air was growing chill, and there were clouds moving fast up the valley. Cath walked to the gate, leaned on it and looked up and down the lane. There was no traffic, no movement apart from the clouds. No jet trails in the sky, no birds on the wing. Not for the first time, she felt very alone.

Across the lane, on the hill overlooking her cottage—a man was standing and watching her.

SEVEN

Drew Hall crested the rise and looked back at his farmhouse.

Summer was on a slow burn, on its way out—and autumn was coming. He could feel it, as only someone who had spent his life in the country could. He stood and looked at the house itself, at the pens and sheds that surrounded it. The house seemed too big, and that was because once—what seemed a very long time ago—his farming operation in this lower part of the valley had been much more widespread, much more like a business. More alive. Now a majority of those pens, sheds and outhouses were semi-derelict. The livestock, the arable income and the whole operation had shrunk. But the house had remained the same. White brick, picture postcard some might have once said. But the fascia was weather-beaten, corroded and unrepaired. There was a hole in the roof, and he felt sure that there were pigeons on the top floor. Why chase them out? They had to roost somewhere. A three-story building, built for a family. But he lived on the ground floor alone and rarely used the other two.

The view from where he stood was breathtaking, but he couldn't remember the last time that he had enjoyed it.

Off to the right of the farmhouse and its cluster of smaller buildings, was the barn. Something was wrong with the main doors. It looked as if there were a gigantic crack in the left one, skewing it to one side, even though the chain that held those doors locked was still in place. He had no idea what had happened there, and had no intention of finding out. He'd locked that barn a long time ago, and it would stay that way. So would the thing that he'd locked inside. Drew looked quickly away again, tried to concentrate on the sky, then the boundary fence a quarter mile below him. Trying to ignore the barn and failing, he wondered—not for the first time—if he shouldn't just put a torch to the damned thing and be done with it. But as much as he'd considered it, the thought of the thing inside prevented him from acting. Maybe it was best if it was destroyed, but in a perverse way he realized that destroying it might also in some strange way destroy him. Sell it? Perhaps. God knows, he could use the money. He was thirty-five and almost penniless, living practically hand to mouth from his farm earnings. Fit and physically well—but not so fit and well in other ways, perhaps.

Drew kept walking, along the ridge and away from the house, looking down to the fence that bordered the main road into Nicolham. There was no traffic this morning, which was a shame. He'd often watched cars come and go. He recognized a good few of the locals when they passed, but liked to spot unfamiliar vehicles with unfamiliar occupants. Then he could guess about what people might be like, where they were going, what they did for a living. Tourists, perhaps? He could wonder if they were happy.

The few friends that he had left—those who still chose to visit the farmhouse on occasion—often urged him to get down into the town more often. They felt that enough time had gone by, and it was important to get on with life and to begin socializing again. Farm work brought him into limited contact with some of the town businesses, but he must surely need more than that. He had to get into the "company" of people properly. Move on. Not just cling to the past. But he was a blank wall on that subject, as much as he would have liked to take their advice. How could he? What had happened back then had killed something inside him. So he stayed and watched vehicles pass and wondered—because, after all this time, it was all he could do. He scanned the hollow down there on the other side of that road and the cottage that nestled in there—where his ex-schoolteacher, the writer and her daughter had tended to him.

"Wouldn't be the first time I'd been run off the road," he said aloud ruefully. "Figuratively not literally, as a writer might say."

He still read books for pleasure. It was his main preoccupation after the chores were over and he was back at home—mainly the classics. But concentration was often a problem when the memories of the past were still so clear. His growing hoard of "specialist" books, however, was a different matter. These were the books he pored over, that he devoured, that he studied with an intensity that sometimes frightened him. He was afraid that it was an obsession, a replacement for life somehow. But he didn't want to think too much about it.

He knew what he had encountered out there that night.

He knew what he had seen.

And he knew they were still out there.

He'd find them.

After all, what else was there for him to do?

In that moment came a familiar smell—a faint and acrid musk that he knew only too well: a trace scent, drifting on the breeze and now whisked quickly away again the moment that it had registered. Drew shook his head, stared straight down and ahead, telling himself that it was only his mind playing tricks again. He'd started thinking about them again and had only imagined the smell. It wouldn't be the first time. But now, he realized that he was waiting for it once more. And when it did come, faint and acrid and sour, he whirled to look back at the long grass by the dry-stone wall, one hundred feet from where he stood. He froze. The scent had gone again. The long grass was stirring, but that must surely only be the breeze.

So close to the farmhouse this time? Could they be daring to come so close after all this time?

Slowly, Drew bent and picked up the gnarled branch that lay close by. Rising again, he waited. The grass barely stirred. Could he be wrong? No, he wasn't wrong. There was something in there, watching him. He took a careful and quiet step forward. A breeze stirred the grass this time. Another step.

What am I doing? What do I intend to do if it's in there?

Another step. This time the sound of pebbles grinding under his boot made him wince. Drew hefted the branch like a club. And this time something did move in the grass.

I just want to see! That's all. I just want to SEE!

Something slithered—and Drew sprang to the edge of the clump of grass, this time yelling at the top of his voice; wanting to make something happen.

The grass instantly thrashed and writhed in a blurred flurry of movement, and whatever was hiding behind it flew out directly into Drew's face. He flailed with the tree branch, lost his footing and toppled— and in the next moment, something wild and squalling was scrabbling at his face. Drew rolled, lashing out—and thrashed back to his feet, arms flailing to protect himself.

Brown and white feathers flew around him.

Squawking in fear, the partridge escaped into the sky in an erratic and awkward flight.

He watched it go, angrily swatting the feathers from his hair, jacket and trousers.

"Damn, damn, damn!"

Drew stood for a long time, watching the bird vanish over the ridge. When he looked back to the boundary road, there were no cars. Clouds were moving up over the valley from the south, and the air was turning chill.

And there was the smell again. The faint and acrid musk now seemed like a taunt. Just as suddenly as it had reappeared, it was snatched away again on the breeze.

You'll never find us.

"Damn, damn, damn!"

Drew walked angrily from the brush, back to the crest of the hill. The clouds were moving faster, and the air seemed even chillier. He looked down to the farmhouse, thought about returning; but he wasn't ready yet. There was a different kind of chill in there, much worse.

He walked slowly along the rise, then looked down at the boundary road.

A woman was standing at the cottage gate far below, watching him. Even from this distance, he knew who that woman was, recognized the sheen of her lovely hair. Startled, unsure and awkward, he stumbled—wanted to make some kind of gesture but could not.

Face burning, Drew turned and started down the rise again, toward the home that was not a home.

EIGHT

"No, darling! Not there. That's right. Don't climb up there. You fell last time, remember?"

Rynne sat cross-legged in the schoolyard, kneading the Play-Doh on the tray in front of her. Sitting nearby, on the fold-out chairs that Faye had brought out of the classroom for the other mothers at the play group, Bianca Fairley and Victoria Marr's mothers continued their nonstop conversation. Rynne watched Bianca climb down from the railing wall in a sulk. She didn't like Bianca; she was mean. And Bianca's mother didn't like Rynne because Rynne knew she was mean.

Rynne returned to her Play-Doh again. She knew what would happen next.

Just because she wasn't looking at them, they'd start talking about her mother again. Like, just because she wasn't looking, she couldn't *hear?*

"So what's she supposed to be writing? Do we know?"

Something about the *we* and the *know*. It was as if Mum were going around talking about her books all

35

the time or something, and as if they were fed up hearing about it, and as if they were supposed to be impressed or something, but weren't.

"Did you see the thing on the telly? That documentary about thriller writers?"

"Last night? No, had a feeling she might be on it, though."

"Thriller writer? No—'*actress* turned thriller writer,' please. Did you see that film she was in?"

Laughter. "*Deadly Impact?*"

"Did it make an . . . ?"

"Impact?" More laughter. "Oh yes."

Laughter. "What kind of *impact* did it make on you then?"

Now the laughter was hysterical.

"Deadly!"

"I can hear you talking about my mum, you know," Rynne said, without looking up. Rynne squashed the Play-Doh with two tight fists, then stood and walked away toward the schoolyard wall, veering away when she saw that Bianca was still—against the instruction of her mother—hanging on the railings and kicking against the wall. Behind Rynne, the laughter had stopped. But she didn't look back because she didn't want to see their faces.

"Rynne!"

Suddenly Rynne was between Shelley and Joe, playing some kind of tag game, whirling between them as they used her to fend each other off. She laughed and allowed herself to be pulled around before they spun away, leaving her dizzy. "Come on then!" Joe shouted back to her as they ran to join the others. But at the moment, Rynne didn't want to play with the others. She wanted quiet time to think. She allowed herself a glance back at the two gossiping mothers, who had now turned in their seats so that their backs were to her. She didn't care. Just 'cause they were mean.

Bianca began sidling along the wall toward her; so Rynne moved away again, this time whirling and spinning her arms as she looked up at the sky. She caught sight of the hills beyond the village, ran to the far wall and grabbed its railings, pushing her face against them and looking at the rolling green and brown. She'd been thinking a lot about the strange man and the crashed car and the Elastoplast on his head. She'd also been thinking about the strange way her mum had looked at the man while Faye put that sticking plaster on, as if she were thinking about someone or something else. Something important and troubling. And that's why Rynne couldn't stop thinking about it. Because if she thought about it lots, then maybe she'd get the answer to what Mum was thinking. She knew she couldn't ask her about it, because it was too important to ask a question—and she wouldn't get an answer anyway. That was Mum. Thinking important things that took her eyes a long way away, and when you asked what she was thinking about, she'd never tell; she'd just change the subject. One thing she knew—Mum wasn't thinking about things she was going to put in her books. This was something else.

Bianca made a sound of delight, and when Rynne looked back she could see why. A cat had appeared on the schoolyard wall, sliding sinuously between the railings as it weaved along the wall, looking as if it had been trained to do so. Bianca kept pace with it, looking back to see if Rynne was watching, then—with a sulk on her face—moving to block Rynne's view, claiming ownership of the tortoise-shell color cat.

NINE

"There's a man at the door to see you, Mr. Dietersen."

Startled at the intercom buzzer and voice, Kapler Dietersen jerked in his seat. Someone moaned under the desk. Dietersen leaned forward and snapped the intercom switch.

"For God's sake, Garvey. Just a minute . . ."

One minute later, Trudi emerged from under the desk, tossing ringlets of blond hair away from her face and moving back to the drinks cabinet. As she poured a brandy, rinsed and gargled, Dietersen readjusted himself and watched her with disgust. Angrily, he flicked the intercom switch again.

"What do you mean, a man at the door? People don't just come to my door, Garvey."

"I don't know, Mr. Dietersen. But he says he wants to talk to you. . . ."

"Have those bloody front gates been left open again?"

"The men were grass cutting. They had to get their equipment out and . . ."

"And so someone just walks right through, past everyone and up to the bloody front door. What am I paying people for, Garvey? I'm supposed to have security here. S.E.C.U.R.I.T.Y."

"I'm terribly sorry, Mr. Dietersen."

Trudi poured another brandy and sprawled out on the sofa by the window as if posing for a fashion shoot. She straightened a dress that didn't need straightening, picked dust motes from it that were not there. Her eyes looked as blank as they usually did. Dietersen pushed back his chair and strode to the lounge door. He could still hear Garvey apologizing as he shoved hard through the door and into the hallway. Garvey—a sixty-five-year-old man in what looked like an undertaker's suit—recoiled in alarm from the intercom system on his own hallway desk. He looked as if apology had become a way of life for him.

"What the hell does he want anyway?" Dietersen snapped. "Is he selling something?"

"I'm sorry, Mr. Dietersen. I really have no idea. But he seems . . . well, all right."

"So if he pulls a gun out and shoots me, at least you can tell the police that he 'seemed all right.' Ask him what he wants."

"He doesn't have to ask me," came a voice from the external hallway door. "I can tell you myself."

Now Dietersen's turn to be startled, he turned to see the man standing there. Casual, gray-black hair, donkey-jacket, farm boots. There was no hint of a threat on his face, but Dietersen didn't like the casual smile. Without looking back at the nervous man in the undertaker's suit, he said, "Piss off, Garvey."

Garvey disappeared into a side room, closing the

door with great care in case the sound of its closing should give offense.

The two men stood and looked at each other. When the newcomer showed no sign of speaking or moving, Dietersen said, "Well, since you seem 'all right' according to my staff and you think you've got a right to just walk in here like you own the place, you may as well tell me what the hell you're after."

"Not a lot. I'm not selling anything. I just want to have a word with you about something that happened last Wednesday."

"Last Wednesday?"

"About ten in the evening. On the Fell Road."

"I don't know what the hell you're talking about."

"My name's Hall. I own the farm west of the Fell Road. I was driving home at ten. Your car was heading down that road and into the village."

"What are you . . . ? Wait a minute. Trudi!"

Dietersen turned to look back at the door into the lounge. When there was no sound or movement, he strode to Garvey's desk and jabbed at the intercom. The intercom buzzer on his own desk inside the lounge sounded like an angry wasp.

"Trudi! Move your arse!"

Dietersen refused to turn and look at the newcomer, each passing second fueling his anger. Eventually, Trudi appeared in the doorway, swinging on the doorframe by one arm, still posing for the photo shoot. Her lipstick was smudged.

"You and your girlfriends took the car out last Wednesday, didn't you?"

"Yeah. We were bored, remember?" Her voice was still bored. "And you were being horrible."

"Shut up. Did you go up the village road?"

"Oh Christ, Kapler. I don't *know*. All the fucking roads 'round here look the same in the fucking dark."

"Well," Drew said, "if you were driving that Lexus parked in the drive, you were doing eighty down that unlit road, and you ran my Land Rover off the road and into a ditch."

Trudi swung on the doorframe, bored as hell. Dietersen took an angry step toward her, and suddenly she wasn't bored anymore.

"Kapler, don't! Look, baby—I don't know what he's talking about. Honest."

"All right." Kapler struggled to remain calm. "All right . . ." When he turned to look at Drew, his smile was fractured around the edges. "Was your vehicle damaged?"

"Scratch on the fender, that's all."

"So how much do you want?"

"Nothing."

"Then what are you here for?"

"Just to give some neighborly advice."

When Dietersen laughed this time, it wasn't fractured, and his composure had returned. "You're here to *threaten* me?"

"Nope. I just wanted to say—next time, take it easy on the Fell Road."

"You came all the way here just to say that?"

"That's all."

"And you're not after anything." Dietersen laughed again like a man in command of the situation. "Come off it."

"There's a cottage on that stretch of road. A widow and a little girl live there. Traveling at that speed, at night—on an unlit road? Anything could happen."

"I'll write you a check."

"I'm told you're a rich man. Good for you. But money's no good to anyone with a broken neck in the ditch. Yours, mine—or anyone else's."

Dietersen turned angrily. "Garvey! Bring my check book."

When he turned back, Drew was gone.

Dietersen turned his glare to Trudi.

"I don't know what he's talking about, Kapler."

The interior door opened and Garvey emerged, sheepish.

"Follow him out, Garvey. And make sure he leaves. And close the fucking *gate!*"

When Garvey had left, Dietersen turned back to Trudi.

"Nobody makes me look like an idiot."

"Come on, baby. Let's finish what we started."

"Trudi, I swear to God . . ."

But Trudi had turned and walked back into the lounge. When she looked back over her shoulder at him—with that *look*—Dietersen cursed himself, and followed.

TEN

Drew wielded the spade with too much anger, blistering the palm of his hand. He cursed, flung the spade down—and then stood with his hands on his hips for a long time, head down and breathing heavily. The sun was hot on his back, just like a taunt given his current endeavor.

Forcing himself to be calm, he carefully and slowly picked up the spade and began digging again at the base of the stone wall. He had often wondered who had built the wall, already there for many years when he had first bought the farm. Dry-stone, stretching for several hundred feet and presumably once forming some kind of boundary around the farm property. But now, apart from this stretch on the southwest corner of his land, it had mostly fallen prey to the changeable weather in this part of the world. Drew continued to dig, trying to clear his mind.

So what was that visit to Dietersen all about, if it wasn't what he said? A threat.

"Shut up," Drew said aloud, the spade biting into the

hard ground. There was rubble here, maybe pieces of fallen wall. He bent, tugged out a rock and threw it aside in a spray of earth.

When is a threat not a threat?

"Con-tra-dic-tion!" Each syllable came with a blow of the spade. Unable to let Dietersen, or his girlfriend, get away with forcing him off the road yet not wanting to threaten him, however justified, Drew had simply *not* been able to let it go, and had been compelled to at least raise it with the businessman. But to what purpose? He felt angry and—not for the first time in his life—ineffectual.

"I should have just let it go."

Throwing the spade down into the hole, he moved to the bag slung over the wall, rummaged for his water bottle and drank. He had worked up a sweat. Leaning back against the rough-hewn wall, he looked down into the valley at his farmhouse—and was instantly reminded by the surrounding outhouses of a series of failed enterprises. Drew kicked the spade at his feet.

And watched a familiar car pull into the farm gate from the main road. The car carefully negotiated the track leading to the house—a test for its suspension—taking a long slow curve around the outbuildings and stopping at the main door. Drew drank from his water bottle again, wondering how long the occupant was going to sit in the vehicle before realizing that he wasn't going to come out. After a while, the door opened—and a familiar figure climbed out.

It was Faye Roche.

Drew watched her walk to the front door, drank again when she rang the bell.

Eventually, Faye gave up ringing, walked back to the

car—her attention still fixed on the farmhouse and surrounding buildings.

"No one at home, Faye," said Drew quietly.

Faye pulled open the car door, leaned in—and the sound of the horn blatted up the sides of the valley. Birds flew from the hedge at the side of the house. Drew sighed and drank again. Faye blatted once more, this time impatiently. Drew watched her move away from the car, looking around and . . .

"Oh no." Groaning, he turned, replaced the water bottle and picked up the spade again.

Faye had seen him and had begun to walk up the side of the valley toward him. She was wearing the same coat she'd worn on the night of the accident, an anorak with fur trim. She didn't seem to have changed since the days she had taught him at Nicolham School, and he could feel her getting nearer as he sweated and worked, digging the hole at the foot of the dry-stone wall. Now he was angry with himself again, for being angry with her—angry at what she had undoubtedly come to say, angry because he knew instinctively why she was here. When he heard the soft footfalls that meant she had reached the top of the rise where he was working, he said, without turning, "Yes, I did go to see him."

"Who?" Faye asked, out of breath.

"Dietersen."

"Really—and what did he have to say for himself?"

"It wasn't him in the car that night. It was his wife, lover, partner—whatever."

"She's definitely a 'whatever.' "

Drew glanced back to see Faye sit on the grass, regaining her breath.

"That's why you think I came up here to see you?

Checking up on ex-pupils like bossy ex-schoolteachers are supposed to do?"

"Waste of time. Don't know why I went. Land Rover's fine. No need for police."

"Well, he shouldn't be allowed to get away with it. The fact that you confronted him about it might mean he—or his 'whatever'—will be more careful next time. But I didn't come to see you about that. How's your head?"

"Fine. No problems."

"I didn't come to see you about that either."

Drew turned and leaned on his spade. "It wasn't me, you know."

This time it was Faye's turn to be perplexed. "What wasn't you?"

"I didn't throw that piece of chalk at Laurie Turner. It was Barry Lomas. But you still gave the detention to me."

"And that's been on your mind for thirty years?"

"What do you want, Faye? What brings you way up here?"

"I got to thinking after that night. About you and what happened here. To your wife, I mean."

Drew's jaw clenched. If Faye reacted to that sudden tension, she didn't show it; just sat watching silently, as if waiting for a response. Drew slowly turned, picked up the spade and began digging again.

"It happened, Drew. It happened, and it was horrible. But you can't just carry on like this, away from everything—away from everyone."

"I'm going to plant pear trees along this wall. Never tried pears before. But I think they'll take, so I'm going to give it a go."

"I was talking to George, Tom and—what's his

name?—Laurence Burns, down at the pub. They've been up to see you again, haven't they? Been trying to convince you about getting more involved in village life again. The way you used to, before . . ."

"They say late autumn, early winter is best time. But I'm doing some preparation now. Get the hard work done, get the soil cleared." The spade hit a rock with a shivering *clang*. Drew yanked it out and sent it tumbling down the slope past Faye.

"They say they're not giving up on you," Faye continued. "They don't want you stuck up here alone. Neither do I. They made me feel a little ashamed, actually. Do you remember when I used to come up to see you—tried to give you the pep talks? I gave up, and I shouldn't have. Your friends didn't give up, though—they still haven't."

Drew wielded the spade again, found another rock and jammed the edge under it, levering it out of the soil. "The key is to choose a sunny, sheltered spot. I'm planting up here rather than the low-lying land by the cottage 'cause that's where morning frost lingers sometimes. Pears don't like that."

"Seeing you that night down at Cath's place—that made me think again. Made me realize that I shouldn't have given up on you."

"They suffer if there's a cold easterly wind. Another reason I've chosen this place. They need more sunlight than apples. See? A sunny, southwest-facing wall for growing and training the trees . . ."

"Not when other things started to go wrong for you on the farm. The Mad Cow crisis—losing all your livestock first. Then the fire."

"Fertile, well-drained, moist soil—got some loam in already. Not a heavy clay soil, and it won't get waterlogged here. If it were chalky soil or light, sandy ground, it wouldn't work. It would stress the trees. And a stressed tree makes for poor fruit. Do it right—there'll be fruit for twenty years. . . ."

"You don't need to be alone, Drew. There's help if you need it."

"Help? Like the help I didn't get from the Farmer's Union when . . ." Drew reined in his anger, resisted throwing down the spade. Instead, he carefully and firmly planted it, dusted his hands and walked over to Faye. He looked past her, out across the valley and down to the farmhouse. "I'm sorry. You mean well, Faye. And so do George and the others. And I never thanked you properly for looking after me—back at school and then that night with Dietersen's car."

"I knew you didn't throw that chalk at Laurie Turner."

Drew turned to look down at her.

"I needed to have you stay behind so we could talk. You've always been stubborn, Drew. If I'd asked you to stay and talk about your mother and father, you just wouldn't have done it. But you always obeyed the rules at school, even when those rules were wrong. And I could see how much your parents' splitting up—so publicly—was doing to you. Might seem strange to hear that now after all this time, but . . ."

"We talked. I remember. And you did help, Faye. You did. Good God—so you stage-managed the whole thing?"

"And then afterwards—when we kept the talking going, remember?"

When Drew spoke again, the anger had dissipated: "You're a remarkable woman, Miss Roche. Always were. And you did help me back then—a lot."

"I want to help you now. And you can start by doing me a favor."

"A favor?"

"Yep, but it involves talking to some people."

"Christ, you want me to go into therapy?"

"Not the way you're thinking. First, a question."

"This is like being back at school again."

"Have you seen them?"

"Them?"

"You know what I'm talking about. Them. The things that you've been hunting and trying to track this last couple of years."

Drew paused, looking long and hard at her face for any sign of derision or humor. There was none. He turned to look out across the valley, to the Fell.

"Yes, I've seen them. They're out there, all right. They're clever, though. Clever in a way that sometimes just doesn't seem possible. But I've seen them."

"Then come and talk about them."

"Talk? To who?"

"Cath's been asked to give a talk on writing to the Nicolham Culture Club. I want you to come and give a talk about what you've been looking for up here."

"They think I'm nuts down there. That I'm chasing shadows up here."

"Tell me who thinks that. Because I don't know anyone who does. Tom lost another three sheep last week. . . ."

"He didn't tell me."

"That's because he hasn't seen you—and you're not answering your blasted phone! Livestock's being taken all the time. You know that. And I don't know anyone who's laughing about it. So I want you to come a give a talk. About *them*—about what you know and what you've been doing up here all this time."

"You're trying to socialize me, Faye."

"Just one talk. That's all. I'll fix everything. Anyone laughs, I'll personally boot them out of the room."

"Or give them detention?"

"I'm retired, remember?"

"You've never retired, Miss Roche. You may have given up the day job—but you've never retired."

"So is that a yes, then?"

"Don't think pears would ever take there. Do you?"

ELEVEN

The Nicolham Culture Club building served many purposes, and had done so since its erection in the center of the village more than a hundred years ago; annexed to the local school. A simple eighty-foot square building composed mainly of the gray stone and slate quarried from nearby and also used for the construction of the school, it had signs over the door that revealed it was also the Horticulture Centre, the Fell Walking Club, the Local Historical Society and Women's Institute.

Cath Lane stood before a maximum crowd of eighty—all seats having been taken when it had become known that Nicolham's own resident novelist would be giving a rare talk on her work that evening; the first time ever since she had moved into the white cottage on the Fell Road. Faye Roche sat at the back with Rynne (there was no school tomorrow, so a late-ish night was okay this evening). Faye had been smiling throughout, and Cath had attempted a few barbed glances in her direction at what seemed appropriate moments without making it obvious. This had been a setup, and Cath had fallen for it.

"Honestly, sugar. It's just a half dozen or so of the locals. Scribblers, you know? Been at it for years, wanting to break through. Needing some good advice. You were like that once. Looking for advice. Remember those talks you went to? The ones you were telling me about that helped you so much. What are their names? Michael Lambton—you know, that lot."

"Faye, you know I don't do that stuff since we moved. I write. That's it."

"You were on that television documentary a few nights back."

"That was cut in from an old interview."

"Well, I think you're being mean. You could at least give a little advice to the really enthusiastic would-be writers in your own village. Not as if it's one of those book-tour thingies that you used to do. This would be half an hour at most. Sort of a guest slot."

"Half a dozen people? That's all."

"Well—maybe ten."

But the hall was packed to capacity, and Cath recognized Faye's handwriting on the block-letter posters adorning the walls that advertised the forthcoming talk of the village's celebrity writer; posters that, by their ragged tape and dog-eared corners had clearly been there for some time prior to their conversation. And in the audience, clearly not local, was at least one journalist she had met years ago when her first novel had made such an impact. The audience appreciation was honest and evident, but a knot of anxiety had fixed in her stomach when they had first arrived. Faye had made the introductions, and Cath had felt anxious enough to throw up. This was the first time she had stood in front of an audience to talk about her work since . . . since the Bad Day. But the sight of Rynne, sitting at the back, brought a sense of resolve. Cath had fought back and had commenced with a question-and-answer session straight from the start, rather than giving a talk. Some of the questions were the standards that she had been asked so often that her reply was instinctively ready:

"Where do you get your ideas from?"

"For thrillers with a harder—let's say more 'horror' edge—from a horror bag I bought for my daughter in Plymouth market. It cost ninety-nine pence and it's never let me down."

"What time of day is it best to work? Morning or afternoon?"

"For me, the best time is later in the day, usually into the evening—when my daughter lets me." Audience laughter—and sparkling eyes from Rynne at the back. "That's a legacy from the days I worked nine to five in an office job, and only got a chance to work after work—if you see what I mean. But for everyone wanting to write, the rhythm and time of day that suits you best is something you have to find for yourself over time."

"What kind of pencil do you use?"

"2B or 3B, any make. They taste better."

They were throwaway jokes she had used before in an attempt to deflect the simple fact that she was no nearer to giving a reasonable explanation of how and why she wrote than when she'd first started to write seriously. She had built up a whole series of what she hoped sounded like convincing theories, even if she remained unconvinced by them herself. She had been born a storyteller, shied away from any real analysis of where her stories came from. They just came, whether she wanted to write them or not.

The journalist she knew had been biding his time with good nature, probably waiting for the standard questions to finish before he began with his own. When there was a brief pause in the questions from the floor, she decided to take the initiative.

"It's a long way from Wales, Matt. And you've been very patient so far."

The familiarity caused a slight stir. The fair-haired man grinned and leaned forward. When he spoke, the Welsh accent was unmistakable.

"There's been talk that the novel you're working on now has been optioned for the movies before it's even finished. Is that right?"

"If it is, no one's told me."

"Can you tell us anything about it?"

"You know better than that. It's bad luck to talk too much about a project in progress because . . ."

I can't make the book come alive.

". . . it might make the magic go away. What brings you all the way from Wales, Matt? Still working for O'Brien and Willis?"

"Yep." Aware of the questioning looks from the audience, the journalist turned to address them. "A literary magazine. They wanted an interview, but Ms. Lane hasn't been giving them since the last novel." He turned back to Cath. "I hope you don't mind me trying a sneaky one?"

She had been avoiding formal interviews, it was true—but despite the anxiety she still felt it was impossible to feel animosity toward an honest journalist who had given her such great reviews in the past, and was so obviously an enthusiast of her work.

"No, but time's up," came Faye's voice from the back. "It's a two-parter tonight. And we must allow our second guest a chance to speak." As Faye pushed forward, Cath could see that there was a facture in her composure. Clearly, despite the organization behind the scenes and the loving manipulation that had led to the event, she hadn't anticipated the arrival of a professional journalist and it was clear from her expression she was worried that perhaps this was a step too far.

"Perhaps another interview later?" Matt was anxious not to lose his chance.

"Well, Ms. Lane is very busy on her . . ." Cath had never seen Faye look this flustered before.

"Have you traveled from Wales for this talk, Matt?"

"Well, yes. I'm staying overnight in the pub, then heading back tomorrow evening."

Cath looked at Faye, smiled and put a hand on her shoulder to reassure her. "And it's a long way to and from Wales, isn't it?"

Matt looked hopeful, and Faye looked relieved.

"We'll organize something tomorrow morning then."

"And I know," continued Faye, addressing the audience, "that we've all appreciated your talk and the insights you've given on the life of a writer."

Cath acknowledged the applause and joined Rynne at the back of the room. She was grinning as she applauded, reaching up to whisper a secret in her ear.

"You're famous!"

Cath hugged her and looked back to see that Faye was now heading for the door, looking for the second guest whom—Cath could see as she looked around the crowd—was not in the room. Her own anxiety at giving this speech, her worries about it after such a long time of enforced professional solitude, had pre-

vented her from thinking about him. The surprise that
the "half a dozen—maybe ten" was actually about
eighty people, had taken her mind completely off the
second guest, whom Faye had also failed to mention
until the last minute. Cath watched as Faye reached the
door, then caught sight of something or someone beyond and began a pantomime, beckoning that whoever or whatever was out there should get inside fast.
The crowd was now taking an interest in Faye's strange
behavior, and Cath began to have other thoughts
about why Faye had organized this whole damned
business.

"Yes—he's here—George, can you . . . ? Good. Don't
let him . . . Tom."

Drew Hall made his entrance as if the two men behind him had pushed him into the room, which indeed they had. Not giving Drew time to turn and
complain, and maybe sour the atmosphere—Faye
grabbed his arm and propelled him down the aisle toward the bottom table where Cath had given her talk.
The two men behind tried to hide their grinning as
they found seats near the back. Overwhelmed by a for-
midable schoolteacher's grasp and now suddenly
aware that he was in the middle of a large, prospective
audience, Drew allowed himself to be led to the front,
fighting to regain his composure.

What are you up to, Faye? thought Cath.

"And we're very pleased to introduce our second
guest of the evening. Some of you will know him already, but I've a feeling that even some of the long-time
residents present will not yet have met Drew Hall, local
farmer and owner of Fell Farm. I've known Drew for
most of his life, taught him when I was the village
teacher. We've asked him to come and talk to us this

evening about something that's been going on around Nicolham for a good many years or more. Something that Drew has taken a keen personal interest in, and which I know has been a cause for concern for some of us in the villages and surrounding farms."

"You're not kidding," called one of the men from the back who had accompanied Drew to the hall.

"So let's have a big round of applause for local lad Drew Hall."

Cath watched Drew's discomfort as the audience applauded, not knowing whether he should stand or sit. From the back, another of Drew's friends gave a wolf-whistle, which was abruptly terminated by Faye's glare of warning. Clearly, Faye's composure had returned. Cath resolved not to let her off the hook later that evening. The applause faded, and Drew cleared his throat.

Cath felt another tinge of anxiety at the silence that followed, found herself willing Drew to speak in a moment of empathy.

"Well," he began, before clearing his throat again. "I've never done this before, so I don't quite know where to start."

"Start at the beginning," said the one called George. "Come on, Drew. Tell us what you know."

"All right . . . all right. I will."

There was another pause, and this time the man called Tom called out: "Come on then, Drew. What's out there on the Fell?"

Drew cleared his throat.

"What's been killing my sheep then?"

Cath was suddenly very interested.

"Cats," said Drew at last. "Big Cats."

He paused for what Cath assumed was going to be an overly dramatic flourish. Instead, when he spoke again, it was quiet and restrained, and with an air of authority that impressed her. "I know it because I've seen them. And in one case—literally, face to face."

Cath was intrigued. On the night Drew had been run off the road, he had been dazed, possibly even concussed according to Faye. It had been a strange evening, and the conversation that night had pushed her back into a dark place from which she had spent a long time trying to emerge. Thereafter, that sighting of him on the ridge, looking down at the cottage also somehow added to the sense of strangeness—that both of those encounters had somehow been with different men. She felt as if this were the real Drew Hall. He was a man, she could now see, in his early thirties, slightly younger than she was, perhaps; with dark curly hair that didn't look as if it had seen a brush for a while. He had a sallow complexion, which seemed strange. Given that he was a farmer, working in the great outdoors or on that wild Fell side, shouldn't he be tanned and windswept, or something? He had a good-looking, if not handsome face. Woolen jersey, jeans.

"They're out there for sure," continued Drew.

"Panthers, leopards, pumas? What?" Tom asked.

"The prints I've found match with panther."

"Not The Hound of the Baskervilles, then?" joked someone else from the audience.

"Well, that's the problem," rejoined Drew. "That's the reason why no one takes the situation seriously. It makes for a good news story, doesn't it? 'Ferocious wild cats at large in the English countryside.' Just the kind of thing that appeals to the media, to the newspapers. And, of course, the media have really hyped the stories up because—well, because it makes good copy.

They'd much rather go along with the myth that what we've got out there is something like The Hound of the Baskervilles—not just in the forests and woods around Nicolham, but all over the country.

"The most famous case—and when I say 'famous' I mean the way that the story really does get hyped up—is at Bodmin Moor in Cornwall. Everyone's heard of The Beast of Bodmin. If it's a slow news day down in Cornwall, there'll be reports of the Big Cat that stalks the moor, taking sheep and livestock. And when the stories do hit the local headlines or television, some journalists prefer to disregard the actual facts and perpetuate the myth. The fact of the matter is that there are numerous zoologists, farmers and experts, including the former Managing Director of Newquay Zoo—an established authority—who are in no doubt that Big Cats are living wild throughout the United Kingdom. And the reason for that couldn't be simpler."

Cath was impressed. Drew had a natural style, very easy, and he managed to talk to an audience with a quiet authority that drew them in. Off to the right, a door opened, and the audience's attention was momentarily distracted by the figure that stepped into the room.

Tall, yet round-shouldered, with an impeccable gray business suit and tie—the figure stood grinning for a moment; clearly expecting the attention that was now drawn to him. Drew stopped talking, and in that moment Cath sensed a tension in the air. The newcomer had a big if not bouffant 1980s hair style that had probably wowed the chicks so much when he was a younger man that he had kept it ever since.

"Don't mind me." His voice was confident and assured, and when he straightened a tie that did not need straightening, Cath sensed that it was more to show off the extravagantly large rings on the four fingers of his left hand. Olive-black eyes and eyebrows that had not only been plucked but waxed and sculpted. Still grinning, and seeming to take pleasure from Drew's discomfort, the man moved to the back row and took a seat. As he carefully crossed his legs, making sure not to damage the perfect crease in his trouser seams, Cath caught sight of Faye and Rynne sitting behind him. The look of displeasure on Faye's face as she watched the back of that man's head suddenly brought everything together.

This could only be Kapler Dietersen, local businessman and entrepreneur—newly arrived to this parish, and not known for his safe driving style on unlit roads at night. Dietersen was scanning the audience now, saw that she was giving him the attention he deserved and beamed a smile of perfect and even white teeth that told her more than she wanted to know. She recognized a predator when she saw one—in more ways that one. Cath looked back at Drew, who had struggled to regain his composure.

"Back in the early seventies," Drew Hall went on, "it was considered very trendy by the rich and famous to have pumas or panthers as house pets. Maybe wandering around the lounge with diamond-studded necklaces. But the introduction of the Dangerous Animals Act in 1976 enforced strict licensing regulations prohibiting this, leaving limited options for the owners. Either give the animals to a zoo, or have them destroyed. Zoos refused to take them, so owners who balked at having their animals killed opted for the only other palatable solution: Let them loose to fend for themselves."

Kapler Dietersen coughed. It was a sound effect from a cartoon, intended to put Drew off. He paused briefly, and then continued:

"And that's just what they've done. With a generally mild climate and an abundant food supply—rabbits, wild birds, voles—they've adapted very well to their new lives."

"Don't forget my bloody sheep," Tom said. Dietersen turned and grinned at him, giving an extravagant nod of agreement that was calculated to show how stupid he thought him.

"Absolutely. If the opportunity is there, or the animal's ailing—or if there's a new litter—the Big Cats may well take the occasional sheep or lamb. In general, though, there's enough small mammals to keep them satisfied. Gets worse in bad weather, right Tom?"

"Too right. Lost six animals this winter."

"In general," Drew continued, "small prides of cats keep to themselves. If they're well fed and sheltered, they shy away from human contact."

"You said panthers?" asked a woman with a notepad from the front row. "But it could be some other Big Cat?"

"It depends which part of the country and where certain prides of Cat have been able to establish themselves. Big Cats are very territorial. I've heard of cases all over the country where there are different types of cats. Black leopard, panther, puma. But here in Nicolham, I believe they're panthers. The animals I've seen . . ."

Cath wondered why Drew suddenly looked troubled at what he'd said. But the moment was gone, as he quickly continued: ". . . look like panthers. The tracks I've seen are similar to panther. Or as they're also called—black leopards. And as Tom knows, they've occasionally taken some of my livestock on the Fell. That's given me a chance to examine the leftovers of their kill—and the nature of that kill suggests panther. Cats like that kill in a very specific way. They remove the innards and leave the pelt. I've taken plaster casts of their tracks—even examined droppings I've found at the scene."

"So if the evidence is so strong," asked Dietersen, making another dramatic pause and so obviously enjoying the attention he was drawing, "why hasn't the government done something about it? I mean, if they're out there taking livestock from farms, they've got to be well . . . dangerous. Haven't they?"

Cath imagined that she could hear something click in Drew's jaw, even at that distance. His voice was so tight and measured when he spoke again that she could imagine a trace scent of testosterone in the air. "There was a Ministry of Agriculture survey a few years ago, after pressure from the Farmers' Union. But the survey only concentrated on a six-month time span— and during that time there were hardly any reports of sightings and no conclusive evidence. The terms of reference were very limited. Sightings and attacks on either side of that six-month period were basically ignored. The big question—the central issue—is this: If the Ministry confirmed the existence of big cats in the wild, they'd have to pay compensation to farmers for lost livestock, and people with licensed weapons would be all over the place shooting at anything that moved—using the control-of-vermin argument."

"That's it exactly, Drew." Tom turned to Dietersen, who smiled and nodded again with a patronizing air.

"There was a case in the papers just last week,"

George said, "about someone being attacked by a Big Cat. Can't remember where, Drew—but that's unusual, isn't it? I mean, why haven't there been more reports of attacks on human beings."

"Yeah, I saw the report. But you see—panthers, pumas, black leopards—they all shy away from human contact. Frankly, they don't like the smell of people."

There was a polite murmur of laughter from the audience.

"I don't mean anyone in particular," Drew said, fixing Dietersen in his sight. Dietersen's smile stayed fixed.

Oh myyy! thought Cath. *Scratch-scratch!*

"Just people in general." Drew smiled. "They can't deal with the scent. But really, it's back to The Hound of the Baskervilles thing again—this idea that they're out there somewhere waiting to pounce on humans. My guess is that the fella who was attacked probably stumbled on the cat by accident, and it reacted defensively. Maybe he got too near to a den with cubs. The facts of the matter are very simple, really. The English climate's generally mild, there's lots of cover in the UK, lots of food. A well-fed cat is a contented cat, in general. They pretty much want to mind their own business—will move out if a human comes near."

"You said that you saw one," said Cath. "Face to face."

Drew turned to look at her.

"Yes."

"What happened?"

Drew looked across at Dietersen, who folded his arms extravagantly and feigned deep interest. Drew shuffled uneasily, leaned back against the desk and said: "It was . . ."

TWELVE

Twilight.

*Drew has spent a frustrating morning on the tele-
phone trying to interest a local developer in buying a
plot on the southern border of his land. It's an acre of
fallow ground, close to Nicolham and the same developer has been building selected and expensive proper-
ties a mile from the site that has always been known as
the Quarter Acre—for reasons no longer remembered.
The developer has been biding his time as he acquires
land site by site, gradually moving closer to the Quarter
Acre boundary. Drew needs the money. In that regard,
things have never been worse. What was once a viable
farming operation is in ruins—on some parts of his
land, quite literally. But he has no intention of giving his
land away at a cut down price. The developer has made
an offer, but it's low—and so the game goes on, with
Drew's fierce pride refusing to allow him to give the land
away for less than it's worth, despite the fact that he
needs hard cash desperately right now. The developer
believes that Drew is playing a shrewd business game,*

has no idea that after the latest telephone call Drew has smashed the telephone receiver down hard and shattered the plastic casing. Infuriated, frustrated and angry to the very core of his being, Drew has spent the remainder of that afternoon feeding livestock and finding practical jobs to do that he has been putting off. Gutters on the back shed. Loose planking in the feed store. When one of the planks fractures at his angry hammering, he yanks it up, strides outside and flings it down a gravel path—scattering hens in a flurry of feathers.

There's a fence up on the valley wall, a quarter mile from the house. Like so much else on his land, it serves no purpose. Originally the fence contained a section of steep grazing land for sheep, but that was a long time ago—when his flock was viable. Now the grass on the valley side up to the fence has grown lush and deep. Last time he was up there, he could see that the fence wire had separated from one of the posts and was flapping loose in the wind. So it's remained these past months. But now, with work bag and tools, Drew sets off up the rough path that gradually ascends the valley wall. Even if the fence serves no purpose, he'll fix it today.

The track takes him past the barn.

The thing that killed his wife is in there.

Not for the first time, he wonders why he just doesn't put a torch to the whole ramshackle building. But then he rehearses what might happen. It'll burn all right—the wood is dried out and it wouldn't take much for the whole building to fall apart. And the thing inside will burn—up to a point. But when that barn does finally collapse into a smoldering ruin, the blackened skeleton of the thing inside will still be there—still a terrible reminder. And then he'll have to set about taking it apart, and removing it piece by piece so it can be taken away.

But this section of his property is visible from the Fell Road down there. What would happen if someone saw the building ablaze? It might be reported. Then people would come. *Maybe the police. Maybe . . .*

"Maybe," he says aloud, "I'm making bloody excuses again."

It makes no sense to Drew that he's kept it locked up in the barn ever since that terrible time. Wouldn't it have been better to try to sell it? Maybe just pay someone to take the damned thing away? Maybe take up the help that had been offered to him from George and Tom and others—just to dismantle it, remove it and take it the hell away? God knows, he could do with the money it might have brought then. But now it's been left to rust and decay, and he knows that he wouldn't even get scrap value for it.

Drew pauses when he draws level with the barn. He stands for a long time looking at it, and knows that just having it here—locked up like that—is somehow like brooding over some terrible festering wound in his soul. He knows that the best thing would be to rid himself of it. Finally, he moves to the barn door, puts his hand on the link chain that keeps the barn doors closed. Somehow, it feels like he has placed his hand on a church altar—and he doesn't like the feeling at all. He dislikes it so much that he drops his work bag, yanks the chain away and then pulls one of the barn doors angrily to one side. The screech of the rusted hinges seems to reverberate from the valley sides, like a murder of angry crows. Dust rises in clouds around his feet, making him choke. When that dust settles in the twilight, he stands and looks at the monster inside.

The beast has not moved since it was dragged in there. But to Drew it somehow seems alive and waiting.

Its headlamps are eyes, its mottled-green cab some kind of hideous head carapace. The deep tread of the huge tires are still packed with ancient mud and brown-dried grass. The threshing baler in front looks like monstrous jaws and spiked teeth—but he cannot bring himself to look there, in case he sees . . . some trace or reminder. A shuddering sigh wracks his body and, head down, he can still somehow recall the Farming Newsletter that reported on what happened that day. The words have been emblazoned on his mind. They replay in his head as the man and the monster stand silently before each other, dust motes and straw swirling in the air.

The accident occurred on the eastern slope of the Drew property, when the 11-ton combine harvester was parked on sloping ground using the hand-operated parking brake. Mr. and Mrs. Hall were attempting to clear a blockage in the auger on the header—used to move the unthreshed crops to the threshing mechanism. It is believed that the vibration of the engine—still running—affected the parking-brake system, which in turn caused the harvester to swing and turn with the result that Mrs. Hall was drawn into the thresher. Parking brakes on combine harvesters should not be relied on for safety, particularly on slopes, since they are not in use for most of the year. Even though the operating lever appears to be in working order, they can become seized in the off position, or debris in the brake may impede its ability to hold several tons of vehicle. Premature wear or glazing can also occur if the brake is inadvertently left applied; the connecting cable may become stretched, or the ratchet mechanism may be so worn it won't stay applied. Anyone working with a vehicle parked on a slope should ensure that it is aligned so that it cannot run downhill, and ensure that the engine is switched off . . .

"It was my fault, Flora," Drew says aloud. "It was all my fault."

The combine harvester sits there in all its idiot bulk, grinning at him.

Drew resolves to do something at last about this great metal monster, lunges back to the barn door and drags it closed again. He twists the chain so tightly around the hasps holding the doors together that he grazes his knuckles in the process.

Twilight is deepening when he continues to ascend the rough track, work bag in hand. He wonders why he is coming up here, why he should need to fix the fence. He struggles to cast off the feeling that he is once again undertaking a worthless and meaningless task— aimlessly fixing the unfixable.

And that is when he sees the familiar tracks in the dirt before him.

Drew freezes and looks around. There isn't a breath of wind, and no tell-tale trace of that scent with which he has become so familiar. He looks back to the barn, then the farmhouse. There's a stillness that feels un-canny. Nothing moves in the valley, and Drew can't shake off a feeling of being watched, or of something about to happen. There are no birds in the sky, and noth-ing makes a sound. He becomes aware of the sound of his own breathing and turns again to look down at the tracks. When he bends to examine them, he recognizes the marks immediately, and when he touches them, the mud track is dry, but the track feels fresh.

Panther.

But too big to be panther.

And this is the troubling thing. He's found these tracks before all over the valley and the Fell, taken plaster casts and studied them back at the farmhouse. They're panther, no doubt about that—but somehow larger than the textbooks or the published data will allow. He sniffs, trying to draw some evidence of that musk.

Nothing.

The tracks move on up ahead, and Drew follows them. Again, the stride between pawprints indicates a Big Cat at its leisure; and again, the length between strides is that of a large cat, bigger than any panther—but a panther, nonetheless. He glances back at the farmhouse as he follows that track uphill. There's a clear sight-line from here down to his home, and these tracks must have been made earlier in the day—in clear sunlight. All he had to do was look out of the farmhouse kitchen window, up the valley side, and he would have seen what had made these tracks. Not for the first time, Drew is overwhelmed by a sense of the animal's confidence; the feeling that this particular beast is utterly at ease with itself, is somehow sure that it can remain aloof and hidden not only from him, but any human eye. Drew also can't help shake off the feeling that this is all somehow a taunt. It's as if the beast is saying: "I'm here. This is my land. And here I am—in plain view. But you can't see me—and you'll never find me."

Drew shakes his head, knowing that this is a crazy thought. The tracks move off the path and into the long grass that leads up to the broken fence. He pauses. These feelings, these thoughts—and now the fact that the tracks almost seem to be leading him to where he'd intended to go.

"Come on, Hall," he says aloud. "Don't get creeped out."

He moves on into the long grass. The ground is steeper here leading up to the fence. The grass hisses around his thighs as he reaches the ridge where the fence posts have been embedded, yanks the loose wire aside so that he can get to the post from which it's become detached. He wonders about the person who erected the fence, a previous owner long forgotten—way back before his time—and drops the tool bag. Bending to open it, he reaches for a hammer, rummages for the fence nails.

And looks up from where he kneels, straight into a huge and silently snarling mask of terror that completely fills his line of vision.

Glinting eyes, utterly alien, root him to the spot. He sees himself in there, a distorted and pathetically small image. He also sees his coming death and cannot move. The eyes are unblinking, as red lips peel back in a monstrous grimace, slowly revealing the solid and savage reality of yellow fangs that are too big, too real— and in that slow moment, the stench from that gaping maw hits Drew full in the face. They are so close that he could lean forward to kiss it, and its opening jaws could take his head from his shoulders, but now—the voices that Drew hears are from the books he so carefully keeps lined in his study back at the farm (and oh God why isn't he back down on the farm and not here?).

"Several Big Cat attacks on humans, both in captivity and in the wild, have been stopped when the victim fought back. There are no known instances in which an attack was stopped when the victim feigned death."

A noise begins deep within that still-gaping maw—so deep that it might be coming from underground. It begins slowly, the stench increasing—full on in Drew's face—a sound and a rumbling vibration, like some

71

nightmare train on its way. As it comes, Drew is aware that there is blood on his knuckles, from the chain across the barn door. The grumbling, shuddering growl has the power of eons, the ever-increasing promise of a death more savage and violent than a mind could withstand. The growl becomes a roaring, and the very vibration of it is shaking Drew's body.

"Avoid rapid movements, running, loud, excited talk . . ."

But Drew cannot move, cannot breathe, as the sound and the smell overpower and consume his body. He can only kneel before that savage widening mask that fills the sky; can only watch the string of saliva that stretches and trembles from one of those monstrous upper canines. The pink and white of that gigantic tongue, the depth of that cavernous mouth, are obscene and fearful beyond sense.

"Look for sticks, rocks or other weapons. Pick them up, use an aggressive posture.

Terror has overcome Drew, and he waits for death as that roar finally erupts from the chasm of the beast. The blast and the stench is from Hell, and Drew's eyes are shut as he waits for those gigantic yellow canines to fasten around his head. He wonders if he will scream as the beast begins shaking and tugging his flailing body into the long grass, ripping his body apart. He knows that the pain will go on and on forever and that he will have lost his mind before he loses his life.

"In the event of an attack, in an unavoidable situation, you need all the threatening display you can muster. The showing of teeth, grinning—which humans translate as a smile—can look like an act of aggression to a Big Cat. Aggressive shouts or other loud sounds also may be helpful when . . ."

Drew screams then—knowing that his scream will be strangled and suffocated by those slavering jaws. He cannot move, he cannot fight back, but he puts every-thing he has into that last act of terror and acceptance of what is to come. As his lungs empty and the scream fills the valley, he waits for death.

But death does not come.

Drew's breath has been completely vented, and as he chokes, he falls across his tool bag—now at last able to throw up his arms over his head in a hopeless attempt to ward off the inevitable attack.

The stench has gone.

Gasping for breath, letting out the terror, Drew sees that the Big Cat is no longer there.

He staggers to his feet, grabbing the tool bag and scattering the contents at his feet as he yanks out the heavy-duty chisel and holds it out before him. Has his scream covered the sound of its departure?

Was it there at all?

Is he losing his mind?

No—there is the massive flattened depression in the grass where the Big Cat was hiding, and upon which Drew had stumbled. There is a broken passage through the long grass that marks the direction the panther—or whatever it was—took off. Or did it? Is it still here, is it—behind him?

Drew spins around, holding out the chisel. Twilight has deepened to early evening and the long shadows have spread over the valley. There is no sign of the crea-ture, and that's when Drew begins running back to the rough track. He halts there, spinning, with tortured lungs and hammering heart. He has to stay calm. An-other voice from one of his faraway books is telling him that he must not act like prey. If he runs, if he panics and the beast is still nearby—then it will come after him and bring him down.

Still with the chisel held out, Drew begins his descent of the rough track toward the farmhouse; now past the long grass and out into the open. He walks backwards now, keeping his attention fixed on the inward boundary of the long grass by the fence. He sees the monster—because surely this thing is a monster, not a panther or any other Big Cat—in his mind's eye, as it suddenly bursts from the long grass and begins its killing run. He sees the black, sleek body close to the ground, coming fast and powerful and hideous. This cat has been playing with a mouse.

The barn appears at Drew's left as he moves.

There is another monster in there.

And that is when Drew stops, breathing hard, sweat streaming from his body making his shirt stick to his back.

The monster in the barn—and the beast waiting for him in the long grass.

Something happens to him, then. Something about the terror he has just experienced; something about the horror of what happened to Flora; something about the long lonely days, weeks and months; the failing farm and all his attempts turning to ashes, and now . . . and now . . .

Drew screams again—his voice carrying over the valley. But this time he is not screaming with fear, he is screaming with rage and defiance. He runs forward, kicking up dust in the early evening air, and jabbing the chisel toward the long grass, defying whatever is there to come out, challenging it to make its stalk and killing run. It may as well kill him, after all. But while it's killing him, he'll use this bloody chisel—and he'll use it well.

He'll make that beast—and all the other beasts that have been eating him since Flora died—suffer, and suffer badly.

But the beast does not come.

The grass is still. There is no wind.

Only the dying echo of Drew's defiance.

He turns his back on the long grass and walks down the track to the farm.

Present Day

"You said that you saw one," said Cath. "Face to face."

Drew turned to look at her.

"Yes."

"What happened?"

Drew looked across at Dietersen, who folded his arms extravagantly and again feigned deep interest. Drew shuffled uneasily, leaned back against the desk and said: "It was . . ."

He cleared his throat again, and Cath could see that Drew's eyes were focused on some strange inner place.

". . . definitely a panther. No doubt about it."

"Yes." Dietersen smiled. "But how do you *know?*"

"Because I saw it. Up on my farm, on the valley side. I was very close".

Cath could feel the animosity building between the men, struggled to think of a question, but before she could think of anything, Faye's voice—a little too loud—came from the back of the hall.

"Tell us about panthers, Drew. Tell us what you know about them. Their behavior, stuff like that."

Cath turned to look at her, saw the steel in her face and that familiar 'look' that Rynne had teased her about just recently. Cath put her arm around Rynne's shoulders and hugged her close as Drew began to talk again on a subject with which he was obviously well acquainted, and wondered what had been going on behind his eyes.

THIRTEEN

Rynne thought of the cat in the play group yard while the man was talking. She didn't know what a panther was, but she supposed when they kept talking about 'big cats' that it meant something like 'bad cat'—and since she knew kittens were little cats, then a grown-up cat must be a big cat, and probably nasty like the one that had scratched Bianca. Not all big cats were nasty, though—so this was all confusing; but in her mind, she was quite sure that the play group cat had paid Bianca back because her mother had been horrible.

Rynne was aware of something else, too; some kind of grown-up something that was going on in the community room while the man was giving his talk. It had to do with that other man, the one with the wavy hair and all the rings on his fingers. When her mum looked at him, sitting there like the cat that'd stolen the cream (that was something that Faye sometimes said), Rynne could feel her body go tense sitting next to her. And it was just the same thing with Faye sitting on the other side. The man doing the talking had also seemed stiff or something whenever the man spoke up. She didn't like the wavy-hair man.

The Big Cat talk was finished, which was good because Rynne's attention had wandered, and she was getting tired. Her mum seemed to have been very interested in the Big Cat man's talk, though; and had asked lots of questions. Everybody clapped lots, and now people were coming up to Mum on their way out and asking for autographs, further proof of how famous she was; and if Mum was famous then that must surely make her famous, too. As Mum smiled and signed, Rynne realized that the play group cat wasn't a bad cat after all. It was just paying back people for being jealous of other people who were famous. Or something. Faye began fussing her, fastening up her coat collar, even though it wasn't even cold outside. And now Mum was talking to that fair-haired man who had wanted an interview and Mum was saying, "Okay then, tomorrow morning before you catch your train," and Faye was smiling and saying "At last," and then promising to pick the man up from the pub so that she could drive him to their cottage for this interview thing. Rynne looked for the wavy hair, ring man—but he was gone in the bustle of people leaving the room, and now Mum was saying, "Sorry, excuse me," and pushing through the people to where the Big Cat man was talking to the two friends who had brought him in. Mum seemed really interested in the Big Cat man and now they were talking and smiling at each other, and when she looked at Faye there was a really funny look on her face. Just like she was really, really *glad* about something.

"I knew it," said Faye to herself. "I just knew it."

"Just knew what, Faye?" Rynne asked.

"Oh nothing, my love. Nothing at all."

"But it must be something. You can't not know nothing at all, 'cause then you wouldn't know it."

"My darling. You were born to be the daughter of a writer."

Rynne looked back to see that the Big Cat man's friends were still back there at the table with him and Mum, and they were laughing at some joke one of them had made or something. She pulled on Faye's hand.

"I need to tell him something."

"Why don't we leave them together for a moment?" Faye said, and when Rynne looked at her, there was a curious sort of smile on her face that she couldn't work out. "Just so they can talk for a while."

"Faye! I need to tell him something." Rynne dragged her back inside, pulling her by the hand all the way to the table.

"Mum?"

All eyes turned to her when they reached the table.

"Yes, darling?"

"Do I call him the Big Cat man or Drew or Mr. Hall?"

Everyone laughed, which made Rynne feel good even though she couldn't understand why they were laughing when she hadn't made a joke.

"What would you like to call me?" asked Drew.

"Dunno."

"Well why don't you call me by my first name—Drew?"

"Okay. I've got something to tell you, Drew."

"And what's that?"

"I know what these Big Cats are called."

"You do? What are they called, then?"

Rynne paused for dramatic effect.

"They're called . . ."

"Yes?"

"Ferocitors."

Drew made an impressed sound.

"Yeah, Ferocitors," Rynne went on. "Want to know where I got that from?"

"Bet I can guess," Cath said, hugging her daughter.

"Go on then."

"Velociraptors?"

"That's right!"

Mother and daughter laughed at the puzzled expression on Drew's face.

"My daughter has a special fondness for certain dinosaur movies. Velociraptors are bad-tempered, man-sized prehistoric monsters."

"Reptiles, Mum," corrected Rynne. "Prehistoric reptiles."

"I stand corrected," Cath said.

"I'm impressed," said Drew. "From now on, that's what they're called."

The crowd was thinning as folks made their way home.

"Come on now," Faye said. She seemed eager to get Rynne away, and Rynne could not understand why. "Let people say their goodbyes. I'll see you out at the car, Cath."

"See you, Rynne," Drew said.

"Bye. Remember—they're Ferocitors."

"They certainly are."

Faye bustled Rynne ahead, out through the community center door and into the car park. Mum was definitely acting different, but in a good way, even though

Rynne could not understand why. Grownups were just too complicated. Faye's car was parked outside the front of the community building, and Rynne watched as she stopped to fumble in her handbag for the keys. Rynne spun in a circle, for no other reason that it was good not to be sitting on a hard wooden chair for a long time—and in half-completed turn, she stopped dead.

The wavy-hair ring man was leaning against their car with his arms folded across his chest. He was smiling at her in a way that she didn't like at all. In that moment, for reasons she didn't understand, the man frightened her.

"Faye . . ."

"Yes, my love? Oh—where are those keys?"

"That man."

Mum and the Big Cat man had walked toward them, still talking lots—and Rynne heard Faye's deep breath being drawn in, like she was disgusted by something (further proof that the man must be really, really nasty). "Never mind him. Let's go home—I'll make a nice supper . . . if I can find those *keys!*"

The wavy-hair man pushed himself away from the car and walked slowly toward Mum and the Big Cat man. Rynne was alarmed. Something was wrong here, and she didn't like it. She broke away from Faye and ran to her mother.

"Rynne?" Still rummaging for the keys, Faye followed.

Rynne collided with her mother—grabbing her around the lower waist, Mum and the Big Cat man laughed. But that laughter was cut short when the wavy-hair ring man stopped in front of them with that smug look on his face. He was smiling at them all, but there was no humor in his eyes when he spoke.

"Interesting talk."

"I'm glad you thought so," Drew replied. "Cath, this is Mr. Dietersen."

"I thought so." Cath's smile was as broad, and with the same humorless return.

"Ms. Lane, I presume? Our famous, reclusive novelist." Dietersen spread his arms out. "Two local celebrities at the same event. Worth every penny."

Drew was not smiling at all. "I understood that admittance was free, Mr. Dietersen."

"That's right. No admittance fee. But the events here are not entirely free. I pay for the hire of the community room, you see. I have lots of interests and enterprises, including contributions to the cultural side of life in the village—which also includes the Nicolham Culture Club. Just my way of paying back into life for all the good things it's given me."

"Admirable," Drew said, as both he and Cath moved to join Faye at the car. Rynne was still clinging to her mother.

"Isn't it?" Dietersen stepped in their way. "I'm still new to the community, but I like to make my mark wherever I go. State my intention."

"And just what is your intention, Mr. Dietersen?" Drew's eyes had grown very cold.

"Well, since you clearly feel you can stroll up to my front door and lay the law down, I thought I might walk up to your doorstep, so to speak—and do the same."

"Lay down the law? What the hell are you talking about? I didn't come on heavily to you, Dietersen—and you know it."

"You turned up on my doorstep, and now I'm doing the same to you. You said you didn't want anything from me. I don't want anything either. You told me to be careful—well, now I'm telling *you* to be careful".

"Mr. Dietersen," said Faye, standing behind them all. Dietersen turned to see her tossing the car keys up and down in her hand. "You're just making yourself look like a twat."

Dietersen colored, turned to look back at Drew.

"Your face has gone funny," said Rynne.

"Just . . . just . . ." Dietersen had lost the moment. He turned to stalk away.

"What's a twat, Mummy?" Rynne asked.

Cath stroked her hair.

"It's something with outdated hair and bad dress sense," she said.

Drew could not suppress a bark of laughter.

Dietersen paused, back still to them—then stiffly continued on his way.

"Really, Cath," Faye said in mock outrage. "What kind of example are you setting?"

"I'm not the one with the bad mouth, madam," replied Cath.

"On the subject of mouths—let's all go and put something nice to eat in them. I recommend the Nicolham Tea Room. Are you hungry, Mr. Hall?"

"Well, I really . . . you know . . ."

"Nonsense," said Faye. "Everyone eats."

Drew shrugged, and smiled assent.

Faye nodded in the direction of Dietersen as he vanished around the side of the community building. "Fat cats—and Big Cats—all over the place, it seems. And I thought Nicolham was a place where nothing ever happened at all."

The adults laughed, and although she did not understand how things had turned from unpleasant to

FOURTEEN

Rynne climbed to the top of the stone wall behind the cottage and looked out across what Drew—the Big Cat man—had called the Fell. It was a funny word because she didn't know what had fallen, unless it was because all those green hills and brown trees and shrubs had fallen out of the sky, or something. Maybe that's what it was. She looked back to the window where her mum was working, and waved. She didn't expect a wave back. Sometimes when Mum was working on her book, she seemed to go inside herself and not notice stuff. That didn't matter, though, because Rynne never felt alone. Even when Mum was busy inside herself and Faye was shopping in the village, and Rynne was all alone— like now, on top of this wall—she never felt lonely. Not in the way that she sometimes thought her mum felt lonely, and there was nothing she could do about it. There had been times when she had seen something in her mother's eyes—when she wasn't working—that seemed lonely, and was troubling.

Maybe when she looked up from her play and found Mum looking at her with a sort of faraway stare, or sometimes looking out of the window but not really seeing anything. This was something grown up, she knew—and even at that age, she knew instinctively that she couldn't do anything to help, other than to love her mum.

Rynne thought back to the day in the play group when Bianca's mother had told her not play on the wall, and took pleasure in the fact that she was on this wall, and her mum wasn't even telling her to get down at all. She thought about the bad cat that had scratched her, and thought again that perhaps she had been wrong. The bad cat wasn't a bad cat—it had scratched Bianca for being mean (no doubt about it) and ever since that day Mum had started being friends with Drew the Big Cat man, things somehow had become—well, *better.* So that would mean the scratching cat was really a lucky cat—a good luck Cat. Rynne looked back to the study window, climbed to her feet on top of the stone wall, waved again and then jumped down to the other side away from the cottage. There was deep grass there, and she plunged through it—heading for the Fell and feeling good at the way that the grass parted before her.

It crouches, watches and waits.

The scent of its prey is strong for one so small. And although it has already eaten and has none of the hunger pain, that musk and the promise of living food so near makes its stomach churn and its jaws slaver. Belly low to the ground, it shifts and flexes its muscles. It will be easy to take this little one; easy to seize and rend and

*devour, to take the life and add to its own life. But this is
food for its own Little One.*

*It feels the breeze through the long grass in its face. It
lies instinctively downwind, and the prey is coming
through the long grass straight toward it, unaware that
it patiently waits. It shuffles again, its sleek black body
pressed down hard to the earth.*

Rynne paused in the long grass behind the cottage. It
was now high above her head, and she loved the feeling of being enclosed. If she wanted to, she could make
her own world here, a place where grownups could
only come if they were invited. When she looked up,
there were no clouds—just unbroken blue sky—and
that made her good feeling even better. She spun,
snatching at the thick green stalks and making a space
for herself. She remembered how Faye had told her
never to go too far from the cottage, watch out for the
Fell Road (which was where the wavy-hair ring man—
the "twat"—had made Drew the Big Cat man nearly
have a bad accident). But she wasn't too far away, was
she? She had made a sort of tunnel, all the way back to
the stone wall, and it would be easy to find her way
back when she wanted. But right now, she didn't want
to—and she plunged again into the deep grass, letting
the good feeling press her on.

*It could hear the prey coming now, through the long
grass—making its way straight toward it, unknowing. It
tensed, ready to make its killing run if the prey should
suddenly scent it, or veer away. There was movement
ahead now, the grass stalks moving as the prey came
on and . . .*

* * *

Rynne stopped.

Suddenly, she had a feeling that she wasn't alone. She looked around at the grass stems but could see nothing. There was a smell now, some kind of musky animal smell, and she didn't like it all. She looked back the way she had come and a growing sense of "wrongness" began to overwhelm her. There was a sort of tunnel through the grass behind, but as the grass slowly moved back into place, it didn't seem as clear or certain as she thought, and suddenly she knew that she was too far from the stone wall and the cottage, and what if that *wasn't* the way back after all? That smell was really strong now. Like a farm smell or something, and the secret place in the grass Rynne had embraced just moments ago suddenly seemed to be closing in around her. Somehow, although she could see nothing, she could sense there was danger here—a danger that somehow had something to do with that smell, which was overpowering now. She backed off, then turned—and as fear overwhelmed her in unreasoning panic, she began to run; clawing at the grass stalks as she plunged wildly back the way she had come.

The prey had sensed something, despite its stillness— and was fleeing from where the thing crouched.

With a shuddering growl, that which lay in wait launched itself forward through the long grass—a slithering black mass of muscle, fur and bone. The grass hissed around it as it saw the prey ahead, fleeing to escape. The food for the Little One looked back once in terror as it ran on ahead, but the black blur of fang and claw hurtled onward, jagging left and right as the prey tried to evade the death that was now upon it.

The food screamed once as it went down beneath the weight and velocity of the immense black predator. Claws raked and fastened in its back, rending the flesh in a crimson spurt that filled the predator with ecstasy as its jaws clamped into the twisting throat. The canine and incisors shore instantly through the windpipe as it twisted and wrenched the torn body from side to side. It tasted the death rattle, felt the shuddering passage of life as its claws sliced away the skin to expose the ribcage. Warm blood in its mouth provided the urge to devour, but the thing resisted the urge. This was food for the Little One. Savagely shaking its head again, the prey flapping and spasming, it took ecstatic pleasure in a final moment of stillness as the quivering ruin that hung dripping from its jaws became still.

Rynne screamed when she heard the horrible shrill cry from somewhere behind her; plunging back through the tunnel of grass, which was now no longer a safe play place, but a place of hidden terror. The stone wall was up ahead and she clawed to the top, throwing herself over and falling to her knees, still believing the hidden thing that had made that terrible sound was right behind her. Sobbing, she ran hard toward the cottage, imagining the hot breath of her pursuer on the back of her neck.

Now upwind, it tensed when it heard the cry—the rabbit dangling limply from its jaws. It caught the scent of the Two-Legs from somewhere up ahead. It snarled, a guttural rumbling that shook its ribcage. That sound was full of disdain, displeasure—and some fear—born from its natural aversion to this unnatural breed. The disgusting scent was of a small female Two-Legs, from the place of stones that the male Two-Legs had as lair.

And then it was gone, away into the long grass—and back to the place where its own Little One could feed.

FIFTEEN

The Welsh journalist sat in Cath's front room, finishing the last dregs of his coffee and trying to balance a notebook and tape recorder on his knee. They had been talking for half an hour, catching up on old times—and Cath was aware from the noises in the kitchen that Faye was pretending to be washing and tidying up without giving the impression of listening in, when in fact she was listening in.

"You all right in there, Faye!" Cath called in a voice calculated to startle. Faye cursed, nearly dropped a plate and attempted a nonchalant reply.

"I'm fine, I'm fine . . . anyone want more coffee?"

Cath looked at Matt, the journalist.

"Not for me, thanks. Three cups will be keeping me awake all the way to Cardiff."

"Mustn't miss your train," Faye called.

"Got the connections all worked out. Now—where was I?"

"Admirers and detractors," Cath said.

"Right. One of the things that fascinates me about

your work is a remark that some of your admirers—and I'm one—"

"Matt, you wouldn't be sitting there otherwise."

"Believe me, I'm really grateful. First interview you've given for—well, years. But this remark that some of your admirers have used, which is that you have the 'common touch' and never lost contact with your roots. They've used it as a compliment. But your detractors have used the same phrase—'common touch'—complaining that your narratives are still, and I'm quoting here again, 'still mired in inner-city areas.'"

"That sounds not so much like a critic who dislikes me, as someone who dislikes 'inner-city areas.' Nonsense."

"Maybe he or she just doesn't like reading about gritty, down-to-earth scenarios? I'm fascinated by the fact that your work as a 'thriller writer' has been lauded for the seriousness of its social concerns and its strong moral tone as much as it has been condemned for glorifying violence."

"I'm not so sure that either view is right," Cath said. "On the one hand, the positive side of what you've said suggests that I'm some kind of social, moral crusader—and I'm not. On the other hand—glorifying violence? Absolutely not."

"So how do you feel about the violence in your novels?"

"What do you mean, how do I feel?"

"Well are you comfortable with the fact that some of your critics have criticized the levels of violence in your books."

"Am I comfortable? Well I'm comfortable with the fact that the violence is an integral aspect to the narrative. I'm comfortable that it's not there as some kind of sadistic titillation—that if it's over the top, then its over the top for a reason. You won't find anything there that's unjustified in terms of how the plot and the characters develop."

"I'm with you one hundred percent there. I'm just wondering why some of the critics have responded so . . . well, violently."

"Matt, violence is shocking. It is horrible. And I've tried to show that. I suppose if anything, I've tried to deglamourize it. There's something specific about human violence, something squalid and horrible—that sets us a species completely apart. Animals kill for food, or to protect themselves or their young. Humans are the only animals that will kill or maim for the sake of it."

"Not sure I agree with you completely on that . . ."

"How do you mean?"

"Well—off the top of my head. We had a cat when I was younger. I saw it with a mouse it had caught. It played with it . . . no, that's not right . . . It *tortured* it before it killed it. We tried to take the poor thing away from it, but the damn cat scratched me. Now that's a little example—maybe a poor example, but still an example—of an animal just killing something for the fun of it."

"That's a domestic cat, not a cat in its natural environment. You want my view? The reason for that behavior? No offense to you or your family—but the reason for that incident was human in origin. An animal's been taken out of its environment, domesticated—tamed, if you like—so that it doesn't have to hunt for food, it's got as much tinned food as it could want, a dry place to sleep, probably petted and indulged. So it has no need to kill for food. But it still has that instinct to hunt. What's happened there is that the instinct has been—

well, I don't want to use the word 'perverted' because that seems a bit strong on you and your family—but it's certainly been bent and misshaped, just by soft living. And it's come out twisted. There you go—a theory according to Cath Lane, wannabe naturalist."

"What about the culture of violence in entertainment? The argument on whether violent novels or movies have a negative effect on society."

"I'm not even going there because the whole debate on desensitization has been chewed to death. In *real* terms, as opposed to fantasy or entertainment, I guess you could say that I'm appalled and fascinated by what people have called the culture of violence, particularly in inner-city areas—and my books have addressed the issue. I like to think that, as a decent human being who abhors violence, I could never bring myself to actually harm another human being."

"There are some who've said that there's money to be made from that kind of writing . . ."

"Yeah, right. That I've made a fortune out of writing about violence and misery and that with all the cash from film adaptations and TV series, I've sold out completely, moved out of the city to a comfortable rural life. I've read some of that crap. There are reasons—personal reasons—why I changed my lifestyle . . ."

"Because of what happened in New York?"

Cath became aware of a stillness in the kitchen.

"Yes."

The journalist was suddenly uncomfortable, not knowing how or whether to continue.

"It's all right, Matt. Go on."

"What happened then—something like that—something so random—it made me wonder if you'd changed your views at all."

"There's a difference between real life and fiction."

"But doesn't one inform or advise the other?"

"Well now we're into the question of writing as serious art, or as entertainment—and I guess that brings us straight back to the portrayal of violence in fiction, and to what purpose it's put."

The journalist smiled. "I'm starting to wonder whether you're a mystery wrapped up in an enigma."

Cath laughed. "Okay. Time to come clean. I admit it. My books—and the violence in them—are one of the root causes for all the problems we're faced with in society. There you are, Matt. You can blame me in your review for all the ills of society."

"Well it would make good copy . . ."

"What I've had to say in the past about my own books isn't a new stance. This is not earth-shaking revelation time. It's like I said before about glamourizing—and deglamourizing violence. Do I believe that glamourized violence in fiction causes problems in society? Well, greater minds than mine have debated that one on and off over the years. Maybe it desensitizes certain individuals; maybe it even encourages others to act out their fantasies. On the other hand, maybe very ordinary, decent and civilized people get some kind of catharsis out of it. That's an argument for psychiatrists and social workers. Violence is real and it's ugly and it's bestial. It exists—and there's a 'beast' in human beings that is so much more destructive than anything in the animal kingdom and leads to so much pain and misery. The cruel ferocity and sadism of our species goes much further than the wildest beast's kill-to-survive instinct. If any theme emerges from my previous books, it's the human struggle to overcome this savagery and rise above the animals. I don't know, maybe that's a contradiction in terms. 'Rising above the animals'—when animals are less violent than humankind. There you are, Matt. How's that for a contradictory and convoluted stance? See what your editorial skills can make of our conversation."

When Cath had waved off the journalist from the courtyard of the cottage, she turned and caught Faye watching from the kitchen window. With a wry smile, she walked back; her body language indicating that she had issues she wished to raise with her. Faye vanished hurriedly from sight.

"Fayyye . . ." Cath called as she walked through the front door and into the living room.

"You're going to tell me off," came a voice from the kitchen. "I know you're going to tell me off. . . ."

"Now what possible reason could I have for telling you off?"

"I don't know . . . I mean, well yes . . . I suppose I have been . . ."

"Economical with the truth? How's that for starters?"

"I really don't know what you mean. Look, I must get the rest of those groceries in before the local store closes so I'll just . . ."

"Only about 'a dozen or so' at the Culture Club. Wasn't that what you said?"

"Milk. I think we need milk. And eggs . . ."

Cath leaned in the kitchen doorway, arms folded. Faye tried not to look agitated. "And it just so happened that Drew Hall was also invited. And then somehow we all end up having a meal together."

"It was a nice meal."

"It was a lovely meal."

"Just a shame that horrid Kapler Dietersen turned up to make trouble."

"Now that's one part of the whole affair that I believe you *didn't* organize. Did you know that journalist was going to be there?"

Faye paused, straightened her dress, fiddled with a lock of hair behind her ear. They were somehow very young gestures, and Cath couldn't help smiling at her discomfiture.

"Well . . . yes. Yes, I did! He telephoned one day when you were out. I don't know how he got the number, but he did. And well, I'd already persuaded you to give the talk, so I just mentioned that—and he seemed very interested, and I said it was open to the public and if he wanted to come along, then no one could stop him, of course . . ."

"Fayyye . . . ?"

"Oh all right—I suppose I did fix it. And yes, I asked Drew to come along and give his talk. But you know, he's very like you in lots of ways, and he—well . . . I've known him a long time—and he *needs* to be mixing with people again. He's too alone."

"And you think I'm too alone?"

"Well, yes, darling—I do think you're too alone. I know you're different from other people . . ."

"Do I take that as a compliment?"

"Yes, you should—because I mean it that way. You're different, but there are times I can see that you're suffering, and I think that just being alone and just working—well, it's all right for a while. But not all the time."

"So you thought you'd be a matchmaker for two lonely people?"

"Oh God—it does look like that, doesn't it?"

"Come here, you." Cath moved to take Faye in her arms, hugging her tight.

"I'm sorry, Cath. I really am an interfering old busybody, aren't I?"

"Yes, you bloody are. But I love you. And I don't know what Rynne and I would have done without you. There you go. Clichés again." When Cath pulled back to look at Faye, she could see that there were tears on her cheeks. "Now, none of that. Or you'll have me blubbering all over the place."

Faye pulled a handkerchief from her sleeve, dabbed her eyes and blew her nose.

"No more interfering. I promise."

"How's Rynne?"

"Napping. She's fine, though."

"Whatever happened on the other side of the wall, it gave her a nasty fright. What do you think she heard?"

"Maybe a sparrow hawk. Who knows? After the talking-to you gave her, I don't suppose she'll be climbing over that wall again."

The telephone rang in the hallway.

Cath looked at it, then back at Faye with one eyebrow raised. Faye held her hands up and turned back into the kitchen.

"If that's another journalist . . ." Cath said.

"I've learned my lesson," Faye called, as she busied herself with unnecessary chores, rearranging plates and cups.

Cath moved to answer. "I'm going to lose my reputation as reclusive novelist, thanks to you. All the mystery will go away and . . . Hello?"

Back in the kitchen, Faye strained to listen—now puzzling at the silence. She picked up a cloth, began wiping a plate that did not need wiping, and moved to the door into the hall. Cath's face was very serious as she listened to whoever was on the other end of the line.

"Slow down," Cath said. "Slow down—and tell me again. . . ." She looked up and caught Faye's eye.

"Who is it?" whispered Faye.

"All right—well yes, I think so. Now? Okay—I'll have to check but . . ."

"Who is it?" Faye mouthed again.

"Just a second, Drew. I'll have to ask Faye."

"Drew? Something's wrong," Faye said.

"Faye, can you stay a little later tonight? To look after Rynne?"

"Well, yes, love. I've no plans. What is it, what's . . . ?"

"Drew wants me to go down to the farm. He's got something to show me."

Faye smiled. Cath put her hand over the mouthpiece and gave her a warning look. There was nothing light-hearted about it now, and Faye wiped that smile away.

"You go on ahead. I'll stay and hold the fort."

"You don't mind?"

"Do I ever mind?"

"Faye, I don't know what . . ."

"I know, I know. Cliché time. You don't know what you'd do without me."

Cath looked at her watch. "All right, I'll be with you in about—fifteen minutes? Up at the farm. Gate locked or open? Open? Okay, then—fifteen minutes. Do I need to bring anything? Okay."

Cath hung up and stared at the telephone for a moment, chewing her bottom lip. Faye didn't know whether to break the silence or not.

"He sounded—strange," Cath said at last. "Wouldn't

tell me what it's all about. But he was excited. Breathless even."

"Doesn't sound like the Drew I know," Faye said. "Big Cat. Bet he's seen one of his Ferocitors."

"Maybe. But the way he sounded . . . I don't know. Odd. He said there might be something there that I'd want to write about. Are you sure about this, Faye? I don't want you to think I'm taking advantage of you."

"Let's just say that I've been a naughty girl, and I owe you one. You go on ahead, and take your time. I'm happy to stay. I'll tell Rynne where you are when she wakes up."

Cath kissed her, grabbed her bag from the hallway stand and was gone. Faye moved back to the kitchen, watched as she climbed into the car. Moments later, the car engine gunned into life and in a crunch of gravel and screech of tires, Cath was gone down the Fell Road.

Faye's big smile was like the cat that had gotten the cream.

"I do love it when things come together," she said, and put the plate in its proper place in the rack.

SIXTEEN

"If you hit me, Kapler, you'll be sorry!"

"Is that a threat, darling?"

"Why do you have to be so mean?" Trudi flinched away from under Dietersen's raised hand and flung herself across the sofa in his study. The maneuver snapped one of her stiletto heels and she wobbled as she fell, taking the edge off the drama of her fall. "Shit!" She yanked the shoe from her foot and flung it across the room. It rattled against the interior door, spinning on the carpet.

Dietersen lowered his hands to his sides and clenched both fists. A nerve was twitching in his jaw.

"If not for you . . ."

There was a knock on the door from the other side. Gingerly, it began to open. Garvey nervously began to put his head around.

"Mr. Dietersen?"

"GET OUT!"

The door quickly shut, and Dietersen turned his attention back to Trudi.

"If not for you and your road-racing skills—or lack of them—then I wouldn't have to be humiliated in my own house."

"It's that bloody farmer again, isn't it? Why are you letting him get under your skin?"

"I am not letting him get under my skin."

"Look at yourself, Kapler."

"You don't understand, Trudi. There are—there are a lot of things happening at the moment. Business-wise, I mean. And the last thing I need is hassle—of any kind. So when you start pissing about . . ."

"I get bored. . . ."

"When you start *pissing* about! And when fucking yokels start turning up at my front door to complain, when I've got sensitive business issues at stake—it gets my goat, darling. Now do you understand?"

"I'm bored, Kapler. Bored!"

"I'll cure you of that darling." Dietersen began to unfasten his trouser belt, knotting it around one hand. "See if I don't." He took a step toward her.

The intercom on Dietersen's desk buzzed. Growling, suddenly aware of his lack of control, he turned back angrily to it; rethreading his belt around his waist as he stabbed the Listen button.

"What!"

"I'm terribly sorry to interrupt again, Mr. Dietersen. But there's a gentleman here who says he has an appointment to see you."

"Is his name Fuller?"

"Yes, sir."

"Let him in. Take him to the library." Dietersen jabbed the Off switch, snatched up a decanter and poured himself a large shot of bourbon, glaring back at Trudi, who had straightened herself on the sofa—realizing once again just how close to the edge she had come. She was pretending a teenage sulk, but Kapler clearly wasn't now in the mood for one his favorite sex-fantasy reconciliations.

"Kapler, why don't we . . . ?"

"*Don't* say a word! Just listen. I've got an important business meeting with our visitor. We don't want to be interrupted for any reason. Do you understand? It's now three o'clock. In exactly three-quarters of an hour—that's forty-five minutes from now, you can't miss it, darling—the big hand will be on the nine and the little hand will be on the four of the fucking expensive watch I bought you last week. When it gets to that time, *then* you can interrupt us. You will knock on the library door with that expensively manicured hand of yours—trying not to break the nails—and you will come in when I say 'come in.' Do you understand so far, darling?"

Trudi nodded.

"Then you will come in, looking just as pretty as you can—and when I say so, you will give our gentleman caller whatever he wants. Do you *understand*, Trudi? Whatever it is that he wants you to do for him—you'll do it. Understand?"

"Yes, Kapler. Then will you be nice to me again?"

"If you're a very good girl, and do just exactly what's required of you."

"All right, Kapler. I'll be a good girl."

"That's right—a very, *very* good girl."

Dietersen finished his bourbon, tightened his belt and rearranged his jacket.

"Business first—then pleasure. Right, darling?"

Trudi nodded.

Just before Kapler left the room, he looked back at her—and emphatically tapped his wristwatch.

When the door closed, Trudi feared to weep—lest her mascara should run.

SEVENTEEN

When Cath reached the farm, she could see that Drew had left the main gates open as he'd said. But there was no sign of him waiting as her car turned up the rough track that led to the main building, pens and outhouses. She'd somehow expected the place to be smaller, given that he was running a one-man operation. But there were large empty pens at one side of the main farmhouse that looked as if they hadn't held stock for quite some time. One of the barns to the rear of the farmhouse was missing its roof, and its interior looked ruined and dilapidated. Cath remembered what Faye had told her about Drew's wife—the terrible accident—and his subsequent withdrawal from life. She could understand that. The haphazard nature of the farmhouse and buildings suggested that the place's days as a real working farm were well behind it.

She stopped outside the farmhouse and honked the car horn.

Invisible hens squawked, but there was no sign of movement from the house. Cath was just about to climb out when she heard an answering car horn. She looked around, but could see nothing. When the horn sounded again, she looked up the dirt track ahead that led up the valley side—and saw Drew's Land Rover parked on the rise. As she watched, he climbed out of it and began to wave.

Cath drove on ahead, past another ramshackle barn with wrecked front doors held in place by an iron chain. Through the wooden slats of the barn door she could just make out the shape of a giant, hulking piece of machinery. A combine harvester, by the looks of it—long retired. She looked around as she drove and could see no evidence of the need for such a piece of machinery.

Drew was hurrying toward her, even before she had stopped the car.

There was real excitement on his face as he held the car door open and she climbed out.

"Thanks for coming."

"How could I resist? I think you've got more of a flair for the dramatic than I have."

"Come on."

"Where?"

"Up ahead. It's not far."

Cath followed as he led the way, waiting for him to say more. When they drew level with the Land Rover, Drew stopped and leaned against it—his gaze fixed on the side of the valley about a hundred feet from them. The area was covered in dense bushes. Cath followed his gaze and could see nothing. She turned a wry smile to Drew as she waited for him to speak. Her attention was drawn to something on the backseat of the Land Rover. There was a long pause as Drew stared. Finally, leaning casually against the vehicle with arms crossed, Cath said:

"So, are you going to tell me why you've got a rifle in the back of the Land Rover?"

"It's not a rifle."

"Well, it looks like a rifle to me, Drew. Are you sure you're allowed to have that?"

"I've got a shotgun licence. Most farmers have."

"That's not a shotgun."

"And it's not a rifle—it's a specialist tranquilizer gun. But it does *look* like a rifle, I'll give you that," he said.

"I was right."

"Right?"

"We both seem to have a flair for the dramatic. But at the moment, you seem to have the edge over me."

"You asked me some questions that night. When we were giving our talks—and then later, you tried again when we all went for that meal." Cath could see that there was sweat on Drew's brow, a glistening of contained excitement in his eyes. He paused again.

"I'm still listening," she said.

"You said you felt there might be things I was holding back on."

"Were you?"

"Yes."

"Drew, if you pause again, I'm going to have to hit you."

"Well, I told them—told you—that one of the things that the press and the media tend to seize on with this Big Cat thing is The Hound of the Baskervilles scenario. You know, mysterious unknown creature wandering the moors—always eluding capture. How come one's never been caught? All that stuff."

"You demystified it. Very well, I thought."

"Well, that's just it. Everything I said—I believe it all. The legislation that made it illegal to keep wild animals as pets. Owners just letting them loose, all of it."

"There's a 'but' coming. I can sense it."

"But there *is* something more to it than that. I told you that I came face to face with a Big Cat on my farm. But I didn't tell you everything that I felt, everything that I experienced back then. I was so close to this damned thing that it could have torn me apart. Why it didn't, I'll never know. And crazy though this might sound—there was something about this thing. Something *different*. Don't know if I can explain it properly, and I know that when—when you're in danger . . . in terror—things can happen to your mind. You maybe see things—not as they are. Do you know what I mean?"

"Yes, I do, Drew."

"But it wasn't like that when I came face to face with this thing. I knew—just *knew* that there was something different about this Big Cat. Not a panther, not a puma—not even a hybrid. Just something else. I know that sounds crazy. But then, as time went by and I became more aware of the evidence of these things on my land—and on the surrounding land—it was impossible to ignore that evidence, and I just became more and more overwhelmed by trying to find one of them. Because there's a pride living out here. I know it."

Drew paused again. His thoughts had consumed him again.

"Drew!"

"Sorry—" Drew exhaled loudly, trying to find the right words. "What I'm trying to say is—it may well be some kind of crossbreed that no one's come across before. I've laid traps, set up cameras, everything. But these cats—well, they've got an uncanny ability to evade detection, and sometimes, just sometimes, a ferocity unequaled by any other Big Cat I've learned about."

"So actually what you're saying here is—well, that the press and media *have* got it right." Cath could not keep the wry tone out of her voice when she spoke again. "That we're dealing with something that *is* like The Hound of the Baskervilles after all—except that it's a *cat?*"

"Yes . . . no . . . I don't know. I just know that there's nothing *supernatural* about it. They're just—different."

"So you've got a bloody big rifle, gun, tranquilizer thingie in the back of the vehicle and something that may or may not be The Hound of the Baskervilles is out there somewhere. And you've called me out to your farm—but you still haven't told me why I'm here."

"I'm glad you came."

"Do you know how to use that thing?" Cath asked, looking to the backseat.

"I've already used it."

Cath looked hard at him. Drew's expression was fixed on the slope and bushes above again. When he snatched a glance back at her, there was a puzzling expression on his face. Something of humor, something of resolve—and something in his eyes that looked like elation and fear.

"Sometimes you spend your life looking for something and can't find it. And yet it's right on your own doorstep all the time. Right under your nose. The moment that you *don't* look for it—it comes and finds *you*. See the fence up there, just before that undergrowth? I was up there, digging. Been thinking about planting pear trees but—well, I don't know. Maybe that's a fool's errand—anyway, I was digging.

"When I turned, there it was—in the bracken, watching me. Obscured, so I couldn't see all of it. But it was . . ." Drew struggled to find the words, and couldn't find them. "I always keep the tranquilizer gun in the back, just in case. I slowly walked back to the Land Rover and—well, after everything that's happened, I was convinced that by the time I got it out and primed it, the animal would be gone. It wasn't. It was still there. It had moved, was still obscured and—Christ, I think it might have been *stalking* me. But this is the thing . . ." Drew was struggling again with the words.

"Go on."

"You can see that the bushes and bracken on that side of the hill isn't that dense. Enough to provide cover for birds or smaller mammals. But not enough to provide cover for an animal that size. This Big Cat—puma, panther, whatever—is *black*. I should have been able to see it at that range—maybe twenty-five yards—in such sparse cover. But I couldn't, Cath. I couldn't see it properly as it moved." The quiver of excitement in Drew's voice raised the hair on the back of Cath's neck. "There's something—I don't know what—but there was something going on. Some kind of camouflage effect that I just couldn't work out. *I couldn't see it properly, Cath!*"

"You said you used the gun."

Drew nodded. There was sweat on his brow again.

"One shot. Snapped it off."

"And you hit it?"

"Yep. I heard the thing cry out. Then it was gone up the hill. Couldn't see it properly—just the bracken and the bushes flailing about. I followed. And I know where it's gone. It's holed up in what I think is its lair. A small fissure, not even big enough to call a cave—and I've looked in that place hundreds of times. Never been any sign, any evidence—so I guess they must have just moved in there recently. Here I am, hunting high and low for these things—and they've moved in right next door to me, in sight of the cottage. Hiding in plain sight!"

"Look, Drew. Is this safe? I mean—shouldn't we be telling someone. The police, or . . ."

"No! Sorry—I didn't mean to snap at you. No, Cath. I promise you that it's safe. The drug in that dart will have worked by now. These are big animals, and it takes time for it to take effect. I rang you just after I'd taken the shot, it's taken you twenty minutes or so to get here—so by now, that thing will be completely knocked out. Completely sedated."

"So what do we do now?"

Drew made a back-thumb gesture to the seat behind him. On that seat, next to the tranquilizer gun was a camera in its case.

"I take photographs. Measurements. Get the evidence I need. Then we leave it. Let it get on with its life. And I—we—get on with ours. That's all I've ever wanted—real evidence that these things exist. If we got the police involved—the authorities—then who knows what would happen. People swarming all over the place. Maybe ruining the habitat for them and us."

"You make this sound so—personal."

"It is. Always has been."

"I was right."

"Right?"

"When it comes to dramatic flair, you definitely have the edge over me."

"Maybe something new for you to write about now?"

"I've a feeling that the manuscript I've been struggling with these past few months is going into the garbage bin."

"What do you say, then? You want to be a part of this adventure?"

"Just don't get us killed, Drew. I've a daughter and an interfering housekeeper-companion to support."

Drew grinned, and led the way up ahead to the gorse bushes.

EIGHTEEN

When the door had closed and Trudi had gone, Dietersen made a mental note to discuss the question of attitude with her when his business associate had gone. She had done as instructed, and done it well enough—but the smile wasn't real. In business and in life, Dietersen had always championed the philosophy that you should always be honest, even if you had to fake it—and when he'd given Trudi her instructions, he'd expected nothing less than full acquiescence and an expression of real joy in the task. Not that his associate had noticed it, but Dietersen had sensed the less-than-happy look in her eyes and later, she would suffer for it.

Bobby Fuller—Dietersen's associate—readjusted his fly zip and reached for the brandy glass again. One designer-jeaned leg hung over the armrest of the leather armchair, Fuller grinned and revealed a gold front tooth. He wriggled in the chair like the twenty-year-old kid he really was, reveling in exaggerated comfort, the leather of his jacket squeaking against the leather of the chair.

"I like your hospitality, Kapler." The accent was Northern Irish. "You know how to treat your guests."

"Nothing but the best for you, Bobby. As always."

Fuller gestured to the three black suitcases he had brought in with him, standing by the drinks cabinet.

"Want to check out the goods?"

Kapler nodded.

Fuller pulled himself from the chair, with more exaggeration at relinquishing such luxury and moved to one of the suitcases. Hefting it to a nearby table, he took a key from his jacket pocket; made a theatrical show of opening both locks, flipped the hasps and made a bowed: "Ta-dahhh!"

Dietersen moved to the suitcase, hefted a plastic bag of white powder and looked back as Fuller returned to his seat and his drink. "This is where I'm supposed to cut a little hole, lick a finger, dip it in and check it out. Right?"

"If you like."

"No, I don't like. I'll like it even less, Bobby, if there's other white stuff that shouldn't be."

"Mr. Dietersen—Kapler—we've done business before. You know my connections. Have I ever been unprofessional before?"

"Never had a deal as big as this before, Bobby."

"You're starting to hurt my feelings."

Dietersen moved to the other side of the drinks cabinet, opened a hidden cupboard and took out what appeared to be a Gladstone bag. Hefting it next to the suitcase on the table, he opened it and smiled. Bobby finished his drink, "pinged" the glass with a finger and gave another look of exaggerated hopefulness at Dietersen when he looked over.

"Help yourself," said Dietersen. When he reached into the Gladstone bag, there was a tinkle of glass vials.

"Great taste in brandy, Kapler." Fuller poured a full glass. "And women. Any chance of a—you know—return visit from Trudi before we complete our transaction?"

"You just concentrate on the happy chemicals from that brandy bottle. I'll concentrate on the chemicals from this bag that will tell me whether we can conclude our business—then we'll see about other arrangements."

"Businessman, ladies man—and a chemist as well, Kapler?"

Dietersen gave a grin like a shark. "I've found that having more than one string to my bow has seen me through."

Fuller was unfazed and confident.

There was a knock at the door.

"Kapler?" It was Trudi.

Enraged, Dietersen's shark grin had turned into something altogether more ferocious. Spittle flew when he snapped: "I *told* you! No interruptions until we're finished in here."

"Please, Kapler . . ."

"Hey, man. Let her in. I can use some more company."

"Not until we're *finished!*"

The door crashed open, and when Trudi was propelled into the living room to land between Fuller's legs, there was blood on her back, blood on her face—and the glass-eye doll look of death in her eyes.

"Oh you're *finished* all right," said a voice from the doorway.

NINETEEN

"It's in there," Drew said. "I know it's still in there. . . ."

Cath drew closer to him, peering through the long grass ahead. The ragged aperture in the side of the hill was perfectly camouflaged by the fissuring of rock. It was only when they were almost upon it that it became apparent there was a cave entrance of sorts here—if cave it could be called in this sloping hillside. There was a rope net across that fissure, pegged into the rock and the surrounding grass slope. Cath looked back at Drew and the intensity of his expression. She had refrained from asking any more questions, had struggled to keep up with him as they climbed to their vantage point; scrub and bushes masking the rock and the aperture.

"So what happens now?"

"There's another entrance, or exit, to the cave there. About sixty or seventy feet around by those bushes. I've blocked it—wedged some boarding I had in the back of the Land Rover across it. The net here hasn't been sprung, and if that boarding is intact around the back, then it must still be in there."

"What do you mean—if the net hasn't been *sprung?*"

"The net's not fixed. It's a trap. If anything hits it with any degree of force, either from the outside or the inside, then those clamps do their work. See them there?"

Cath followed his pointing finger and saw the dull glint of mental hasps or stanchion fastenings in the fissured rock around the entrance and in the ground at the base of the cave.

"Those clamps are sprung—the net instantly contracts and wraps around whatever hit it. Then the cat is in the bag! So it hasn't sprung, which is good. Let's check the back."

They made their way around the side of the hill. A wind had begun to rise, ruffling the bushes and gorse. Cath couldn't shake the feeling that this was somehow nature's way of saying that they shouldn't be here. Suddenly, she began to feel ridiculous—less than an hour ago she'd been at home; now here she was on a big-game hunt in the middle of the English countryside. She laughed as they moved, and Drew looked back quizzically.

"Could have used that net on Kapler Dietersen," she said.

"Don't think anyone could net something as slippery as that."

When Drew shoved aside a dense patch of undergrowth and gorse, Cath saw the boarding he had jammed into the rock on the hillside. The gap that it was covering was barely large enough for a Big Cat or a human to squeeze through. She pushed on after him. Drew yanked the boarding out, and as he did so she could hear a dull and hollow echoing from this fissure, like the sound of a deep well—evidence of the cave beyond.

"With the noise we're making," Drew said, "if that cat was still awake, we'd know about it by now." He discarded the boarding into the bushes. Cath could feel cold air coming from the gap. Drew pulled a flashlight from his belt, switched it on and leaned forward—shining it inside the gap.

"You got the camera?"

"Yes."

"I'm going in. You still up for this?"

"Drew?"

"Yes?"

"What if there are other—things—in there? Other Big Cats, I mean. I'm not an expert—like you—but isn't this a bit like, well, going into the lion's den?"

"Believe me, if there were another cat in here we'd already know about it."

"Shouldn't we be *armed,* or something . . ."

But it was too late. Drew had already squeezed through the aperture into the darkness.

"Oh God—what on earth am I *doing?*" hissed Cath.

And in the next moment, she squeezed into the darkness after him.

Drew's beam criss-crossed the darkness, and Cath could see that the cave was not large. They were on an incline here, leading down into the hillside—but already it was possible to see daylight shining in through the entrance on the other side; the criss-cross shadow of the net on the ragged stone and damp earth ahead. There were loose stones and pebbles beneath their feet, and when Drew stumbled and grabbed for a

119

handhold, the torch beam swung crazily. Cath grabbed for his arm, and as he righted himself—they both became aware of the smell.

"Oh God," Cath said, gagging: "What on earth is *that?*"

"Big Cat musk," said Drew. "They *have* been using this place for a den. I can't believe it. I was in here— oh, maybe three weeks ago—and they'd never been in here before. But that musk tells me they must have moved in shortly after I'd searched the place."

"Drew, if there's a *live* one in here . . ."

Drew had rounded a ridge of rock and moss and was bathed in daylight from the other entrance. Cath saw the look of frustration and weariness on his face as he switched off the light and jammed it into his belt. He bent double, exhaling—looking like someone who had just finished a sprint.

"What is it?"

"I don't believe it . . ."

"What?"

Drew pointed ahead and up, beyond Cath's line of vision—and when she rounded the ridge, blinking at the sunlight, she followed his pointing finger.

On the other side of the ridge was a shale incline, leading to what amounted to a ragged chimney of rock, leading up and away from the cave. Loose stone and clumps of grass and earth were scattered on that slope and at the top of that chimney-incline, thirty feet from where they stood, more daylight was shining down on them from a small aperture fringed by grass.

"That wasn't here last time," Drew said wearily.

Cath looked at the unbroken net in the main entrance, still secured.

"It got out up there," she said.

Drew yanked the flashlight from his belt again, shining it cursorily around the cave, checking the darkened corners. The space was too small to hide any animal lying in the debris of rock, shale and earth.

"Yep." He sounded deeply crestfallen. "It scrabbled up there, and clawed its way out. See all the loose rock and those fresh clods of earth and grass. They came from ground level on the hillside up there. Must have sensed a draft of air coming down. Damn it! These things manage to stay one step ahead of me every time."

Cath moved to put a hand on his shoulder, also feeling his keen sense of disappointment—and stepped on something soft in the darkness.

Something shrieked and hissed—filling the cave with a sound of terror and rage.

And Cath screamed as that something attached to her leg and she staggered back at Drew. He clutched at her, dropping the torch, and the thing adjusted its grip on the fabric of Cath's jeans—a razor claw slashing at her boot, slicing the leather clean through to her ankle. They fell against the dark side of the ridge, Cath frantically kicking out at the weight on her left. Drew snatched at her in the darkness, suddenly had two handfuls of fur and yanked hard. The shrieking and spitting reached a new edge of ferocity as Drew yanked again.

The thing came free of Cath's boot, taking strips of leather with it. Something wickedly sharp had snagged in the seam of her jeans and when Drew dragged the weight of it from her, the seam snagged and tore— ripping the denim away in a clean slice ten inches long. Cath heard Drew's grunt of exertion as he flung whatever it was away from them into the cave, and as they both staggered involuntarily into the light cast by the main entrance, they saw the thing bolt out of the darkness across the lightened cave floor in a flurry of fur and manic rage, the strip of denim tangled in it.

The thing—too small to be a Big Cat—raced lopsided in a hissing tangle of fury away from them, moving too rapidly to be seen properly. In a blur of motion, it ran for the light—and straight into the net across the cave entrance. Instantly entangled, it thrashed and struck and hissed—each strike, each slashing blow entangling it further. Claws locked and knotted in the rope. A long, loud hiss—like a release of steam, but with an edge of fury that was chilling—and when that hissing had been fully expressed, there was another sound: a *yowl* that began low and threatening and now was rising in pitch to a caterwaul of pure hate that filled the cave.

Cath and Drew stood in the light and watched as the animal ceased to struggle; now hanging in the net above the ground, as if caught in some web.

It watched them with gleaming opal eyes. Utterly motionless, those eyes shone with what seemed to be a mixture of calculating awareness, fear and hate—waiting for their next move.

"Christ," said Drew.

"That's your Big Cat?" Cath asked incredulously. The black cat was about two feet long and a foot high, with a jet black, shiny coat—and with features that were clearly those of a panther, but not The Hound of the Baskervilles creature that she had been led to expect. There were two small streaks of white fur above each of the cub's eyes.

"Sort of," Drew said.

"Your net didn't spring."

"No . . ." Drew couldn't take his eyes off the cub.

Cath looked at him, then down at her leg. Miraculously, despite her ripped denim jeans and the chunk sliced from her boot, she was uninjured. Drew dropped to his haunches and quickly checked her out when he saw the damage.

"It's fine," Cath said. "It didn't get the skin. What do you mean—'sort of'?"

Drew looked back, took a step forward toward the net—and then stopped again when the animal began another furious struggling. It writhed and twisted, yowling with a sound that was both fear and threat. When it ceased again, exhausted, Drew said:

"It's a cub—a Big Cat cub. Maybe three months old. They're breeding out here—just like I always said."

"What are we going to do?"

Drew edged closer to the net, prompting the cub into another frenzied struggle—fangs bared and hissing.

"Let me have the camera."

Cath passed it, and Drew took off the casing—adjusting the lens and flash.

"Well, Mum and/or Dad is somewhere sleeping off the tranquilizer. The other parent isn't around, but could be due back. So I guess we have to free Junior—keep out of his way, and then find somewhere to wait for the big'uns coming back. But first . . ."

Drew began snapping off shots of the cub, the interior of the cave seeming to leap and dance in the flash. The light sent the cub into new paroxysms of frenzy as it lunged and thrashed in the net that still, despite Drew's confident description of its effectiveness, had not 'sprung.' Cath supposed that even wannabe big game hunters got it wrong sometimes, and watched in fascination. There was a new gleam in

Drew's eyes that she hadn't seen before. This was the evidence he had been so desperately seeking for so many years and—not for the first time—she wondered what the search itself was actually all about, and whether there were other reasons for his obsession in finding these Big Cats.

"That's it," Drew said at last. "That'll have to do. I don't want it getting any more stressed than it is now. It might hurt itself."

"Best untangle it from the other side of the net," Cath said. "Once it's loose again, we might want to have that net between us and it." She gestured to her ripped jeans leg and boot. "Next time mightn't be so lucky."

Drew smiled. "You've got a hunter's instincts."

"When it comes to avoiding personal damage or injury—I'm an expert."

Drew saw something else when she spoke, something that made her wince at her own words. "Come on," he said, guiding her toward the rear entrance of the cave. "I'll need some heavy-duty gloves from the Land Rover, and something to cut the net. It's got those claws well and truly stuck."

Half expecting one or other of the Big Cats to be waiting for them there, Cath allowed herself to be led back into the sunlight. Drew quickly jammed the boarding into the aperture, kicking down hard on it and jamming it into the fissure. He staggered back; momentarily off-balance—and Cath proffered a steadying hand. Drew took it, smiled—

And in the next moment, Cath had reached to touch his face.

"I guess my improvised net just doesn't work," he said, smiling. "Thanks for not saying anything."

"Maybe you're trying to catch the wrong thing."

Cath hadn't meant to say anything, hadn't meant to use those words that seemed clumsy to her ears but which she'd expressed instinctively in a way that now startled her in their meaning.

Drew's arm was suddenly and gently around her waist.

Their embrace was urgent, their kisses hungry.

When Cath pulled away, she was breathless and unsteady.

"I'm sorry," Drew said, now not knowing where to look.

"Why?"

"I don't know."

"I didn't know how much I wanted to do that," she said.

"Cath. I shouldn't . . ."

When she looked into his eyes again, there was pain. He seemed about to say something else; something that he'd hidden deep inside himself for a long time, but had been unable to release.

"It's all right, Drew."

"I wanted . . ."

"Drew, it's okay. . . ."

"The cub," he said at last. "We can't leave it like that. It'll get hurt."

And now Drew was striding off, around the ridge toward the main cave entrance. Cath followed, watching as he hurried down the slope toward the Land Rover. She watched him go, and wondered at what had just happened. Part of her wondered whether it had really happened at all. Somehow, that wintry morning in New York and that terrible blood-stained sidewalk seemed a long, long way away. Part of her wanted to cling to it; part of her never wanted it to go away, but an equal part lived in mourning and in fear of it. The contradiction was crushing. Cath knew that she had never properly mourned for her husband; knew she was still clinging to the memory of him. This was the reason why she couldn't work and why the new novel just wouldn't come. She was frozen; still rooted to that cold and dreadful morning when the man in the woolen cap had demanded their money.

Cath watched Drew yank open the Land Rover door, saw him rummaging in the tool kit on the backseat, watched him sprinting back up the slope. She realized how vulnerable he was too, dealing with his own grief. Was that why she was so attracted to him? Was that a good reason for what she realized now was such a strong attraction? Could two fractured people make themselves whole, or was this a foolish and dangerous situation in which to become embroiled?

She moved to meet him as he came, watched as he pulled on the heavy-duty gloves. There were pliers in his back pocket, for the netting, and now it seemed as if he couldn't bring himself to look her in the eyes. Was he really trying to pretend that what had just happened had never taken place at all? Unsure, vulnerable and struggling to come to terms with these conflicting feelings, Cath followed him around the ridge to the main cave entrance.

The cub was still entangled in the netting, and it began a renewed and frenzied attempt to free itself when it saw them approaching through the bushes.

"Cath." When Drew spoke, it seemed as if he was still trying to avoid her eyes. "If I get it by the scruff of the neck and force its head down—show you where to cut—do you think you could manage the pliers?" He fumbled the pliers from his back pocket and handed them to her as they drew level with the cave entrance and the struggling cat. She took the proffered hand and held it with both of hers—not allowing him to pull away. This time he looked her full in the eyes.

"It's all right, Drew," she said.

"It is?"

"Yes."

He placed his free hand on hers and squeezed. "It's just—it's been such a long time, that's all."

"I understand."

When he smiled, it was as if a shadow had come and passed—and Cath knew that there would be time later to understand what had just happened between them.

"Come on then, kitty!" Cath knelt down before the netting. "Let's get you sorted out."

Drew crouched beside her, pulling the gloves on tighter. Slowly he reached out his left hand toward the animal. It saw the hand coming, thrashed and squirmed. When it hissed, Cath felt a fine mist of spray from the animal's mouth, winced at the fetid animal smell. When it arched its body away from that approaching hand, Cath almost cried out in surprise when Drew's right hand suddenly flashed out and caught the cub by the scruff of the neck, forcing its head and jaws down toward the ground. One if its rear legs was free now, raking soil from the ground as Drew maintained the pressure.

"Okay, Cath! There—and there!" Cath quickly changed position, moving the pliers to the spot where Drew indicated with the pointing finger of his other hand.

Hand trembling, Cath snipped at the netting as the cub thrashed and squirmed. Drew shifted position as part of the net tore and came away, now seizing the cub near the base of its tail; trying to ensure that as its claws came free of the net that it wouldn't be able to slice chunks out of them.

"Okay, I think that's going to be enough. Back off to those shrubs behind us, Cath. I'm going to chuck it back into the cave and then come to you. It's scared, and it'll head back there into the dark rather than come at us."

"Sounds like a good theory. Why don't I believe it's going to happen that way?"

Drew looked up at her and smiled. The shadows seemed to have gone.

She smiled back—

And saw that expression suddenly change; saw a wild, unfathomable look of anger or hate or fear or alarm transform his face; saw his eyes wide and staring—and shrank back from him in a moment that had suddenly transformed beyond understanding. She cried out as he roughly seized her shoulder and pulled her close; so close that she had a sudden crazy glimpse of her face in the iris of his eye, as he yelled:

"Christ! Look *out*, Cath!"

Now she realized in that split second that he was not staring wildly at her—but at something *behind* her. Off balance in his grip, she turned as he stumbled and shoved her hard, just as—

Something smashed hard into her back, slamming her against Drew and knocking the breath from both their bodies as they were flung hard into the bushes. Cath fell hands flat; felt the pain shudder through her arms and shoulders and neck in a way that instantly catapulted her back into being six years old again, when she had fallen the same way from a tree. The muscles in her neck and shoulders yanked and jarred, but there was no air in her lungs and she couldn't even gag. The air was filled with a sound of great rending, like sailcloth ripping and shredding, and the rumbling roar of a great wind. Branches thrashed and tore at her face. Drew was gone from her and she clawed to rise, with that roaring and bellowing sound filling her head and now suddenly an overpowering *animal* smell that simultaneously terrified her and now did at last make her gag and retch. She spun, still winded and disoriented, the surrounding hillside spinning and tilting as her arms windmilled and she tried to regain her footing. Groping for balance, she heard—

Drew, yelling and kicking and screaming hoarsely at something that flailed and battered and roared on top of him in those bushes. Something that simultaneously threw ragged clumps of grass and bush wildly into the air as it struck and roared and swung savage blows on him. The rolling bodies slammed into her—and Cath's legs were swept away beneath her. She felt an impossibly hard and powerful back, grabbed for it. She clutched and grabbed and hung on, still trying to find her feet.

And took a clump of what felt like fur in both hands as the rolling bodies tilted again, catapulting her away from that incredibly powerful and lean black blur of whatever-it-was. Drew was still yelling over the sound of that ferocious roaring and bellowing and spitting, and Cath—her eyes filled with whirling images—tried to rise again, and tried to make some sense of what was happening.

She became aware that the struggling cub in the cave net was adding its own caterwaul to the dizzying sounds of fury, saw it thrashing and twisting with insane energy in the netting—and recoiled as a huge, sleek black shape exploded from the gorse bushes past her and flew at the netting. Drew's clutching hand connected with her ripped boot and she leaned down to help him as he emerged from the bushes. His jacket was shredded; one sleeve and the shirtsleeve beneath was gone completely—and there was blood streaming down his arm.

"Oh God . . ."

Drew clambered to his feet, hair awry and blood on his chin. Both staggering, they looked back at the netting and could only watch in awe as the fearsome black shape reared, swatted and lunged at the web that had ensnared its cub. Lean, but huge—this Big Cat was bigger than any puma or panther in captivity, and the ferocity of its onslaught was paralyzing. One side of the netting, pegged into the rock-fissure, was suddenly torn away. But as that netting sprang free, it flipped over—further wrapping and entangling the cub as it squirmed and thrashed, hissing and caterwauling. Its parent leaped back on its haunches at the sudden movement, landed—and turned its gleaming opal eyes on the humans that were threatening it.

The Big Cat was silent now as it stared at them. Now no longer swatting at the netting, it crouched motionless and huge, low to the ground. Tail twitching, the look of hate in those incredible green and gleaming eyes was unmistakable and terrifying. The bared jaws revealed deadly, yellow curved fangs—and the hissing that issued from that cavernous throat was like the hydraulics of some terrible killing machine.

"Back downhill," Drew said quietly. "Back off with me—slowly—and don't turn your back on it . . ."

Cath could not move.

Drew pulled at her arm, and suddenly—she was moving with him; unable to take her eyes from this night-black and gleaming creature. The sense of power, of threat and malevolence, was overwhelming.

The cub thrashed and flopped in front of the Big Cat. It flinched, taking its eyes away from them momentarily; now raking one claw into a fold of the net and shredding it; now rearing back and yanking that net as its own claw snagged, dragging the cub with it. A boiling, shuddering roar of anger—impossibly loud—seemed to shake the bushes around them. Drew tugged harder at her arm and now they were back in the cover of those bushes again, branches obscuring their view of the Big Cat and its cub as they retreated down the slope of the hill. The animal's claw was still snagged, and now it seemed that the force of its fury was directed at the rope as the cub was dragged again—and the Big Cat reared back on its haunches, as big now as a bear.

"Come on!"

Drew dragged Cath with him as they ran down the hillside—the sounds of roaring and hissing still filling the air.

"You mustn't have hit it," gasped Cath as they descended. "With the tranquilizer, I mean."

"I hit it, all right. I saw the dart go in and lodge. I can't understand it. There was enough of the drug in there to have knocked it out completely by now . . . my *God*, how could I have been so bloody stupid!"

"Stupid? How?"

And then Cath realized what Drew now understood—the simple fact of the matter that had been obscured by the fear and the dazedness.

"It's not the cat you shot. It's the *other* parent."

The Land Rover was in sight now at the bottom of the slope.

Drew nodded, wiping blood from his chin. "The one I shot is up there somewhere sleeping it off."

"I don't think I'm going to apply for any big-game hunter vacancies."

"Me neither." Drew held up his bloodied, sleeveless arm. "Wouldn't be able to keep up with the tailor's bills."

"That arm looks bad. We're going to have to get you to a doctor before . . ."

"Christ!"

Stumbling as they reached the bottom of the slope, Cath looked back up the rise at what had so alarmed Drew. They froze at the sight that met them.

The Big Cat had emerged from the gorse bushes. Sleek and black—and still impossibly huge—it was crouched low to the ground, tail swishing. It was slowly and stealthily coming down the rise of the slope, haunches shifting from left to right as it moved with deadly intent. There was no sign of the netting or the cub—and there was no sound now—no roaring, hissing or caterwauling.

Drew stooped, grabbed up a tree branch—and shouted: a wordless, breathless yell that startled Cath.

The Big Cat was motionless. Even from that distance, they could see its jaws silently open wide in a grimace of anger that seemed not only animal, but also somehow a horribly human mask of hate.

Drew yelled again, waved the branch once more.

The Big Cat came on—still low, faster than before; sleek and gliding down that grassy slope, bunched and powerful muscles working on its shoulders as it moved.

"Damn it!" Drew pulled away from Cath, ran forward a few steps, still waving the branch. The Big Cat did not falter as it descended, gathering speed but still staying low. Drew yelled again. The animal paused only briefly, and came on again. Drew glanced back at her. "We're not scaring it. Keep moving back to the Land Rover. If that's a death stalk—it means the damned thing is going to come at us. . . ."

"Drew!"

The Big Cat was speeding up in its descent, head raised and eyes fixed in their direction. Yelling again, Drew flung the branch hard over arm. It spun end over end in a spray of old bark and moss—hit the earth at the base of the hill and flew straight at the Big Cat. The animal reared aside, let the branch shiver to pieces, raised itself from its low stoop and came at them at a full run. Drew charged back to Cath, grabbed her hand again and pulled her on as they ran to the Land Rover, fear giving them added strength. Cath could *feel* the animal at her back as it reached level ground and came at them in a black blur at full speed. They had gotten away with it the first time, but surely this time it was going to take one or both of them down and tear them to pieces.

Drew slammed into the Land Rover.

The nearside passenger door was locked.

"Christ!"

No animal on earth could be capable of making the scream-roar behind them. That all-enveloping, terrifying sound had slowed down time, and Cath was somehow watching herself and Drew desperately dragging themselves around the front of the vehicle—too slowly, much too slowly. And now in that dreamlike slow motion, Cath was somehow aware that as Death came down upon them, the horror-sound seemed to be shaking not only the vehicle but also the trees around them. She could feel the beast right behind her, knew that she would be the first—that the Land Rover door on the driver side was also locked, and as Drew struggled with it, those hellish jaws would fasten around the back of her neck. The impact would slam her to the ground as those yellow-curved fangs met in her throat and the immense claws would rend the flesh from her back, rip her lungs and her heart and . . .

Drew yanked open the other door as they both turned simultaneously.

The Big Cat, no more than twenty feet away on the other side of the Land Rover, leapt directly at the cab. Cath cried out as they both ducked and the animal hit the roof of the cab with a resounding *BOOM!* The vehicle shook on its suspension as the animal rebounded from the roof, the impetus of its charge carrying it straight over their heads. It landed twenty feet from them in a sleek black blur that was both beautiful and terrifying. Whirling in a flurry of torn grass and earth, it slid in a semi-circle and came right back at them.

It meant to rend and kill them with an intensity that was paralyzing.

And yet—suddenly—Cath was inside the cab, not understanding how she had moved; and Drew was with her now, yanking the driver door shut and flinching from the window against her as the Big Cat slammed hard into the door panel, rocking the Land Rover again. Its vast black-furred and demonic head filling the glass, its breath instantly misting it. Drew fumbled for the ignition key, found it and jammed it home. The ignition screeched, but the coughing roar that filled the air was not the engine turning over—it was the beast, now leaping up onto the hood of the Land Rover. It lunged at them, double swatting the windshield with its gigantic paws. A crack chased across the length of the shield as the engine turned over and Drew jammed the Land Rover into reverse with a lurch. The Big Cat skidded backwards on the hood, claws screeching on the paint as it regained its hold and came at them again, its jaws impacting on the glass and smearing it with saliva.

"Get in the back, Cath!"

Cath scrambled over the seat as the vehicle jounced backwards, was flung facedown across the backseats in a tangle as the Land Rover skidded in a semi-circle, the windshield suddenly clear of black nightmare as the Big Cat slid from the hood and out of sight. Cath struggled to rise, heard Drew yell: "*Christ!*" as another impact on the driver's side shuddered the Land Rover. Drew fought with the steering wheel, dragging it hard over as he made for a turn. Cath pulled herself up, just in time to see—

The Big Cat leaping back onto the hood, its front claws gouging into and denting the metal with two heavy *clangs!* Thin shavings of paint and metal sprouted between those curved yellow claws, and now the animal was dragging itself across the hood and roaring hellishly directly into their faces as Drew threw the gear into first and gunned the engine again.

Cavernous jaws spread wide, the Big Cat lunged at the windshield again. The impact cracked the glass again and Cath screamed as Drew yelled: "The gun! Get the gun. . . ."

The windshield imploded, showering the interior with glass.

Cath watched in horror as Drew tugged at the wheel, fought with the gears—and the hellish thing that covered the hood reared back again, shaking its head as if the blow had stunned it. Glass flew from its black and glistening mane as it fought to keep its purchase on the hood of the jouncing vehicle.

Cath saw its eyes refocus as Drew struggled.

She saw its head steady, even as its body slid from side to side, still anchored by its claws in the metal of the punctured hood. It roared again, a coughing scream of malevolence and anger, its jaws wide, its breath blasting them with the stink of death. When it next lunged, it would be in the cab with them.

"The gun!"

The Big Cat braced, and came at them.

And suddenly, again with no conscious effort, the tranquilizer gun from the backseat was in Cath's hands as she too lunged forward across the passenger seat— the barrel of the rifle jamming straight into the thing's jaws and throat. The Big Cat shrieked and gagged, an explosion of sound. Drew swatted at that great black-furred head as it twisted.

Cath pulled the trigger, the rifle jerked in her grip— and the Big Cat screamed as the Land Rover lurched into a ditch, flinging her up against the roof of the vehicle.

Brilliant white light and stars exploded in her head.

The rifle was ripped from her grasp, her hands slamming painfully into the dashboard. Cath was still dazed by the blow to her head, everything spinning before her as the Land Rover jounced and flung her from side to side. The sounds of roaring and screaming continued, but now Cath could not be sure whether it was the animal or the vehicle. The Land Rover bucked to a halt.

"Cath, are you all right? Speak to me—are you all right?"

Cath's vision cleared. When she moved, broken windshield glass crunched all around them. The Land Rover was canted at an angle, and now Drew was clambering into the back, hastily hunting for something as he continued to speak to her. "Are you hurt? Are you okay?"

"I'm not hurt—I'm fine. Drew, where the hell is that cat?"

Still hunting, and throwing aside the detritus that littered the rear of the Land Rover, Drew hastily pointed out through the passenger window. Cath followed the sight line.

The Land Rover had run up the side of a small mound and was tilted precariously in a stand of trees. As if the sudden violence had affected their surroundings, the trees were now shaking furiously in the wind, as nature itself seemed to be venting its anger at what had happened. Even over the sound of that wind, Cath could hear a coughing roar. Fifty feet from where they had ended up, the thing making that sound was walking in an erratic circle, just on the fringe of the trees. The Big Cat was lurching from side to side, swatting at its jaws with both forepaws, now dragging its great head on the ground as if trying to dislodge something—the dart. There was no sign of the rifle, either in the Land Rover cab or lying outside on the ground. The animal was in clear distress, now rearing back as if it had trod on live coals, leaping into the air with incredible agility despite its size, emitting that shuddering, coughing roar.

Drew found more of the boarding that he had used to shore up the rear exit of the cave, slammed it into place against the shattered windshield. There was not enough of it to cover the gap.

"Hopeless!" he spat. "If that thing comes back at us, we've had it."

"Then let's get the hell out of here!"

Drew lunged back into the strewn rear of the vehicle, throwing boxes and plastic containers to one side. "Got it!" He clambered back into the driving seat, thrusting his discovery into Cath's hands—now twisting the ignition key and revving the engine. The noise was not that of a healthy engine. As he twisted and revved, Cath looked at what he'd given her. A thin metal cylinder, rounded at one end and with a drawstring threaded into a screw around its circumference.

Drew cursed and kept revving. The Land Rover began to jerk backwards, rear wheels spewing back clods of earth and soil.

"That's a flare," he shouted above the noise of the engine. "If that cat does make another run at us, I want you to pull the string there and stick it through the windshield. Keep it well out when you do, or we'll burn. That should deter it."

The Land Rover screeched from the mound, the chassis protesting. The engine growled and shuddered. Cath looked back at the Big Cat, still immersed in its own agonies and paying no attention to the vehicle as it finally reversed until it faced the animal.

Drew struggled to get the vehicle into first gear.

"Damn gear box is shot!"

Cath stared ahead, watched the animal walking in circles; waited for it to suddenly focus its attention back on them again and make another horrifying dash to the vehicle. She held up the flare, grabbed the drawstring and waited as Drew finally got into first gear, and the Land Rover began to trundle forward.

The Big Cat keeled to one side, went down on one foreleg.

"Look!" cried Cath.

The creature tried to rise, but its haunches seemed to give way. Its massive head bowed and went facedown to the ground. In the next moment, it keeled over to one side and lay very still.

Drew wrenched the wheel to the left, began to drive—and then stopped.

"We can't leave it like that, Cath."

"What?"

"We can't leave it," he repeated.

"Why not?"

"Cath—that's not the *other* parent. That's the one that I shot with the tranquilizer dart. The other one is still out there somewhere."

"What do you mean—it wasn't the other parent? How could you know that?"

"Because when it came at us, I saw that first dart still stuck in its hide." Drew pointed out through the shattered windshield, pulling aside and discarding the ineffective boarding. "Can you see? There—on the left side of its belly. A small flash of yellow? That's the dart."

Cath could see it now. Despite everything that had happened, the dart had not dislodged.

Drew continued: "I don't know how it managed to stay on its feet for such a long time, because I'd worked out the body weight ratio and quantity of the drug I used in the dart really carefully. I didn't make any mistake. But somehow, this animal's much more resistant to the drug taking effect than any other Big Cat I've learned about. I don't understand it."

"I shot it. In the mouth . . ."

"I think the shock of that was what threw the thing off. But Cath—that second shot of the drug's topped up the first, instantly. And the drug could kill it—or it could choke to death if that dart is still in its mouth. I've got to do something, or it may die."

"Like what?"

"Well, I've got stuff in the house. And I know about animals. But damn it—I'm not a vet. . . ."

Cath saw a change come over Drew, watched as thought and emotion registered on his face as he quickly considered the options.

"I've got an idea."

Quickly, he headed back to the Land Rover, flung open the rear doors and climbed in. When he emerged, it was with a sheet of tarpaulin. The wind had begun to gust now, making the sheet flap and flurry as he walked on past her toward where the Big Cat lay. Cath grabbed an end, pulling tight to stop it flying loose in the wind. It snapped and cracked as they walked.

The black fur of the creature that lay before them ruffled in the wind. Its tongue protruded from its mouth, between those savage yellow fangs. Its opal eyes were half closed, glazed and unseeing—but its ribcage was moving as it breathed in short, sporadic gasps. For a moment, they were both transfixed as they stood looking at this incredible, dangerous and beautiful creature. From its snout to the tip of its tail, the cat seemed enormous. She felt dwarfed in its presence; small and weak and utterly diminished by the sight of this sleek, wild and immensely powerful engine of destruction that had no place in the English countryside.

"It's a male," Drew said.

"Obviously," said Cath. "But there's something . . ." She struggled to find the words, raising her voice as the wind snatched them away. "Something . . ."

"Something about its face," Drew said, now having to raise his voice as the wind buffeted the valley side. "Something that makes it look . . ."

"More than a panther or a puma. God, Drew, it looks—demonic."

The word was inadequate, but the only word that she could find to describe that savage and primal mask of a face; with its slitted opal eyes, the curvature of its jaw and protruding fangs, the angle of those jet black pointed ears. Cath looked at the cruel and massive claws on one of its forepaws and felt colder than the gathering wind. She looked at Drew and knew that he was feeling something similar. He flapped the canvas on the grass next to the animal, and looked at her. Cath understood, moved to stand on one end to stop it flying away in the wind and watched as Drew braced another end with one foot, grabbed the beast by its rear legs—and hauled its bulk over onto the canvas. It was not an easy job, and when he had managed to completely pin an edge of the canvas with the Big Cat's weight, Drew quickly moved around it, braced himself and knelt down next to the sedated animal. Cath felt a thrill of anxiety then, staring at the animal's dulled eyes. Drew knew what she was thinking.

"It's not going to wake up. Hell, Cath, it might not wake up at *all.*"

In the next moment, Drew had braced himself against the animal's side and with enormous effort, rolled the great beast over onto the canvas. The smell of animal musk and urine was overpowering. Its bladder had emptied. They both recoiled, but the wind had quickly snatched away the worst of it, and when Drew rejoined Cath, he grabbed a free edge of the canvas and looked first to the Land Rover—then back to the farmhouse, two hundred yards away at the bottom of the dirt track.

"We'll never get it in the Land Rover. Too heavy, too awkward—and I'm worried about its breathing."

"We're taking it to the *house?*"

"The cellar. See there—the double doors, like storm doors—at the side of the farmhouse? They lead down to the cellar. There's a cage in there."

Cath just looked at him.

"I know, I know. In my less enlightened days—I was intent on catching one of these things. So I built a cage, it's on a track so that it can be moved. I was going to catch one, keep it in the cage. Study it and take pictures. Then I was going to get in touch with the so-called experts who've ridiculed the whole idea of Big Cats being loose in the wilds of the UK. I was even more of an arrogant bastard then than I am now. This was going to be me showing the whole world that they were wrong, and I wasn't just some stupid bloody obsessive who was chasing shadows after his wife had . . . Well, I was wrong. What I told you back there was true. All I wanted to do was take the pictures, maybe some blood samples—and let the thing go. But now . . ."

"But now I've given it a double dose of that drug and might have killed it."

"You saved us, Cath. I was shouting at you to get the gun. It nearly killed us both." Drew looked back down to the farmhouse, then up to the darkening sky and the ever-building wind. "I don't like the look of that sky. . . ."

"So let's get kitty here back down into your cellar. Then you can call a vet, and we can take your pictures—and you can tell everyone that you've caught the shadow you've been chasing out here on the Fell."

Drew looked at her for what seemed a long time, the wind plucking at his ragged clothes and hair.

He kissed her then.

And when they moved apart again, both took an end of the tarpaulin and began dragging it down the dirt track to the farmhouse.

TWENTY

News Night: BBC 18.00 hrs

"*And now it's over to Brian Falkener of the Met Office to tell us more about the storm that's coming in from the North Sea and causing so much damage already. Hello, Brian?*"

"*Hello, David.*"

"*There are speculations already, Brian, that we're due for another great storm like the one we had in 1987 and the Burns Day Storm in January 1990. Do we need to batten down the hatches?*"

"*Well, we certainly need to take precautions. There's an unusually strong weather system, with very strong winds already hitting the Northeast Coast and due to continue through the night. But I should point out that the storms you've referred to in 1987 and in 1990 were not technically hurricanes—even though they've been referred to as such over the years. We just don't get hurricanes in England. The storm winds then—as we predict now—are expected to be equivalent to a Category*"

2 on the Saffir-Simpson Scale. As I say, this is coming in from the North Sea, and since it's non-tropical in nature, we refer to it as a European windstorm."

"Not a hurricane then—but twenty-three people were killed in 1987. . . ."

"Yes, but it has to be said that the warning systems we have in place are much more advanced than we had back then. And of course, we've been advising about this weather build up for the past couple of days now. So people are recommended just to be sensible. Not to travel until this has blown over. Stay inside in the more remote areas, and just stay safe."

"The storms in '87 and '90 were considered a rare event, Brian—with a severity that experts at the time said could only be expected every several hundred years on average. And yet, here we are again, with a similiar storm just about to hit the mainland. I'd like to bring in Sylvia Prentiss, who is a member of ECO—a group whose concerns about global warming and environmental issues have been well publicized of late. Sylvia—another 'European windstorm'—when we're told that they shouldn't really be happening with such frequency?"

"Good evening. Well, yes . . . I was particularly interested to hear Mr. Falkener say that we'd been given improved advance warning of the storm hitting landfall today, but I'm afraid I can't really agree with him. It's a well-known fact that due to financial cutbacks, there's actually a lack of automatic buoys and weather-reporting ships out there in the North Sea—which means that they're relying too heavily on satellite data. What we're dealing with here, as a result of climate change and industrial pollution of the environment, are storms that are incredibly difficult to predict despite the technology available. . . ."

"I'm sorry but I can't accept that, David. Following the great storm in '87 and the Burns Day storm in '90, there were considerable changes in systems control at the Met Office and the reporting of severe weather. I think the record shows that there have been considerably more warnings about the landfall of this particular storm—something we take very seriously given the loss of life and damage experienced previously. Our tracking devices are very sophisticated and . . ."

"Rubbish!"

"Please, Miss Prentiss. I think it's unnecessary to cause alarm here. The Met's Cray mainframe supercomputer and in-depth simulations actually provided warnings for the Burn's Day storm in 1990 accurately and in sufficient time to enable people to take precautions."

"But you'd still recommend us to 'batten down the hatches'?"

"Definitely—yes. . . ."

TWENTY-ONE

The cellar of Drew's farmhouse seemed much larger than the building that stood above it. Amidst the clutter of workbenches, cupboards, broken farm equipment, shelves, chain link and general clutter—Cath could see the cage in the center of the room from where she stood.

The outside storm doors had both been pulled open, and Drew had slipped down into the darkness while she stood up top waiting. He'd crashed into something and cursed, making her flinch—and when a light came on, she saw that he had pulled a string hanging from the ceiling that had operated cobwebbed strip lights running the length of the cellar. The storm wind outside had whipped up a sheaf of yellowed papers in the cellar that flew through the air like startled birds. Shelves rattled, tins clattered and rolled. There were floor rails at each side of the twelve-stair entry down to the cellar, and Drew had installed sheet metal to cover those rough-hewn stairs. Overhead, more rails—and a block and tackle—with overhead

147

and ground-floor rails leading down and away across the cellar floor and ceiling to where the cage was anchored. The cage itself was a dozen feet square; rough hewn, but solid. Even from here, Cath could see blobs of solder on the solid chrome bars. Apart from the incongruous old-fashioned iron bolt and hasp used to lock the cage door, it looked like a professional job—and she wondered how long he had spent in isolation, crafting this holding pen for a creature that most people believed only existed in the fevered imagination of a misguided few.

Drew appeared at the bottom of the slope/step and held up a hand. Cath took it and, using that hand and one of the rails at the side, Drew ascended again—stepping over the enormous black bulk of the animal on the canvas that they had dragged to the top of the stairs. Its breathing was still erratic and wheezing, and Drew stooped to turn its massive head—studying those huge, glazed opal eyes.

"I don't like it."

"Now what?" Cath asked.

"We slide him down—across the floor and into the cage."

"And if he wakes up while we're doing that?"

"Like I said—there's a chance he might not wake up at all."

Between them, they maneuvered the tarpaulin to the top of the stairs—the wind tugging at their clothes. When the creature was right on the edge, Drew jumped over it onto the sheet-metal of the stair slope. His foot skidded, and he grabbed for a rail to steady himself.

"Careful!"

Grabbing an edge of the tarpaulin, Drew shimmied to the bottom of the stair-slope—tugging hard. The tarpaulin and the beast came quickly after him, the tarpaulin hissing as the gigantic bundle slid to the floor of the cellar, making Drew jump out of the way as it slithered to a halt. Cath winced again, expecting that movement to wake the creature from its slumber. But the massive black shape lay still as Drew clambered back up the slope, grabbing for the interior handle on the nearest storm door. Cath moved down, grabbed the door ridge and eased it down into Drew's grasp, struggling as the wind snatched at it—threatening to yank it out of her grasp. Drew slammed it into place— Cath winced once more—looked at the immobile Big Cat, and then hauled in the second storm-door. The flapping sheets of old yellow paper settled at last on benches, shelves and floor. Drew secured the trap door, and they both slumped back against the stair rails—looking at each other.

"I don't know what I'm doing here," said Cath at last.

"But you're glad you came?"

"Yes."

"Come on then."

They seized the edges of the tarpaulin and hauled it and its burden across the concrete floor to the cage. Cath watched the Big Cat's head lolling from side to side as they moved, its great muscular tongue still protruding between those thick, solid fangs. When a foreleg flopped over the side, claws raked three parallel grooves in the concrete as it was dragged. Drew flipped the huge paw back onto the tarpaulin, and when they had reached the cage—hurried to slide the fastening iron bolt in its hasp. The gated door swung open with a screech. Cath looked back at the creature again. Was this the time it would choose to wake up— just before they got it inside the cage?

There was a raised ridge on the gate, eight inches from the floor. Drew stepped into the cage, lifted an edge of the tarpaulin and hoisted it and the Big Cat's head over the ridge. Cath followed suit, moving to take the rear edge of the tarpaulin. Between them, they began to hoist their burden through the gate and into the cage.

"Fancy work," Cath said as they grunted and hauled. "The rails and the hoist and everything."

Drew laughed. "Whiled away the long nights, I can tell you. I wanted to make sure I could get the cage in and out. I'd gotten this kind of . . . conceit, I guess you could call it."

"Conceit?"

"Yeah. Once I'd—" Drew smirked at himself, shaking his head. "Once I'd 'shown them all,' I was going to attach the hoist, drag that cage back along the rails to the storm-doors, use the pulley to get it back up top—open the cage and let the thing go again."

"Very 'Born Free,' Drew. Back to the wild and all that . . ."

"Yeah, I know. Naive. I had a point to prove."

"But you don't have to prove it anymore, do you?"

The thing was inside the cage, and so were they.

"Okay," Cath said. "This is where it wakes up and we get ripped to pieces."

"Nope. This is when I give kitty something to help it with that tranquilizer—and telephone the vet."

"You going to tell him that you've caught The Hound of the Baskervilles?"

"Do you know—I think I might."

"Not before I've cleaned that cut on your arm. Have you got a first-aid kit?"

"Upstairs. Think I might need a stitch or two . . ."

"And some kind of jab."

"Let's see what the vet says first."

"Well, come on. Let's get the stuff, and you can show me around."

Drew closed the cage and pulled the iron bolt into its hasp. Inside the cage, the Big Cat slumbered, snorted and wheezed.

"Cat's in the bag at last," said Cath.

Drew smiled again, and led Cath up a wooden flight of stairs to the kitchen of the farmhouse above.

TWENTY-TWO

Faye looked anxiously from the television screen to the windows of the kitchen. They were rattling even louder than before, and there was a great rushing from the driveway beyond, which seemed so much more than a storm wind coming. She couldn't get the images of disaster abroad out of her head; in particular, news footage scenes of tsunamis, with tidal waves of water and debris crashing into holiday resorts, tearing houses apart and deluging people on the streets in a deadly tangle of shattered woodwork, brick and foaming water. The sound out there now was like that—not a storm wind, but like the rumbling approach of a tidal wave, about to crash into the house. Faye rose again, crossed to the windows and looked out into the darkening sky. The trees beyond, on the Fell Road, were thrashing and twisting wildly; like living things, trying to uproot themselves and escape. When she turned to look back across the kitchen, the room seemed so vulnerable. Above the sound of the storm wind she thought she could hear the roof joists and ceiling beams creaking and groaning. Back at the television, one of the people being interviewed was saying:

"We're not anticipating that there will be anything other than superficial damage in the towns and built-up areas, but we are advising that those living in the Northeast in rural areas, villages, farms—and outlying districts to the Northwest, should take extra precautions. . . ."

"Oh God." Faye checked her watch, but could not now remember how long Cath had been gone. Rynne was still asleep, despite the rushing wind and the groaning beams and walls—and for the moment, that was perhaps a blessing. She looked around again at the benches and shelves, at the pile of ironing on the table—looking for something, anything, to take her mind away from her anxieties. Normally, she was much more level-headed than this (perhaps *too* level headed, Cath had often accused her). But there was something different tonight—something, despite the severity of the approaching storm that rang loud alarm bells in her head. Cath had asked her to stay, and that was what she would do—but she felt helpless, and the anxiety was churning her inside. Decided now, Faye marched into the hall and snatched up her handbag from the stand. She found her mobile, switched it on—found Cath's number and dialed.

"We are not able to connect you at the moment. Please try again later. Alternatively, leave a message."

"Cath? Are you all right, darling? Just with this wind coming on and everything—and the news reports about a hurricane that isn't a hurricane—I was worried about you. Give me a ring back as soon as you can. Everything here is fine, nothing to worry about, and I'll be staying put until you . . ."

TWENTY-THREE

"That's one hell of a wind building out there," said Drew as Cath dabbed more of the antiseptic into the wound on his arm. The scratch had been a bleeder, but it looked as if no stitches would be necessary. She began carefully winding the bandage around his arm. Drew watched her. "Well, you're a good doctor, but I'll still need a tetanus and anti-bacterial shot."

"Don't you trust my tender care?"

"Yes, I do. But some of these cats have bacterial infection under their claws. Even a simple scratch could lead to blood poisoning."

Cath looked down to her shredded boot. Standing on it with the heel of the other boot, she pulled and kicked. The damaged boot came off cleanly, clonking across Drew's living room floor. Throughout, she continued to bandage without interruption.

"You're a multi-tasker," Drew said.

"What was she like?"

Drew looked at her as Cath continued with the bandaging. She didn't look up, her expression still fixed on her task; but Drew could tell by her body language that she *was* watching for his reaction from the corner of her eye—intensely. And, of course, he immediately knew whom she meant.

"She liked the farming life. Perhaps more than me. But you would never have been able to guess if you saw her—out of her environment—that she was, well I nearly said 'a farmer's wife,' but that's a cliché as well, isn't it? No, I mean, if you saw her in town or if we visited the city—family, friends—you might have thought she had a job in advertising or big business or something. She was very classy, very stylish and very funny. She liked to laugh."

"There aren't any pictures. Of her, I mean. In this room."

Drew laughed. It was a dry, humorless sound. "No, you're very perceptive. There used to be. But sometimes—well, sometimes it was just too much to see them. You know?"

"Yes."

Cath knew that he was waiting—and that it was her turn.

"David liked to laugh, too. That's one of the things I remember really well. When things started to happen for me—in my writing—he used to keep me grounded when the media bullshit kicked in. Television interviews, documentaries, the movie version of the book. He said he'd never allow all of that to go to my head—and he'd make excuses to do outlandish things just to . . . to . . ."

The man in the woolen hat. The New York sidewalk. The pool of blood.

Cath suddenly pulled herself back. "I'm sorry—what did you say?"

"I was just saying—it's difficult to laugh now."

"Yes, it is difficult."

"They never caught the guy who killed him?"

"No. We were in the wrong place at the wrong time. I used to think that the man who did it was really evil, you know? But he wasn't. He was pathetic, really. Just after a handful of change for a fix. He's probably dead of the drugs or hypothermia or pneumonia—or a combination of all three."

"Faye told me about it."

"Faye does a lot of talking behind the scenes, doesn't she?" Cath had finished bandaging, but her fingers were still on Drew's arm. "She told me about your wife, too."

"Faye saved me. Really. Some of the things she said. Things haven't been—well, you know—good. All a bit of a mess, really. Not knowing which way to go, whether to stay and make a go of this place—or at least change direction—or whether just to give it up and move on. This thing with the Big Cats—I suppose it's about something else, really. But after we get kitty sorted out—I've realized what I've got to do."

Cath gently squeezed his arm.

"Flora—my wife—the thing that killed her . . ." Drew stumbled to a halt, bowed his head. "I'll start again. Because it wasn't a *thing* that killed her. When I say it like that, it sounds like I'm giving an inanimate piece of machinery a personality, like it was a living thing. That's just what I've done. It was an accident. Stupid. The combine harvester. I should have got rid of it, sold it or burned it. But it's still out there in the barn. As soon as we've got tonight sorted out . . ." When Drew looked up, Cath saw that there were tears in his eyes. "I'm going to get George and Tom up here with tractors, and we're going to drag the bloody thing off my land and get rid of it."

Cath squeezed his arm again.

"And I'm going to help you do that."

From the cellar below came the long, low sound of an exhalation of breath. It was a sound that was not human, but which carried with it a dreadful expression of life lost and extinguished, even above the sound of the wind outside. Emanating from the cellar stairway, it seemed to fill the kitchen with cold shadows.

A death sigh.

Cath's grip tightened on Drew's arm.

And suddenly, they were both at the top of the stairs, looking down. There was no further sound, and although it was not possible from where they stood to see the cage—they knew that the sound had come from there.

Now, only silence.

They started down the stairs, Drew leading—so that Cath saw the expression on his face as he drew level with the cage before she did. She knew from that expression what had happened, and the new anguish on his face was heartbreaking.

The Big Cat was dead.

Its labored breathing had ceased. Its chest no longer rose and fell. The tongue still protruded from those deadly jaws, and its eyes were glazed in death.

"Oh no . . ."

Drew dropped to his knees before the cage, put his hand through the bars and touched the sleek black fur on its neck. Cath came up behind him, her hand resting on his shoulder in a similar gesture.

"What have I done?"

"Oh God, Drew. It wasn't you—it was me. I was the one who shot it again, gave it the overdose."

"I should have left them alone." Drew stood up. The tears that had been glistening in his eyes had spilled onto his cheeks. "All this time. All this searching, and . . ." He gestured hopelessly at the inert beast in the cage. "What the hell have I been doing all this time?"

"You were looking for something," Cath said. "So was I."

When they came together, there was hunger and a savage joy that surprised them both. There was no feeling of betrayal or loss of things past as they hurriedly undressed; no sense of the past or the present or the future. Just the hungry and passionate *now-ness* of their need for each other, and the need to burn out the pain that had excluded the laughter and the pleasure from their lives in such a long, long lonely time.

TWENTY-FOUR

The wind gusts through the open front door of Kapler
Dietersen's opulent house, blowing leaves from the surrounding trees into the hallway; each gust making them
rise in whispering clouds to settle on the antique chairs
and bureau, now swirling in a miniature whirlwind,
now resting on the window sills—each blast of air
through that doorway stirring them anew. The oil paint-
ings on the wall lift and clatter in their ornate frames
against the walls; lace curtains billow and flap—but no
one comes to close the front door.

A side door in the hallway, which once led to ser-
vants' quarters, constantly opens and slams shut in the
draft. In the days of this house's real glory, there was a
staff of seventeen. But now, only three people have
served Dietersen: Mr. Garvey and his wife, and a taci-
turn groundsman called Jeffrey—meaning that only two
of those rooms are in use; one for the married couple,
one for Jeffrey. In the married couple's quarters, Mrs.
Garvey lies on the bed, her eyes fixed unblinking on the
ceiling. The wind gusts and rattles the windowpanes,

but she does not heed it. There is a spider on her face, moving slowly across her cheek to her hairline, now vanishing into the gray strands of her hair. She does not move to brush it away.

In the kitchen, Mr. Garvey—who had that day decided that he and his wife could not possibly work for Mr. Dietersen any longer—is sitting cross-legged on the floor, his head bowed. For ten years, he has not been able to stoop properly because of his rheumatism and arthritis. But now he sits cross-legged and uncomplaining, one hand stretched out before him as if he has just thrown a die.

On the grounds at the front of the house, behind the bushes fronting the main drive, Jeffrey lies facedown in the grass and out of sight.

In the living room—a phrase now redundant—Trudi lies across a sofa, now stained the color of the red wine spilled on the floor. Bobby Fuller's eyes are wide open and startled, still fixed on the door.

And Kapler Dietersen, a wide red smile in his throat, white powder in his lap and stirring on the floor at his feet—sits bolt upright in his armchair. His eyes are screwed shut, in a hopeless attempt to ward off the reality of what was about to happen to him. One of his hands grips the armrest of that armchair, wrinkling the fabric.

The other hand—and its ornate rings—has been hacked off, and is no longer in the room.

TWENTY-FIVE

"Give me your fucking money," says the man in the woolen hat.

"I don't like this man, Mummy," Rynne says, clinging tightly to her hand.

"That's not what you said the first time," Cath says to the man in front of them. His head is down, and Rynne can't see his eyes or his face. He sways from side to side on the rain-washed street in his long, dirty coat and bare chest. But this time, there is no knife in his hand— both of which swing back and forth at his sides, like some kind of ape contemplating its next move.

"Money," says the man in a guttural and dragging voice.

"Give him some money and make him go away," says Rynne.

Her mum just stares at the man. Blank-faced, she says: *"The first time you said: 'Give me the money'— then you said: 'Give me the fucking money.'"*

"Money," says the man again, and he makes a sound that could be laughter, or just the sound of him clearing

phlegm from his lungs. It is an intensely horrible sound, more like an animal than a human—and Rynne still cannot see his face.

The man raises a hand and points beyond them. Mum continues to stare straight at the man, but some terrible and irresistible force makes Rynne turn slowly back to see—

The playground cat that scratched her is lying in a spreading red stain on the sidewalk.

Rynne doesn't want to be in this dream; but she cannot wake up. She wants this man in the woolen hat to be gone, but everything is moving too slow and dragging in the way that nightmares do. The irresistible force is turning Rynne's head away from the ruined corpse of the playground cat—back to the man in the woolen hat.

A thrill of terror envelops her.

He is standing right next to them. Somehow, he has quickly and horribly closed the gap between them in a dream-blink. Inches away, his head still hangs, breath rising around it in that freezing cold air. She can smell his breath—horrible and familiar, and the same smell she encountered in—

A cave, somewhere? But she's never been in a real cave before.

It's an acrid animal smell—the smell of death.

The man in the woolen hat slowly begins to lift his head to look at them, horribly close and intimate.

Rynne tries to screw her eyes shut in this dream, tries to will herself awake. Because she does not want to see what that man's face has become. But she is frozen and terrified and must look.

"Cath . . . Rynne?" It is a dragging and awful voice that comes from the man's mouth as he finally lifts his head.

The face is black furred and sleek.

There are droplets of dew on those sprouting whiskers, sharp as porcupine quills.

There are curved yellow fangs in that sleek black face.

And the eyes are gleaming glass opals—somehow dead and alive at the same time, and with a ferocious and hungry purpose. The thing's jaws widen in a rumbling hiss. Somewhere deep in that maw, hell is waiting for them. She cannot scream, and she cannot wake— because this is not a dream at all.

The face lunges at her mother's throat.

And Rynne woke with a scream in her bed—and screamed again as something beyond her bedroom window shattered and crashed in the storm-blown night.

TWENTY-SIX

"Oh my God!"

Drew was the first out of bed and at the bedroom window, looking for any sign of whatever had caused the crash. Cath, for some reason only now aware of her nakedness watched, mesmerized by the sight of him standing there in silhouette. It made the breath catch in the back of her throat. After the heat and the hunger of their lovemaking had come the even closer intimacy as they lay together in each other's arms, both utterly satisfied by the act of love—and, not talking, not needing to express anything in words, they lay listening to the wind gusting around the farmhouse as their own hurried breathing had settled. The voice of that wind seemed somehow to speak of the passion and the longing and the pleasure they had experienced; now somehow released into the night.

And then, something out there had shattered that peace and broken them out of that spell.

Cath realized that she was holding the blanket to cover her breasts. Throwing it aside, she was beside

Drew in a moment. The heat of their bodies together again as she slipped her arm around him, and he did the same, made her feel alive in a way that she could barely understand.

"It's the damned feed shed," said Drew—and when Cath looked out the bedroom window, she could see what the rising storm was doing to the outhouses and buildings at the rear of the farmhouse. Night had fallen during their lovemaking, and only the details of the nearest buildings could be seen—the remainder now blanketed by darkness. Two fences were down, a water barrel had been torn from its hasps in an outhouse wall and was rolling wildly back and forth on the ground—and the roof of the feed shed had been torn away, now only connected to one supporting wall, so that the corrugated metal flapped and crashed up and down with each gust like some huge, demented jack-in-the-box lid. From somewhere beyond, hens were squawking and flapping; the few livestock that Drew possessed lurching and crashing against their stalls as the wind gathered strength.

"This storm isn't going to blow out," Drew said. "I've got to secure the animals."

The romance and the intimacy were not broken, but suddenly practical need had snapped both of them into a completely new moment.

"Where's your telephone?" asked Cath. "My mobile's in the car." Anxiety was now beginning to rise inside her as another fence by the outhouse was suddenly yanked from its posts by the storm wind and went flapping end over end to vanish in the darkness.

"Living room downstairs. Your mobile wouldn't be any good here."

"Why not?"

"You can't get a signal. The farm's in the hollow of the valley." Drew's voice mirrored her own anxiety as he stared out into the night, now moving quickly from the window to the bed and where their clothes lay scattered and intertwined on the floor. He caught Cath's arm as she passed him—pulled her close, and kissed her fiercely on the mouth. She seized the back of his head as she hungrily returned that kiss.

What had happened between them had not—would not—disappear.

They pulled apart. Drew reached for his clothes as Cath hurried naked from the bedroom and down the stairs to the living room. For one brief and puzzling moment, it felt as if she were back in her own home and knew the layout of Drew's own home intimately, even though she had seen no details as they breathlessly clung to each other on the way to the bedroom. But there was no time to reflect as she quickly descended and flitted through the darkness like a ghost to the telephone on the table.

The telephone line was dead.

"Drew!"

Cath snapped the telephone back into its cradle and tried again. The line was still dead.

Drew appeared at the top of the stairs, hopping on one leg as he pulled on a shoe.

"The telephone's not working. . . ."

He clattered down the stairs, shirt unbuttoned and flapping. At the bottom, he stabbed the flat of a hand on the light switch. Beyond the farmhouse walls, something groaned and cracked. The rushing wind seemed to make the very walls shudder.

"Drew—I've got to get back to Rynne and Faye. This is more than just an ordinary storm. I need to know they're safe."

"I know. Get dressed, and I'll drive you back . . ."

"No. You've got those animals to see to. I'll be okay."

"Cath—this bloody wind . . . and those country roads . . ."

"There are things you have to do here." Cath rushed past him, quickly ran her hand across his face as she passed. "The thing is—can you manage? Do you need me here?"

Drew grabbed her and held her.

"The thing is—do *you* need *me?*"

Cath kissed him again—and they didn't need to say anything more.

When she broke away and hurried upstairs for her clothes, Drew watched her go; watched her disappear into the bedroom. He listened to her hurriedly dressing, and then looked around the living room.

Living?

With the wind rushing around these four walls of the farmhouse and with the renewed sounds of splintering wood from somewhere beyond, Drew realized in that moment that he had not really been living at all for years. His life had been put on hold and this room— this house—had not been a home at all. It had been a prison cell of his own making. In that moment, the wind could pull it all apart if it wanted to. It could shatter the walls, tear off the roof; it could blast everything in here, away out into the night—take it all. There was no way of knowing what would happen next; whether anything at all would develop between them. Life was sometimes too cruel and too random to take anything for granted—but for the first time in many years, Drew felt that he was truly alive, and if this storm wanted to destroy and smash everything away, then so be it.

But the animals needed protection—and he could not leave them at the mercy of the storm.

Beyond the living room, on the porch, Drew could see and hear the glass panels on either side rattling. The bushes behind the car and the Land Rover were alive with movement. He moved onto the porch and opened the front door, the strength of the wind taking him by surprise. He staggered back as magazines and newspapers in the living room took to whirling flight.

Cath was suddenly there, now pulling that living room door shut and joining him as they looked out into the tumultuous night.

"Cath, I can't let you drive alone. This bloody wind . . ."

"And I can't go if you're not sure you can do what needs to be done here alone."

"I've been alone a long time."

"Me too. Be careful."

"If I've found you, I don't want to lose you."

And in the next moment, Cath was headed toward her car, the wind snatching at her clothes.

"When will we . . ." began Drew. But the wind blew away his words, and she did not hear. Drew watched her climb into her car. The engine turned over immediately, the headlights stabbing straight ahead up the rough track that had taken them to their rendezvous with the creature now lying dead in the cellar. Drew felt a stab of guilt, now overcome by a feeling of loss as Cath's car reversed and then slewed to one side facing the main road. Was this all too good to be true? When she left, would it be forever? Would everything be changed tomorrow?

The car door opened and Cath leaned out to look back at him.

Her smile allayed his fears.

Then the car door slammed, and the vehicle screeched down the main drive to the road, headlights piercing the wild night; shrubs and trees alive with wild movement.

Drew watched the car go; watched the headlights recede into the night, listened as the sound of the car engine was finally swallowed by the sounds of the storm wind.

When she had gone, he grabbed the heavy-duty flashlight from the bench in the porch, slammed the door behind him—and with his heart full of a fierce joy, ran into the night toward the sounds of cracking timber and the hoarse sounds of frightened livestock.

TWENTY-SEVEN

Cath drove, and she didn't care.

She didn't care now that the wind just seemed to be getting stronger; didn't care that she was having to grip the steering wheel hard to keep the car from veering to the roadside as the lanes twisted and turned. She'd always prided herself on being a careful driver—but care had been cast to the wind tonight. She was driving too fast and knew it. It was as if the storm wind had seized her, plucked her out of the life she had come to know. She was in a whirlwind that had already carved the road ahead; she was being dragged along in the tail of its ferocious undertow; hurtling onward through the night in those ferocious wind currents. That storm might smash her against a tree; might crash her through the hedges or snatch the car up into a crushing maelstrom of shattered windshields and rending metal. It might tear her apart; rip the life screaming from her throat—to be swallowed by the storm.

But not tonight—not now.

If the car's wheels did leave the road, a tidal wave of

roaring black night sweeping under the chassis, it wouldn't spin and twist in the vast throat of the tornado like the other cars she'd seen on television news footage. No, it wouldn't be like that, at all. She'd be in control, flying *with* the storm. She was so much a part of what was happening tonight that she'd be controlling the very air currents themselves with a twist of that steering wheel.

What the hell am I doing? demanded the sensible woman inside as her headlights swept from side to side in the storm.

I'm running like a kid, answered the other side of her. *It's stupid and it's foolish, and I'm not a teenage girl in love for the first time. But I can't help it. And I don't know what's going to happen next, but something IS going to happen and now I can't stop it.*

You'll run off the road, you idiot! And then what? Do you want to kill yourself? Think of Rynne.

The wind's going to take me. And I know it could smash me if it wanted to—know that what's happened tonight might smash me just as badly in the long run.

Then why . . . ?

Because tonight I've got wings. Tonight, at last, there's a chance that I'm going to FLY . . .

And then Cath saw the tree across the road, just as she took the bend much too fast.

She slammed on the brakes, tires screeching above the storm wind as the car slewed sideways on—and kept sliding broadside toward the tree. She knew then that the car would keep traveling sideways, aided by the wind from behind, and that she would collide with that thrashing mass of branches and solid wood. Gripping the wheel so tightly that her hands looked skeletal, Cath gritted her teeth, braced her arms and waited for the sickening *crump* of metal.

The car kept sliding, the headlights spinning in a wild arc, flash-illuminating a shattered roadside fence, clods of spattering mud and thrashing foliage.

She screwed her eyes shut, waiting for the side windows to implode as those spiked branches stabbed through the glass.

But the car slid to a halt, rocking on its suspension only inches from the tree; branches scratching furiously at the bodywork.

Still frozen behind the wheel, Cath stared ahead through the windshield at the slashing rain in the headlights. They remained pointing out into the night, their illumination fading to nothingness, as if the car were suddenly suspended in space. When she realized that she wasn't breathing, she let out a great gasp and was finally able to turn and look out the side window at the branches thrashing at the glass. Fingers trembling, she turned to look back and saw what had happened. The tree—a tree she'd probably driven past a hundred times and never noticed—had been torn out at the roots. Matted clods of earth lay heaped around the root crater on the other side of the road.

Steadying her breathing, she threw the gears into reverse.

Something was dragging at the rear axle. Cursing, she kicked open the door—cursing again when the wind snapped it back at her. Squeezing out, hanging on to the door lest the wind rip it from its hinges, Cath struggled out into the howling night. Had she wrecked the bloody car, after all? The wind buffeted her against the bodywork as she made her way to the back, hand-over-hand. At the rear, through tear-blurred eyes, she saw what had happened. A branch had snagged under the bumper. Sod's law dictated that the damn thing must have also entangled in the wheels and that she'd be stranded. But to her immense surprise, the branch yanked out on the second attempt. She tried to see if there was more stuff snagged under there, but it wasn't possible in the dark. With no flashlight in the car, she'd just have to try again. Maybe being a professional cynic just brought its own bad luck with it. A renegade thought came to her; one of the unrehearsed things she'd said at an after-dinner speech somewhere: I'm not a cynic—I'm just a disillusioned optimist.

"Who will shortly be lying under another fallen tree if I don't get the hell out of here fast," she said into the storm as she reached the driver's door. She was just about to yank it open again—when she saw movement from the embankment below her. The headlights must have dazzled her when she first got out of the car, probably the reason she didn't see what was below. But now, with those twin beams stabbing off into the rain-whipped darkness, they gave enough illumination beneath to make a kind of shadow show in the gully.

There was a man down there, staggering with both arms out—as if he were walking on a tightrope—but something much bulkier than that. Now, he was jumping down from the raised edge of that bulky, indeterminate shape—and someone else was clambering up into silhouette relief. Although Cath had no way of knowing what had happened, or what was going on down there, instinct told her that it was bad. When someone cried out in agony from the darkness, her instinct seemed to be confirmed. Cath moved quickly to the roadside, edging around the headlight beams.

Shading her eyes from the glare, she called down to the shapes. Later, she wouldn't remember what it was that she'd cried.

"Hello? Anything wrong? Can I help? Are you in trouble?"

Later, it would seem to be important—almost vital that she could bring it back to mind—because perhaps if she'd said something else, something different, maybe everything would have turned out differently.

The response from the shapes down below was immediate.

The first silhouetted figure wheeled to look up, arms pin-wheeling at his sides; as if he was still on that tightrope and Cath's voice threatened to unbalance him. Indeed, it did seem to unbalance him as the shape fell to its knees on the embankment and then staggered upright again. The second shape looked up from the tangled mass. Then a muffled voice that didn't seem to belong to either of the men shouted up to her through the storm:

"Yes! For Christ's sake, give us a hand."

Another voice now: the tightrope walker: "Have you got a car . . . ?"

And before Cath could answer, a torch beam stabbed up out of the darkness directly into her face. Cath recoiled, shaded her eyes; saw a third figure blundering around on that dark mass as the second man jumped down out of sight into the darkness.

"What's happened?" she called down. "Are you all right?"

And now that third voice called up to her again; this time she could make no sense of it above the storm wind. But as the third man clambered about in the wind, his torch beam flashed over and around him.

And in those brief moments, the light gave Cath a jigsaw piece-by-piece view of what had happened; each flash revealing another piece of evidence.

The dark mass at the bottom of the gully was a wrecked Land Rover.

It was lying on its side, the roof ripped, luggage rack tangled. Glass from a shattered windshield sparkled and glittered around it in the torch beam.

Now Cath realized that the three men had been climbing out of a broken side window when she'd arrived on this storm-driven scene.

There were two tire-track gouges over the edge of the embankment. Then a ragged gouge about twenty feet down where the tires had impacted in the soil after roaring over the edge at speed. Further tire gouges and then an explosive flurry of soil where the Land Rover had impacted and rolled.

The tree behind her, lying across the road.

The storm.

All the pieces fit.

Moments earlier arriving on the scene, and perhaps that falling tree would have sent *her* car careering off the road and over the embankment, and those silhouettes scrabbling around down there in the dark from their Land Rover wreck would only now be arriving on the scene to ask the same questions of her—if she hadn't broken her neck in the process.

Behind her, the night seemed to split apart.

Whirling, heart leaping, Cath saw another tree on the other side of the road tilt over into the rain-slashed night. This time it didn't come down across the road. It fell away into the darkness, branches thrashing as if it were alive and trying to keep its balance. Cath recoiled, shielding her eyes as a flurry of clotted mud and pebbles clattered and burst on the roof of her car, thrown up by the roots ripping from the ground. Now, it seemed that the girl who had flown in on this scene—the one who'd wanted to take off on a wild romantic flight into the night—really had flown away. Now she was a woman alone, faced with the urgent, practical task of helping these people. This stretch of the road was on a promontory, the road raised high and starkly exposed. On a night like this, with a storm wind unlike anything she had experienced before, this was surely the worst, most exposed stretch of road anyone could be on. How long before another tree came down? How long before her own car was blown off the road?

Staggering back to the edge of the embankment, Cath looked down. And now, in the torch beam that slashed and dissected the night, she could see that the two men were pulling a third away from the wreckage of the Land Rover, and it was clear from the way that he took all his weight on one leg and threw back his head in silent agony as they threw his arms over their shoulders, that he was badly hurt.

Cath swayed from side to side as the wind dragged at her, not knowing what to do for the best. Should she go down there and help? Or wait for an instruction? Or call something else out, just let them know that she was still here?

No, you wait. They'll drag him up. ("Have you got a car?" one of them had called.) *And then you'll help them into the car, and then you're going to get off this road and into the village as fast as possible.*

The men started to climb the embankment.

Down there in the gully, there seemed to be natural shelter. The storm wind still raged and tore at their fluttering jackets, but did not prevent them from climbing. Here at the top, with Cath constantly looking over her shoulder to check that another tree wasn't coming right down on top of her, she had constantly to step back to the edge and look down; the wind constantly pushing and dragging her from sight.

"Come on!" she cried needlessly, when they were about halfway up, the wind snatching her voice from her mouth. The figures were still silhouettes, even though they were less than fifty feet below her. And although she could see no details of the injured man's face, she could see and imagine that agony as his head twisted from side to side as they climbed.

When they reached the top of the embankment, Cath held down both hands to help. And at that moment, the storm wind decided to send her cartwheeling back away from them. Sprawling in the mud clots and the whirling air, Cath was overwhelmed by her own shamed anger at such helplessness. On all fours, knees skinned, and snatching the hair out of her eyes, she turned back to see the two men hauling the injured third over the rim and toward her. At last she could see their faces, and in that moment a first lightning flash seemed to take a photograph of the scene; indelibly imprinting it in Cath's mind. Every detail of the three, frozen in place, fixed in her mind. A portrait, perhaps, that she should never forget.

The man on the left must be about Cath's age. A black woolen cap on his head, and oh God wasn't it so much like the woolen cap that the guy had been wearing on that New York street so long ago?

Give me the fucking money! he'd said, knife skittering from his hand and into the snow. Somehow, in that same moment, she saw David; looking up at her, his hands clenched to his middle, trying to keep the life inside him; that terrible lost and lonely look in his eyes, and the cold reflection of snow flakes in his wide and dreadfully frightened eyes . . .

No!

This man wasn't like that, at all. Did everyone wearing a cap have to be a potential murderer? No, this man was staring hard at the man supported between them. A mustache, an aquiline nose, heavily gloved hands. A smear of blood above his right eye. The man on the right was younger, perhaps twenty or twenty-one. Stockier than the other two, heavy knitted pullover beneath his quilted jacket, like a fisherman's gear somehow. Thick, curly hair; blowing all over the place—like a perm job gone badly wrong. Small eyes were hidden in the round pinkness of a puffy face that was also somehow a baby's face.

And the man in the middle. Just as Cath had thought, a man in agony. The eldest of them all, perhaps forty or forty-five had short, cropped hair. Either the designer stubble of a vain man or perhaps he'd just not had time to shave. His face was screwed in pain. His leather jacket was torn down one side, from armpit to hem. But Cath's gaze in this infinite moment went to the real horror of that frozen tableau. To the man's left leg. The jeans were torn above the knee, a ragged and horribly nasty hole ripped there—and when the wind flapped at the torn fabric, she could see a glistening, dark redness beneath. She didn't need a medical degree to guess that the man's leg was broken, the way it hung so horribly unconnected below the kneecap.

"Car!" yelled the man with the woolen cap, seeing Cath at last.

At first, she thought he was yelling about the wreck

of their own car, down there in the gully. Sharing his anger at the terrible bad luck they'd had. For a second, she stared at him, waiting for him to say something else; then realized that he had been yelling at her about her own car. Suddenly galvanized, she clambered to her feet and hurried to the vehicle as the three men staggered through the wind blur toward her. Someone was yelling again as she flung open the passenger door and looked back. But now there were only two men—the injured, older man sprawled on the trunk, facedown, letting it take his weight while the younger man looked anxiously back to the embankment. The man with the woolen hat had gone.

"Where . . . ?" Cath started to say, and the words were cut off by the squealing creak of wood, like a sailing ship running aground. The younger man flinched, his shoulders hunching in anticipation as Cath whirled around, waiting for that expected tree to come down on them. The creaking squeal became a roaring crash as the unseen sailing ship exploded through invisible foam onto a beach that was still twenty miles from where they stood. Another tree, somewhere in the dark. Cath dragged the car door open and hung on to it, beckoning urgently as the younger man dragged his older and injured companion away from the trunk and along the side of the car toward her. She held the door and hung there with fierce impatience. Had the man in the hat run off?

The older man swatted out at the young man, yelled something through his pain that the wind swallowed. When the young man tried to help him again, he pushed him back with surprising strength; so much so that the younger man had to throw his arms to either side to regain balance. Then the older man flung himself back hard against the car, flattening his back there to take the weight off his damaged leg, breathing heavily. He turned his attention back to the embankment and this time, Cath saw how the young man seemed to be keeping a wary distance from the older man. Was he afraid of him?

Why the hell were they taking so much time?

"Will you for Christ's sake get in the car?" Cath yelled.

Something about the last few minutes—seconds, moments?—had seemed to rob her of any initiative, any strength. She was used to being an observer; she was a writer for Christ's sake, she was supposed to observe. But something that was happening here seemed to be stealing her soul away. The older man turned to look at her. Was it because she'd felt so free a little while ago, as she'd flown down this road? Was it because of the special thing that had happened between Drew and herself? All those dreams of a new and liberating love—without any guilt about David. Had she let her defenses down somehow?

The older man, the man with his back to the car, turned to look at her. Rain was streaming down his face, dripping from his nose.

For the first time, she got a proper look at his eyes.

They were black, and they rooted her to the spot.

Because for one horrifying moment, she seemed to be seeing the eyes and face of a dead man. Someone who had been dragged from a river, even down to the rivulets of water streaming from his face. There was blankness there, a frozen white mask without any emotion at all. That blankness and lack of emotion was somehow dreadful.

"Got them!" yelled a voice from the edge of the embankment, breaking Cath out of that terrible moment, as Cath's eye contact with the dead-faced man was broken. The man with the woolen hat was hurrying toward them once more; this time carrying three small suitcases—one in each hand and the third under his arm; small, but heavy enough to make him round-shouldered as he ran. Had he gone back for their bloody *luggage?*

Angry at her ineffectiveness, angry that she'd been reacting like a frightened rabbit, Cath leaned into the car through the passenger door open and popped the lock on the rear door. Then, hurrying around the front of the car, shouting: "Right! Get in the car. The next tree coming down could be right on top of us!"

By the time she'd angrily clambered behind the wheel and slammed the door, the baby-faced man had maneuvered the injured man into the backseat. That dead face was a screwed-up mask of pain as he sat and shuffled backwards, now moving his bleeding leg gingerly after him, both hands gripping his upper thigh as if he could strangle the agony in his flesh. Cath flinched as something bumped the rear of the car. Expecting the shriek and grinding crash of another falling tree, she flashed a look in the rear view mirror to see that the man in the woolen cap was yanking at the trunk of the car.

"Leave it!" she snapped. "Leave the bloody cases. We can come back for them."

"Gimme the fucking keys!" snapped the younger man—and God, didn't it sound like *Give me the fucking money!* Before she could react, he jerked over the seat, snatched the keys from the ignition and lunged from the car back out into the night.

What the hell was happening here?

Something was going wrong with her Good Samaritan act.

Angrily, she twisted in her seat to see the younger man rounding the back of the car, jamming the keys into the trunk. The trunk swung open, obscuring her view—and the car bumped again, rocking on its suspension as the cases were thrown in. In the backseat, the injured man winced, breath hissing through his teeth.

Their eyes met again.

This time, he was trying to smile. It just didn't work.

"S'alright about the cases," he said through pain-clenched teeth. "We need them."

Now the man with the cap was climbing in beside him, the baby-faced one sliding into the passenger seat and handing the ignition keys back. Cath snatched them from him, and in the next moment the car screeched in a U-turn away from the uprooted tree, and back in the direction she'd come from.

"Where you taking us?" asked the man in the woolen hat, and then—as if he'd been perhaps too brusque considering that she was their rescuer: "I mean, which way."

"Your friend needs medical help," Cath replied as the headlights swept away down the embankment, picking out the trees on either side of the road on the way down. They hissed and thrashed as if they were alive. "Best bet is Stamford. But we'll have to go the long way round 'cause of that tree blocking the road."

"Can't," said the injured man through clenched teeth. Cath looked to see him bowing his head in pain as he kept that pain-stranglehold on his leg.

"No can't about it." said Cath. "That leg's broken and you need help."

The other two men looked as if they were going to

object, but quieted when the injured man said: "Okay, you're driving."

Now Cath was driving into the wind and was fighting to keep control of the steering wheel. On the way up there, the wind had been behind her, promising to give her wings. Now it was a downhill battle to keep the vehicle on the road and prevent from slamming over the roadside and into the darkness.

"Tree knocked us clean off the road," said the woolen cap. "One minute nothing. Next thing, wham! Straight in the gully."

"Yeah," said baby face. "Wham!"

Cath didn't have to turn her head to see that he was smiling. Something was wrong with him. *A penny short of a shilling*, as her mother used to say.

Cath gripped the steering wheel tight as the wind buffeted the sides of the car. She remembered this downhill stretch. There were cracks and ruts in the disintegrating tarmac on either side. If she hit one in the dark, with a wind like this, the wheel could easily be yanked out of her hands. Maybe she could slow down, but the thought of another tree coming down out of the darkness kept her foot on the accelerator. The needle wavered around fifty. Dangerous to go slower, dangerous to go faster. On the fringes of the headlight beams, she could see the bushes and trees thrashing and writhing. It was as if herds of wild and invisible animals were rampaging in the night. More than that, it seemed that the night had come alive.

"Bad night to be out," said Cath through gritted teeth. She was being ironic, trying to make some kind of bond with these ungrateful strangers.

"Could get worse," said the man in the woolen cap, turning to look at his friend in the backseat.

Cath didn't like the way he said it. Was there a suggestion of threat? It had come out in the sly and sexually suggestive tones of Kapler Dieterson. No, she was overreacting—just the way she had when she'd flashed back to the woolen-capped man who'd killed her husband. She snatched a glance in the rearview mirror. The dead-faced man was glaring forward—and now, somehow, the man in the woolen hat spoke again, but with an air of forced bonhomie that seemed to be an attempt to cover lost ground.

"We been working this building contract. On the new housing estate. Pinchill? Just north of Stamford."

"Yes, I know it. About half-finished, isn't it?"

"Yeah, 'bout that."

"You're builders?"

"Nothing so grand, love. Transient labor, that's us."

"Trans-yent," laughed the baby face, staring out of the side window into the night and fogging it with his breath. "Hah."

"Shut up, Crip," said the injured man.

"Shutted," said the baby-man, nodding his head with gravitas—an important instruction understood and registered.

"Been staying at a pub in Osford," continued woolen hat. "Six-week contract. Bad bloody luck from the start. Pick a pub with the cheapest lodgings—a tenner a night—shared bath. Good grub, though. But the lousiest beer. So tonight, of all the bloody nights we coulda picked, we go out looking for another boozer with better beer."

"Tree fellers," Crip said, turning back to grin at them. "Get it? Irish, see? Tree fellers—that's us. And there's this tree, and it falls on the road. Tree fellers. Is that a joke, Tully?"

"Shut up, Crip. . . ." The injured man—Tully—groaned, leaning forward in his seat to hug at his thigh.

"Is it still bleeding?" asked Cath from the front.

Tully did not reply. But when the woolen hat leaned back to look, he said: "Christ, yes."

"Then you need a tourniquet on it."

"Turn-the-key." Crip grinned.

"What?" groaned Tully.

"A belt," Cath said, braking gently as a tree branch flew disintegrating across the road, then putting her foot down when it swept from view. "Are you wearing a belt? Is he wearing a belt?"

Woolen-hat looked at her stupidly—but now Tully was emerging from that spasm of pain, and Cath caught a glimpse of him in the rear view mirror; nodding to himself as he yanked his belt free from his jeans, wincing again. Finally, when it was free, he looped it around his leg, then through his buckle, before pulling it tight across his thigh.

"Look," said Cath at last. "You should loosen the belt for a few seconds every couple of minutes or so. You don't want to cut off the circulation."

"Yeah," Tully said, now staring up in agony at the roof of the car. "Right."

"Any of you got a mobile phone?" Cath asked.

When there was no reply, she glanced at the baby-faced man next to her, who was grinning as if she had just made a really good joke.

"A mobile phone," she said again—and this time, when she looked in the rear view mirror for some kind of response from the other two, she did not like what she saw. The woolen cap was looking intently to the injured Tully with an uncertainty that seemed to be waiting for instruction. Tully was clutching the belt, still struggling with his pain.

Finally, Tully said: "No. I mean—we've got one, but we left it back in the Land Rover. Never thought. Just had to get out of there."

A flurry of leaves blocked the windshield. Cath adjusted the wipers to maximum speed and cleared them.

"Here," she said, reaching into the glove compartment and retrieving her own mobile, now quickly readjusting her grip on the wheel as the car hit another rut in the road and the vehicle jounced on its suspension. Tully hissed in agony.

"Sorry!" Cath made to hand the mobile to the baby-faced man, who continued to grin and made no attempt to take it from her. Cath tossed it over her shoulder into the woolen hat's lap. Clumsily, he caught it.

"I think this warrants an emergency call, don't you?" she continued. "The nearest hospital is in Marsham, which might be too far out—but there's a clinic where they treat emergencies in Westerby. That's about eight miles or so." Glancing briefly in the rear view mirror again, she could see that the woolen-hat man was simply staring at the mobile phone in his hand with a blank expression on his face. "Look," Cath went on. "You best make that call now. You see those lights down below? That's a friend's farm. Once we get there we're in the hollow of a valley and we won't get a signal until we drive out of it again."

"A friend's farm?" asked Tully. "He's got a family— wife and kids, I expect?"

"No, he lives alone. Look, you'd better make that call before . . ."

187

"Is that right?" said woolen hat. "You hear that, Tully."

"I hear," said the injured man.

"What do you think?"

"I think we need somewhere until this bloody storm blows out."

"What about the boat? Will he wait?"

"Look at it out there, Pasco. . . ."

Pasco, so that's his name. . . .

"You think that boat's going anywhere in weather like this? He'll wait. He doesn't get the rest of his money otherwise. And believe me, he likes money."

"What are you talking about?" Cath suddenly felt a tightening knot of anxiety in her stomach.

"And he's a friend of yours, you say?" Pasco went on. "The man who owns the farm."

"Yes, but look—we have to get that leg of yours seen to. Urgently. You can't . . ."

Then Cath saw what had suddenly appeared in Pasco's hand, and suddenly the wild terror of the savage night was right there in the car with them.

TWENTY-EIGHT

With sodden rope, left lying in a loose pile by a nearby fence, Drew had made a noose; lassoed the flapping corrugated metal roof of the outhouse and—using his body weight to haul it down—secured that roof around the door lintel and open window frame. There was a controlled and yet fierce strength of purpose in that task—and he knew that it had to do with what had just occurred between Cath and himself. But it was something that he didn't want to think about too intensely—because he was afraid to think about it too carefully—and this brute strength of purpose in securing the roof in the midst of this wild storm was serving that purpose.

Don't be afraid, said a voice in his head. *This is good—and it's important. Don't shy away from it.*

"I'm not!" he shouted into the storm, and meant it.

The storm doors leading down to the cellar were secure but rattling, as if something were trying to get out, and as Drew hurried to the cattle stalls at the side of the farmhouse, he felt another pang at what was lying in the cage down there.

The cattle and horses were secure but frightened. There was nothing he could do about that other than to tighten the fastenings and hasps on loose doors and gates; move amidst them and make calming sounds and gestures as he laid out more feed and hay— unnecessary, given that the animals had more than enough—but resisting the urge to move too quickly and suddenly lest he ruin the calming effect he was try- ing to achieve. The pigpens were quiet, with all of the animals obviously taking refuge inside, the concrete structure safer than the stalls, stables and barns. One of the henhouses had been destroyed, and there was no sign of the former occupants—not even a feather. The birds inside had been blown away into the storm. Fences were down everywhere, and it would mean a hell of a lot of work when the storm had blown over.

I don't care, thought Drew as he battled around to the front of the farmhouse. *Whatever the storm does to the property, I'll fix it. I'll fix everything as good as new—because it'll be like starting again. Starting afresh and . . .*

"Starting new!"

As if in answer to his cry, there was another sound— a regular *crash-whump-crash, crash-whump-crash.* It sounded like the outhouse roof—but that was defi- nitely tied down and secure—and this sound was more distant, coming from somewhere up ahead on the rough track leading to the valley side where they had first encountered the Big Cat, and where every- thing in Drew's life, he now realized, had begun to change. He strained to see in the darkness, swung his flashlight beam way up ahead—but the light diffused in the storm blur and he could not make out where it was coming from.

Drew ran on ahead, past the front of the farmhouse and up the rough track.

At last, he knew where the sound was coming from.

It was the shattered door of the barn.

The place where he kept the monster that had killed his wife.

And as the storm wind snatched and tugged at him while he ran, it was as if he were being called up there by the hideous thing that had destroyed his life. It had held him back from ever being able to move on with his life and was even now trying to turn him back to the farmhouse—the prison cell of his own making.

So Drew ran full tilt toward that barn, denying that once-powerful urge of withdrawal from life; because now that strait jacket was in shreds and tatters—and he was running to confront the beast.

Now the torch beam revealed what he knew it would reveal.

One side of the barn door had blown open and shattered, its boards and planks flapping loose in the frame or lying scattered on the ground.

Gasping for breath, bent double with hands on thighs, Drew finally raised his head and pointed the light directly into the barn.

The storm wind had blown the dust and cobwebs from the huge, hulking carapace of the combine harvester. The once grimed-over "eyes" of the beast had taken on a new and lustrous shine of life in the torch beam. For a moment, it seemed that the wildly flapping and shattered half door was being propelled by some invisible energy from the thing inside the barn, rather than the storm wind.

"Except that you're not alive!" shouted Drew.

The combine harvester remained fixed in its idiot grin.

Drew moved slowly and carefully forward, shining the torch beam over the bulk of the machine.

And then, shoving the torch into his belt, he moved quickly to the shattered door, grabbed it with both hands and yanked it wide open on its rusted hinges. The top hinge cracked away from its support straight away. Drew slammed it back again, yanked down hard—braced a foot on the bottom rim—and tore it away completely. Flinging the half door aside into the night, he stood back and stared at the machine again for a long time as the storm snatched at his hair and clothes.

Then—stooping—he picked up a rock.

Straightening again, he hefted the rock in one hand.

"You're dead!" he yelled—pitching the rock straight at the thing. The rock punched a hole through the windshield, cracking the rest of the glass. "You were never alive!"

He turned his back on the barn, and on the lifeless thing inside.

"I'm sorry, Flora."

Drew fell to his knees then, and wept.

They were the sounds of grief that had been pent up inside since the accident, and Drew gave them up to the fierce energy of the storm. His voice called and howled in a once-suppressed, now-released agony that was animalistic in its pain and ferocity but deeply human in its heart-rending expression—fiercer even than the storm itself.

Finally drained, and with no sense of how much time had passed in that limbo of pain and storm and loss and letting go, Drew looked up and then down into the darkness of the valley hollow where the wind was raging around the farm.

"Take it all if you want to," he said. "I'm starting again."

And out there in the night, that which had taken tempo-rary refuge from the storm, heard the howling cry of an animal that was not of its kind—even above the savage wind—and recognized something within that call that it also felt deep inside.

The loss of a mate taken away.

The storm had stolen the scent, but its acute hearing had pinpointed the source and location of that cry and even now, it slithered from its hiding place—uncaring of the wild night, so alive with movement—and headed at once toward the place whence the sound had come. But whereas this Two-Legs' cry had been the cry of loss, it lacked something that now surged through the breast of the creature which sped through thrashing under-growth toward the hollow of the valley.

It lacked the fury and the anger and the ferocity of that which was hell-bent on retrieving what had been stolen, and of exacting a terrible and ferocious vengeance on the creatures responsible. With a savage intent, it streaked blacker-than-night through the storm—with a terrible power neither human or inhu-man, but infinitely ruthless and deadly.

TWENTY-NINE

"It's all right, darling! Everything's all right. It was only a dream."

Faye held Rynne tight, feeling the sweat on her brow and her heart hammering.

Outside in the wild night, the sound of the rushing wind around the eaves had become a shrill whistling moan.

"It was the man," Rynne cried. "The man who was a cat. He wanted money and he wouldn't go away."

"It was a dream, Rynne. That's all. Just a nasty dream."

Faye settled Rynne back into bed, and moved to the bedroom window. There were no trees close to this side of the house so the chances of anything coming down on this side, or branches snapping and coming through the window, were unlikely. The tree at the front of the house had been uprooted in the storm, the source of the terrible crash that had so alarmed Faye and also woken Rynne from her bad dream. But even though the tree had fallen away from the house, Faye was still filled with a dreadful anxiety about what might happen next in this terrible and violent weather.

"Where's Mum?" Rynne asked.

"She's gone out for a while, dear. She'll be home soon."

"Where did she go?"

"She went to see Drew."

"The Big Cat man?"

"Yes."

"The man in my dream was like a cat, Faye! And he was going to *get* us! Will Mum be okay, Faye? Is she safe?"

Faye hurried back to the bed and took Rynne in her arms again.

"That was just a nightmare. That's not real. Your mum will be home any moment. Now—come on downstairs and I'll make you a nice drink."

Rynne was still hot, her brow sweating, as Faye led her downstairs. She hoped that the child wasn't developing a fever.

"Why did Mum go out?" Rynne asked as they descended the stairs to the living room. "Why has she gone to see Drew?"

"Something . . . I think something to do with the book she's writing."

"Bad people can't turn into bad cats—and cats can't turn into people. Can they, Faye?"

"Only in dreams," said Faye. "Only in nightmares . . ."

And then the lights went out, and Rynne screamed as night invaded the house and the storm wind shrieked new fury around them.

THIRTY

Drew had almost reached the farmhouse, had paused for breath that had been stolen away by the wind—when he realized something was wrong.

He looked around in the wild darkness of the night, at the wind-thrashed trees and braches. He had lashed down the feed shed's roof, had seen to the animals, had secured what could be secured—had even faced down the beast in its den—but there was something else, something now unsettling and disturbing in a more immediate and *dangerous* way.

Could it be something to do with Cath? Was she all right? Had something happened to her on the drive back to Rynne and Faye?

"I should never have let her go back in all this!"

Despite his anxiety and concern for her, something instinctively told him that this wasn't it. Drew pulled out the flashlight, breath regained, and battled on through the wind toward the farmhouse. No, this was something else. Something still formless and shapeless but nevertheless something that was growing in threat and becoming more palpable and real with every step that he took.

Something is coming.

Something is coming here on the storm.

That something, Drew felt, was traveling fast, and he could not shake the feeling that its sole purpose was to harm him.

The front door of the farmhouse was open, banging back and forth in the wind.

It had not been open when he'd left it.

A curtain on the porch beyond had flapped out through that front door and was snagged in the top frame, beckoning to him as he ran toward it.

"Cath!" he called as he reached the doorway. Her car was nowhere to be seen, but the feeling that someone or something had entered the house was overwhelming. There was mud on the mat in the entranceway, but this could have been blown in by the storm. Drew stepped warily inside. The feeling of imminent danger was still palpable.

The interior door to the living room was open.

Could have been the wind . . .

Drew struggled to close the door behind him against the wind, which now had a different sound; moaning and whistling like a living thing. Drew moved through the porch, stood in the interior doorway and looked around the living room. Sheets of newspapers and magazines had been scattered all over the room, but he remembered that from the time that Cath and he had first opened the front door and gone out into the storm. It seemed like a very long time ago.

There was a stillness in the room, an air of expectancy and watchfulness. It made Drew's flesh creep.

"Who's in here?"

Drew moved across the room to the staircase, half expecting to see mud on the stairs as a sure sign that someone had come in. There was none. He strained to look upstairs, resisting an urge to run up there.

In the kitchen, the door to the cellar was open.

But surely that had been open before?

From the cellar, he could hear the rattling of the storm doors as the wind plucked at them. Mad light and shadow danced in the kitchen as bushes thrashed and clutched at the window beyond. The mud on the kitchen floor leading to the cellar door must surely have come from his and Cath's shoes? God knew— they had been too preoccupied in each other to have noticed something like that. Drew moved into the kitchen, stooped to examine the mud marks. They were still fresh and damp.

Something behind him—*now!*

Drew whirled, instinctively holding up the torch like a club to ward off whatever was about to launch itself upon him.

The living room beyond was as empty as before.

A sheet of newspaper slithered slowly from the sofa to the floor.

Was there something crouched behind that sofa— something watching and waiting to pounce?

This was ridiculous! Drew rushed to the edge of the sofa and pushed it hard.

He recoiled as something screeched. He raised the flashlight high in defense.

It was the castors on the sofa. That was all.

Quickly dodging to one side so that he could see what was behind the sofa, Drew kept the torch raised high like a weapon to see—

Nothing at all.

Cursing himself for a fool, Drew straightened, pulled the sofa back to its original position and then froze.

Something *scratched* in the kitchen.

Drew whirled back, but could see nothing. He strained to listen for further sound.

There was only the rattling of the storm doors below.

A trickle of sweat between his shoulder blades also served to raise the hair on the back of his neck as he moved slowly back to the kitchen. He paused in the doorway—and the noise came again.

A long, deliberate *scratch*—like a single claw dragging on a concrete floor.

Now he realized that it was coming from the darkness of the cellar doorway.

Drew rechecked the living room, scanning the kitchen for movement as he moved to the cellar doorway. Leaning into the darkness, he flicked on the light switch. The sudden illumination received no response, did not serve to alert any intruder or whatever was making the noise. Drew carefully stepped into the doorway and looked down into the cellar.

It was as before. The storm doors were still locked; still rattling as the storm wind pounded at the hasps. There was no sign of anyone or anything down there. But could someone or something be hiding beneath one of the workbenches?

Drew started down the stairs.

Now it seemed as if it were more than the storm trying to get in through those rattling double doors beyond; it was as if some wild animal was trying to break in.

Drew paused on the stairs, stooping low now to see

if anything was crouched in the shadows. He flinched when the overhead lights flickered.

"Christ, Drew! Pull yourself together."

At the bottom of the stairs, he heard the *scrape* again—off to his right, from the cage.

For a moment, he could not move.

When he did, he turned carefully and slowly.

And looked.

"Good *God* . . . "

The Big Cat snarled at him, revealing its long yellow fangs. The sound filled the cellar, louder than the storm. The fetid smell of its breath was the same as the smell from the cave. Its opal-glass eyes seemed to radiate hatred as it shifted position, pushing closer to the bars—as if willing its sleek black body to press through the bars to the other side, where it could rend him to shreds.

Drew staggered back, bumping against a workbench. The torch dropped from his hands and rolled across the concrete floor.

The Big Cat shifted back, away from the bars and onto its haunches, as if it could now launch itself forward and smash its way through those bars. Its gaze never left him.

Something moved between its forepaws.

The Big Cat looked down briefly to acknowledge the presence of the thing that emerged from the sleek black fur of its underbelly, before returning its deadly opal-eyed gaze to Drew. He watched, mouth open, as the thing pushed forward between the Big Cat's paws and rubbed itself against the bars. When it saw Drew, it pulled back and hissed.

"Good God *almighty* . . . "

It was a cub.

"How . . . ?"

And now Drew could see the streaks of white fur above this creature's eyes that was so like the white flashes of fur on the cub they had caught in the net back at the cave. The fact that the Big Cat should now suddenly be alive in the cage when it had been so clearly dead was—impossible. But that there should now somehow be a cub in there with it was even more impossible. The bars of that cage could not possibly be wide enough for it to squeeze through from outside. But the Big Cat *was* alive, and somehow the cub *was* in there with it. For a crazy moment, he wondered whether the Big Cat had given birth. But this was the *male* cat, damn it! Drew struggled with his thoughts, unable to take his eyes from the white fur on the cub's brow and telling himself that this could not possibly be the same cub they had encountered in the cave. Could this creature have followed them, made its way down to the farmhouse through the storm? Could this cub have been the presence he had sensed as it made its way back to its parent?

"It can't be. . . ."

The cub slithered and shifted.

On the dewclaw of its right forepaw was a snagged fragment of netting.

There it was—and there they were—alive and so full of what seemed to be a wild and naked hatred for what he had done to them. Somehow—impossibly— Drew now had what he had been hunting for, and more, all these years.

He could not believe it.

And now—God help him—he did not want it.

Stunned, unsure what to do, Drew retrieved the torch from the floor. He never took his eyes from the creatures, nor he they. They spat and hissed as he carefully placed the torch on the bench behind him; as if this mundane act could somehow undo everything that had been done.

"I'll . . . go . . ."

They were the only words he could find as he stumbled away from the cage and back to the stairs.

He turned back only once, as if expecting the vision in the cage to have disappeared. As if in answer, the Big Cat roared defiance at him; the cub shrinking back and burying itself in the black fur between its parent's forepaws and chest.

Drew froze.

Beyond the shuddering cellar storm doors, there seemed to be an answering roar in the night. A snarl of sound which was like a hellish echo of the Big Cat's fury—but which must surely be just that—some bizarre echo, or maybe the storm's thunder.

Drew waited for that sound to come again.

There was nothing but the storm, raging and buffeting.

Drew ascended.

At the top of the stairs, he paused in the kitchen doorway; one hand braced in the doorframe—and felt the storm shuddering the very fabric of the house.

"What have I done?"

In the living room, he picked up a sheet of newspaper—something for his hands to do—and continued to struggle with the reality of the creatures downstairs in the cage.

Headlights swept the glass windows of the porch.

"Cath!"

Drew cast aside the newspaper and hurried to the front door. As he moved, he heard the crunch of gravel as the car came to a halt, heard the car door open. At least she was safe! She'd seen that Rynne and Faye were safe, and she had come back to him through the storm. As he opened the door, he realized just how much he wanted her.

"Drew!"

He recognized her silhouette running toward him, as the storm gusted through the front door and into the house.

"Cath, thank God! You're safe. . . ."

"Drew, go back! Don't . . ."

Something was wrong with her voice. There was a jumble and flurry of movement behind her, but Drew couldn't make out what was happening as he took a step forward and—

Cath was suddenly propelled forward into his arms from behind. He staggered back as they embraced, instantly recognizing her smell and her warmth, the impetus of Cath's forward momentum throwing them back into the porch. She lost her balance and clung to him, his foot skidded on leaves and Drew fell clumsily back against the porch shelf. A blur of silhouetted movement, Cath was shoved hard against him again, and this time they both reeled and staggered—back into the living room, as shapes filled the porch and the front door slammed shut.

"Honey!" said an unfamiliar man's voice. "We're *home!*"

THIRTY-ONE

*That which had followed its prey back to the Two-Legs'
stone lair and had slithered low through the darkness
as the Two-Legs managed to close the entrance before it
could make its killing run, hissed at the vehicle in the
driveway and retreated to the feed shed to hug the
ground, watching.*

*It had heard its mate calling from the cellar and had
clawed at the cellar storm doors, answering its mate's
cry and knowing that its cub had joined its father in
captivity, instead of waiting in the lair for its return.*

*The rushing, roaring sound of the Round-Leg Beast
approaching had made it retreat to the darkness again.
It had watched as more of the hated Two-Legs had
emerged and entered the house. Its mate and its off-
spring had been taken then, not by two of the Two-
Legs—but by three more, who had now come to savor
and gloat in the capture.*

*The She Cat growled long and low as the storm wind
continued to grow in strength and ferocity. It was a*

sound of fury and intent. Once there had only been two, now there were five.

Five hated Two-Legs.

Its mate and its cub were held by them.

Five would die.

THIRTY-TWO

The first face Drew saw was the face of a baby, atop a man's body. He was grinning, standing with his hands held at each side as if he were hoping Drew would rush him. Drew made to pull away from Cath, baffled and enraged by the sudden rough entry of these intruders—but Cath clung tight to him, holding him back.

"What the hell do you think you're doing? Get the hell out of my house!"

The man in the woolen cap was half carrying a third man, arm-over-shoulder, moving quickly to the sofa in the center of the living room. Now Drew could see that the man was badly injured, one leg at an unnatural angle below the knee. He cried out in agony as the man in the woolen hat rested him back on the sofa.

"Cath, who are these people?"

"These people," laughed the baby-man, looking back at his friends to see if there was a joke.

"Not funny, Crip," said the man in the woolen hat.

Drew pulled away from Cath and seized the baby-man by the shoulder.

"Get the hell out of here!"

The smile vanished from the baby face.

Drew did not see the blow, but in a flash of white light he was suddenly on the floor and Cath was kneeling beside him, holding him close again. Everything had suddenly become a blur of slow motion.

"Now that," said the woolen-hat man, standing suddenly in Drew's line of vision and smiling down at him. "*That* was funny."

He lashed out with his foot, connecting with the side of Drew's head.

White light exploded, and Drew was suddenly not there anymore.

Cath flew at Pasco, fingers clawing at his eyes.

Pasco seized her wrists, stumbling back—and Crip began laughing and whooping at the fun. Cursing, Pasco collided with the sofa and the sudden jolt sent a spasm of fresh agony through Tully's leg.

His scream was drowned by the pistol shot he fired into the ceiling.

Cath pulled away, Crip was no longer laughing— and all three remained frozen as flakes of plaster drifted down on them like a single flurry of snow.

"You," said Tully through gritted teeth, pointing the gun at Cath. "Painkillers. For Christ's sake. Get me some painkillers."

Cath stared at the gun. When Pasco had taken it out of his jacket in the car, Tully had cursed as if he had shown their hand, and snatched it from him. She had known then that everything was going to turn bad.

"Now!" Tully shouted—and Cath backed off into the kitchen, and started looking through the cupboards and cabinets. Tully turned the gun to Pasco. "And *you!*" Pasco's hands clenched and unclenched at his side.

"You will fucking behave yourself, Pasco. You'll keep your hands off the both of them."

"You pointing a gun at *me?*" Pasco asked. His face was blank, an expressionless mask. But that very blankness, and the tension in his words, conveyed a menace that Cath could feel as she rummaged through a cabinet and found a red cardboard box.

"I'm telling you," Tully continued, "that we don't need any more hassle than we've already got." Tully turned to Crip, who was looking back and forth between the two men, alternately smiling and frowning. "And you, Crip."

"Yes, Tully?" Now he was smiling broadly and eager to please.

"Get back to the car. Bring the stuff in here."

"Stuff?"

"The suitcases, Crip!"

"What do you want them in here for?" Pasco asked. "Leave 'em in the car."

"I want them in here."

"Why?"

"Comfort!"

"For Christ's sake!" Pasco turned—the threat and the tension dissipated. "We'll both go."

Cath hurried back, throwing the red cardboard box onto the sofa next to Tully as she moved quickly to Drew. Groggily, he was rising on one elbow, a livid weal on his temple.

"What are these?" asked Tully.

"Solpadeine. That's all I could find in there."

"What's solpadeine?"

"Painkillers."

Drew groaned as Cath pulled him into a sitting position, his back resting against a chair.

"Aspirin? Is that what this stuff is? Soluble aspirin?"

"Drew, are you all right . . . ?"

"I'm . . . okay . . ."

"You're giving me *aspirin* for a broken leg?"

"Damn it!" Cath stood erect, fists clenched, glaring at the man on the sofa. "That's all there is. Which is why you should be in a *hospital,* not here! What do you want? What the hell are you doing here?"

The front door gusted open, admitting the storm.

"Pasco! Shut that bloody door!"

The door slammed, and Tully looked back at Cath—now examining the box in his hand and nodding, as if he had solved a problem.

"You and your boyfriend behave and you'll be okay. You mess around, cause any trouble—and I'll turn Pasco loose on the both of you."

"What do you want?"

"First off—I want the car keys. For the Land Rover."

"Land Rover's damaged," Drew said.

"Yeah, right. Where are they?"

Drew pointed to a side table. When Tully gestured, he swept them up and tossed them to him.

"We're going to stay here until the storm dies down," Tully continued. "And you're going to be nice and polite and behave yourselves. Then we're going to leave and you and your boyfriend can carry on with your lives as if we'd never been acquainted."

"That leg needs proper medical attention."

"And now—would you be so kind as to get me a glass of water? It says on this box that I need some water to dissolve these things in."

Drew rose shakily and Cath helped him into a chair. As she went to the kitchen to get water, the door banged open and shut again as Pasco and Crip returned. Cath handed the glass to Tully. He smiled up at her; a ghastly rictus of mockery and pain—now holding up the gun in one hand and the painkiller box in the other to show that his hands were full.

"Why don't you be a mother?"

Cath took the box and watched as Pasco and Crip brought three suitcases into the living room. She put the tablets into the glass as they placed the luggage—almost reverentially—in the middle of the room. Pasco had a small bag with a drawstring over his shoulder. She handed the fizzing glass to Tully, watched as Pasco slid the small bag off his shoulder; quickly sliding it to one side beneath a writing table. There was something too nonchalant about that movement. She became aware that there was an expression of alertness on Tully's face now as he watched him. Tully sipped from the glass.

"Good idea," Pasco said. "A drink. Got any booze in the house?"

Tully downed the painkiller.

"More. Give me more."

"Hello?" continued Pasco. "Booze? In the house? You deaf?"

"I don't know." Cath headed back to the kitchen with Tully's empty glass.

"You don't *know?* What the hell kind of girlfriend are you, then?"

"Kitchen," Drew said. "Second shelf . . ."

"That's more like it." Pasco swung from his chair and loped to the kitchen.

"I don't want you getting pissed, Pasco." Tully grimaced.

"You just going to tell me what I can and can't do all night?"

"I don't want you losing it, that's all."

"After what we've been through, you're not gonna say I can't have a drink?"

Returning with more water for Tully, Cath was suddenly confronted by a grinning Pasco. She tried to side step him. He moved with her, blocking her way.

"Excuse me!" Cath moved around him, squeezing past.

"Nice manners." Pasco turned to watch her go. "Nice arse, as well."

"Pasco, I'm telling you . . ." Tully took the water, and Cath moved back to Drew, now coming out of his grogginess at last.

"Okay, okay!" Pasco gave a whoop of delight when he found a whisky bottle on the shelf. Quickly unscrewing it, he drank deeply. "Christ, that's good!" He screwed the top back on and threw it across the room to the child-man. Clumsily, Crip caught it—then greedily took a hefty swig.

"Don't hear you telling Crip off."

"Drinking makes him cleverer. Just makes you more fucking stupid."

The blank expression was on Pasco's face again.

Cath waited for something bad to happen.

But that blankness didn't hold. Pasco's face suddenly cracked into a grin; now he pulled off his woolen hat and ran a hand through thick curly hair as he guffawed. He returned to his chair, still laughing—patting the suitcases lovingly as he passed—sprawling and beckoning again for the whisky bottle. Dutifully, Crip brought it over; now sitting cross legged and grinning next to those suitcases—eager baby face studying the faces of his two "friends" for instruction or approbation.

"So what now?" asked Drew.

"Like I said." Tully shifted position again, grimacing. "We wait."

"So you're alone here?" Pasco asked. Without waiting for an answer, he slid from the chair again and moved to the telephone on the table by the door. Pausing for a quick swallow of whisky, he lifted the receiver. "Hello? Hello—room service? What kind of hotel is this, anyway? Service is useless. Just been 'serve yourself' so far. You get it, Crip? 'Self service'? Okay—room service? Tell you what you do. You send up some sandwiches, please. Nice ones, eh Crip? With the edges cut off." Pasco slammed the receiver back down, drank again and moved back to his chair. "She was right. The line's dead."

Outside in the storm, something cracked and splintered.

Pasco paused, listening—exchanging glances with the others. Then he slumped back into his chair.

"Crip?"

"Yeah?"

"Get yourself into that kitchen. See if there's anything to eat."

Crip quickly did as he was told.

Pasco drank again. "So what are *you* then?"

"You talking to me?" Drew asked.

"Well, I'm looking at you, aren't I?"

"I'm a farmer."

"Right. A farmer. You don't look like a farmer. And what about you, sweetheart?"

"Nothing," Cath said.

"Nothing?" Pasco laughed. "You're a 'nothing'? Hear that, Crip? She's a nothing."

"Yeah," laughed Crip, opening the refrigerator door. "There's chicken in here, Pasco."

"That'll do it. Find a plate. Load it up."

"There's them little red tomatoes and stuff."

"Load it all up. Bring me a plate. So, Mr. Farmer—what's she like in bed, then? She go down on you?"

Drew tensed, saw Tully shift on the sofa—and the look that he gave to Pasco was instantly registered by him.

"Okay, okay!" laughed Pasco, holding his hands up in mock surrender. He drank again. "You want something to eat, Tully? Keep your strength up?"

"I couldn't keep anything down."

Crip brought the plate over to Pasco, chewing on a chicken leg. Pasco took it, began stuffing it into his face. "Looks good, tastes good. Could have been presented a little better on the plate, I believe."

Drew and Cath watched him eat in silence. Crip sat cross-legged on the floor again, next to the suitcases; chewing on the chicken leg. When Pasco had finished, he dropped the plate on the floor and wiped his hands on his front.

"Should check the house out, huh?"

Tully nodded.

"Okay, I'll check upstairs. Crip, there's a door over there in the kitchen. Looks like it leads down into a cellar or something. You check that out."

Drew exchanged a look with Cath. What would happen when they discovered what was in the cage down there? In the intensity of their predicament, should he—or would he—tell Cath of the strange and confounding appearance of the cub in the cage? Drew decided to keep his mouth shut and see what happened.

Pasco sprinted quickly up the stairs and was gone from sight. Drew and Cath watched Crip move to the kitchen. He paused in the cellar doorway, looking down into the darkness, as if unsure about venturing down there.

"There must be a light switch," Tully said. "Find a light switch."

Crip groped in the dark and found the switch. Grinning back at Tully, he turned and clumped down the cellar stairs. Cath felt Drew's grip tighten on his arm. When he looked across the room, he could see that Tully had been watching them and had noticed their tense body language.

"What's wrong with you?"

"Nothing much," Drew said. "Just three guys holding us hostage."

"And one holding a gun on us," said Cath.

"Life gets shitty sometimes, doesn't it?"

"I'm not a doctor," Drew continued. "Like I said—I'm a farmer. But I know enough about animal injuries to see that leg of yours is in a very bad way."

"You going to give me a lecture about the hospital, like her?"

"No. Probably too late for that."

"What does that mean?"

"You're bleeding pretty badly. Every time you loosen that belt."

Tully realized that he hadn't been loosening and tightening the belt as Cath had suggested back in the car. He put a hand down by this thigh. When he lifted it, the hand was covered in blood, as was the sofa where he was sitting. Convulsively, he tightened the belt again—grimacing in pain. "Get me some fucking towels, then!"

"Where?" Cath asked Drew.

"On the bench. Just there."

Cath moved quickly, snatched up tea towels from the bench—opened a kitchen drawer and found more; now holding them out to Tully with cold anger in her eyes. Cursing, he snatched them from her; threw them down next to him, grabbed a fistful and jammed them up against his leg. It stained instantly.

"You'll bleed to death by morning," Drew said.

"You better hope I don't. I'm the only thing that'll stop Pasco carving you up and raping your girlfriend."

There was a clattering on the stairs as Pasco descended. He was grinning again.

"Nice big bed up there. All mussed up. Wonder what *that* means?" He was still swigging from the whisky bottle, which was now almost empty. "Where's Crip?"

"Still downstairs in the cellar," Tully replied, looking at the tea towel to see that it was stained bright crimson. The grin vanished from Pasco's face. He stared, and drank again. Tully took another handful of towels and pressed them to his leg. Pasco walked past, fascinated by the sight of all that red, into the kitchen and to the top of the stairs. Cath realized that she had seen something like that look before, on the faces of people passing by some horrific car accident with morbid curiosity. But there was also something else in Pasco's expression. He was enjoying it. At the top of the cellar stairs, still staring back at Tully, he called:

"Crip? Anything down there?"

Cath had returned to sit on the edge of Drew's chair. Drew waited, stiff and tense, for Crip's discovery of the cage and what was—or was not—inside. They both had the same thought. What might they be likely to do?

"Crip? You still alive or not?"

215

"Yeah." Crip suddenly appeared at the top of the stairs, right next to Pasco.

"Christ!" Still staring at Tully, Pasco had been unaware of his presence and flinched away at the voice right next to his face. "What you trying to do? Scare me to death."

"I scare you then, Pasco?" laughed the child-man. "Did I really give you a scare?"

Ruffled, Pasco slapped him flat-handed on the chest. The blow didn't move him. Crip stood there, solid and grinning.

"Find anything down there?" Pasco asked.

Drew and Cath waited.

And then Crip said: "No. Just stuff. Benches and shelves and stuff."

Cath looked back at Drew, brow creased. Drew returned the puzzlement.

Pasco nodded, lazily sauntering back to his chair—staring again as Tully loosened and retightened the belt. Crip returned to the fridge, found a carton of orange juice, ripped the top off and guzzled.

Back in his chair, drinking again, Pasco said: "So you're a farmer who doesn't look like a farmer. She's a 'nothing.' What do *we* look like, then?"

"You really want me to answer that?" Drew said.

Pasco laughed. "You're good. You're funny. But go on—tell me what you think we look like?"

"You look like someone who likes to make people suffer," Cath said.

In mock outrage, Pasco replied: "Me? No! I'm a lover—not a fighter."

Drew fingered the weal on his brow and forehead. "Yeah, I've had some experience of that."

"You're very good, you are. Very funny. But you've got me wrong. I'd rather love than fight any day." Pasco rubbed his crotch, grinning at Cath. "Know what I mean, darling?"

Cath deliberately held his grin with a blank stare.

"Now those suitcases there," continued Pasco. "They're going to buy me a lot of loving." He paused, looking across to Tully—whose eyes were closed. Had he fallen unconscious with the pain? Was he sleeping? Being careful, he corrected himself: "Sorry I mean *us*— not just me. *Us!* You wanna know what's in 'em?"

"No," Drew said.

In mock disappointment again, Pasco asked: "Why not?"

"Because we don't want to know," said Cath. "We just want you out of here and gone."

"You're no fun." Checking out Tully again, Pasco leaned behind him and grabbed the drawstring of the shoulder bag that he had slid under the writing table, dragging it out and swinging it up to his lap. He held it there in his lap, grinning again, and keeping a watchful eye on Tully—whose head was now down so that his chin was resting on his chest. The gun was still tightly held in his lap, barrel pointing out. Had he really passed out? Cath and Drew's attention was riveted on Pasco. Was he going to make a move? Maybe try to take the gun away from the injured man?

"Crip?" Pasco said at last, still keeping his eyes on Tully.

"Yeah . . ." answered the child-man through a mouthful of cold chicken.

"Anything else to drink over there?"

Pasco was still fiddling with the drawstrings on the

bag as Crip returned to the drinks cabinet and found another bottle. "Yeah." He spat chicken skin on the floor. "Tek . . . tek . . . something."

"Tequila," Drew said.

"Exotic," exclaimed Pasco. "You a Mexican farmer, then? Bring it here, Crip."

Dutifully, the child-man brought the bottle as Pasco finished the last mouthful of whisky and exchanged the empty bottle for the new one. Crip moved the empty bottle from hand to hand, unsure what to do with it.

Drew watched Pasco, still keeping a careful eye on Tully, whose head remained still. The towels by his legs were soaked in red. He watched Crip puzzling over the empty bottle, exchanged a glance with Cath—whose face was white and drawn with anxiety—but was unable to communicate what was going on in his head.

What the hell had happened down there in the cellar? Why hadn't Crip said anything about the cage, the Big Cat and its cub? He slavishly did everything he was told, so why hadn't he said anything when Pasco had asked if there was anything in the cellar?

Just stuff, he had said. *Benches and shelves and stuff.*

And a ferocious black panther in a cage, thought Drew. *With a Big Cat cub that just can't possibly be in there!*

Drew watched Pasco watching Tully—watched Pasco drink and then wince at the taste. "Fucking lighter fuel!" exclaimed Pasco, and drank again.

So what were the options? Perhaps Crip had literally *not* seen the cage? Impossible. It was hidden by the turn at the bottom of the stairs, but it was in clear view when you'd reached the bottom—or were heading back to the stairs to ascend. Did he *see* the animals then, but it just hadn't registered? Clearly, he was mentally challenged, but even an adult with the mind of a child—albeit a violent if not psychotic mind—would react to the sight of those wild and exotic creatures. By rights, Crip should have come thundering up the stairs in excitement, telling the others what he had discovered. Or was it possible—and now Drew could not get the thought out of his mind—that Crip had seen the cage, but . . . ?

No, that's not possible!

But he really *hadn't* seen what was inside the cage.

Could it be that he had seen an *empty* cage?

Some inner logic was telling him that perhaps the cage door was unlocked; perhaps the cats had escaped the cage. Perhaps they had escaped out into the storm-driven night again, through the cellar storm doors—which had finally blown open? Perhaps he *really* didn't see them, and that this was the logical answer. Crip didn't see them because they weren't there. But, no—Drew could hear those doors, still rattling and banging as the wind raged around the house. Perhaps the beasts were loose from the cage and hiding in the cellar when Crip had gone down there?

No, thought Drew. *That cage door is still locked. I know—because I made that bolt and hasp myself, I fitted it myself. And when we left that Big Cat in the cage, I slid the bolt on that cage and I made SURE it was in the hasp. Nothing could get in and out of there . . .*

Except, impossibly, a Big Cat cub?

It MUST have followed us back. It MUST have got in through the open front door. It MUST have found its parent in the cellar—and squeezed through those bars to get into the cage.

Have you seen how narrow those bars are? Even if it

did follow us back, how on EARTH did it get back in there?

He became aware that Cath was looking at him again, trying to read his mind.

The cage door IS locked. Those cats are in there.

Cath could see that there was something in his eyes; something he was trying to convey to her, but could not.

They're in the cage—but Crip couldn't see them. He just couldn't SEE them!

When Drew had gone down there himself, when he had discovered the cub in the cage, the Big Cat had responded with threat. It had roared, it had snarled guttural fury. But since the arrival of these intruders, when Crip had gone to the cellar, they had remained completely silent. Not one snarl, not one hiss, not one rumbling roar to reveal their presence. Even the sounds of the storm, of the rushing wind and the crashing night, wouldn't have covered up the sounds that animal and its cub made.

That's because they're not there, said the inner voice. *They can't be there.*

They're there, thought Drew with utter certainty.

He remembered what he'd told Cath when she'd first arrived on the scene, before they had ventured into the cats' cave lair—something that until now, in the rush of excitement and terror and love and the whirlwind storm of emotion that had followed their capture of the Big Cat—he had forgotten until this moment.

"I told you that I came face to face with a Big Cat on my farm," Drew had told her. "But I didn't tell you everything that I felt, everything that I experienced back then. I was so close to this damned thing that it could have torn me apart. Why it didn't, I'll never know. And crazy

though this might sound—there was something about this thing. Something DIFFERENT.

"Don't know if I can explain it properly, and I know that when—when you're in danger . . . in terror . . . things can happen to your mind. You maybe see things—not as they are. Do you know what I mean?"

"Yes, I do, Drew," Cath had said.

"But it wasn't like that when I came face to face with this thing. I knew—just knew that there was something different about this Big Cat. Not a panther, not a puma—not even a hybrid. Just something else . . ."

And then:

"It may well be some kind of crossbreed that no one's come across before. I've laid traps, set up cameras, everything. But these cats—well, they've got an un-canny ability to evade detection and sometimes—just sometimes—a ferocity unequalled by any other Big Cat I've learned about."

Cath had said: "So actually what you're saying here is—well, that the press and media have got it right. That we're dealing with something that is like The Hound of the Baskervilles?"

"Yes . . . no . . . I don't know. I just know that there's nothing supernatural about it. They're just—different."

The storm rattled and whistled at the kitchen win-dow, banged and rattled at the storm doors in the cel-lar. Pasco looked up. For a moment, Drew wondered if he would send Crip down there again to check out the sound—and that maybe this time, Crip would descend and then *see* what he had missed the first time. But Pasco returned to the tequila bottle and his slow watch of Tully, who remained in the same position. Had he died? Drew could not see his chest rising and falling as he breathed.

And Drew remembered:

"When I turned, there it was—in the bracken, watching me. Obscured, so I couldn't see all of it. But it was . . ." He had struggled to find the words. *"I always keep the tranquilizer gun in the back, just in case. I slowly walked back to the Land Rover and—well, after everything that's happened, I was convinced that by the time I got it out, primed it—the animal would be gone. It wasn't. It was still there. It had moved, was still obscured and—Christ, I think it was stalking me. But this is the thing. You can see the bushes and bracken on that side of the hill aren't that dense. Enough to provide cover for birds or smaller mammals. But not enough to provide cover for an animal that size. This Big Cat— puma, panther, whatever—is BLACK. I should have been able to see it at that range—maybe twenty-five yards—in such sparse cover. But I couldn't, Cath. I couldn't see it properly as it moved."*

He remembered now the excitement of that moment.

"There's something—I don't know what—but there was something going on. Some kind of camouflage effect that I just couldn't work out. I couldn't see it properly, Cath!"

And Crip hadn't seen it at all in the cage!

How was that possible? Could this somehow be the same thing? Drew's mind was spinning with the crazy implications, the bizarre aspects of what he *hadn't* seen out there in the bracken—and what Crip had now so obviously *failed* to see in the cage.

So you're trying to tell me, Cath had said. *That we ARE dealing with The Hound of the Baskervilles? Except that—it's a CAT?"*

"I know what you're thinking," Pasco said, and Drew

was startled out of his spinning thoughts to realize that he had been watching him for some time. "I know just exactly what you're thinking."

Drew did not answer, knowing anything he might say would just be used and fed into whatever sick fantasy Pasco might have in mind. He gritted his teeth, feeling the tension in Cath beside him.

"How do we get out of this?" Pasco continued. "That's what you were thinking. How will we get through the night in one piece?" Pasco looked carefully again at Tully. "Well—I've got an idea. But I don't want to feel as if I'm making anyone do anything against their will. Know what I mean?" He drank again and belched. "Pardon me. Awful thing—house guests without manners. Where was I? Oh yeah—how to get through the night. What do you think, Crip?"

"What?"

"I've got an idea."

"Yeah?"

"Yeah." Pasco fixed his eyes deliberately on Cath. "What do you say we have a party? Would you like a party, Crip?"

"A party? Yeah?"

Pasco turned his gaze back to Cath. "You be nice, Nothing Girl. And we can pass the time. And no one will get hurt. And the Mexican farmer can watch, and if he's really good he might get to play at the party as well. . . ."

"Tully!"

Drew's yell had an immediate effect.

Tully's head snapped up, raising the gun.

Pasco glared at Drew in rage.

"You said that we'd be all right if we co-operated," said Drew tightly. "But if you don't get that leg seen to,

223

you're not going to last the night. And in the meantime, your lunatic friend is just going to do whatever the hell he likes. Do yourselves a favor, Tully. Just get the hell out of here."

Pasco started to rise from his seat, anger flaring. Drew was on his feet first, enraged and ready to go, aware now of Cath's hand on his arm.

"Let me have him," Pasco said.

"Come on and try it," said Drew through gritted teeth. "I've had all I'm going to take from you."

"Sit down, both of you!" Tully snapped, grimacing again as he struggled with the belt around his thigh. The towels packed in around his thigh were now completely red.

Neither man moved.

"Now!" yelled Tully.

Pasco sat back.

"Pretty please," Tully said—and Drew reluctantly sat back again. On the other side of the room, Crip watched intently with his mouth open. When Drew had finally settled, still rigid and angry, Tully turned to Pasco.

"I told you to behave yourself."

"What am I supposed to do? Just sit here? We got a whole fucking night of just sitting here?"

"Have another drink, and think about tomorrow."

"Tomorrow, yeah. If that bloody boat is still there."

"Shut up."

"Right—shut up, do this, do that. I'm telling you, Tully. I'm getting pretty fucking sick of being told what to do. If you'd listened to me when I said . . ."

"What's that? In the bag."

"What?"

"You know what I mean. That bag in your lap."

"Nothing."

"Tell me, Pasco."

Pasco picked up the bag from between his legs, began fiddling with the drawstring like a schoolboy who'd been caught by a teacher with stolen goods.

"Nothing."

"You tell me nothing again, I'll put a bullet in your kneecap."

"All right, all right—that leg of yours has turned you mean. It's a keepsake."

"Show me."

Pasco's expression slowly changed. A smile crept over his face as if a new and deeply appealing idea had occurred to him. "Anything you say, Tully. You're the boss. I really have to hand it to you. You know how to do the bossing. And I really have to hand it to you . . ." Pasco pulled the bag open, took what was inside and tossed it across the room to Cath.

Startled, Cath caught it—then cried out and dropped it in horror and disgust. It hit the floor with a curious *flopping* sound.

"Oh my God," said Cath, backing into Drew. He held her, and looked down at the thing as Pasco burst into mocking laughter.

It was a severed human hand.

"See what I meant?" laughed Pasco. "Got to *hand* it to you! Get it? Got to *hand* it to you!"

Crip was laughing too. "Hand, yeah! Hand!"

"Good Christ," Drew said—recognizing that hand, just as Cath had done. The elaborate, over-ostentatious rings on each finger were only too familiar.

"Kapler Dietersen," said Cath, struggling to control her nausea.

Suddenly, Pasco wasn't laughing anymore. Tully was

sitting higher, the mask of pain on his face now more alert, more dangerous.

"Shut up, Crip!" Tully snapped—and Crip was silent again.

"What did you say?" Pasco asked.

"Kapler . . ."

"Cath, no!" warned Drew.

". . . Dietersen."

"You *know* Kapler Dietersen?" Pasco's humor and drunkenness seemed to have disappeared immediately. "How the hell do you *know* Kapler Dietersen?"

"Shit," said Tully.

"They know him, Tully. They only fucking *know* him! What the hell are we going to do now?"

Tully shook his head angrily. "I knew after we offed him you were doing something. When I was checking those cases. You idiot!"

"I always take something. Always take a keepsake after a job. You know that."

"I've told you *not* to do it. Told you!"

"Yeah—well, done it now, haven't I?"

Tully raised the gun to Drew and Cath. "Crip? Take them both upstairs, in one of the rooms. Me and Pasco have to talk."

"Don't you wanna talk to me as well?"

"Crip—just do what the hell you're told."

Sulking, the child-man moved to Cath, reached to take her arm. Angrily, she swatted it away.

"Go with him—and don't cause any trouble. Now."

Drew and Cath moved on ahead, Crip following up the staircase behind them—looking back like a child being sent to his bedroom.

"So what do we do?" Pasco's voice came up the stairs behind them as Crip pushed them both on ahead into the bedroom. "They know—knew—Dietersen. That changes everything, doesn't it?"

They were the last words that Drew and Cath heard as Crip slammed the door shut behind him.

THIRTY-THREE

It crouched beneath the kitchen window, the storm wind ruffling its sleek black fur—and listened to the hated voices inside. The wood of the cellar storm doors had been gouged and splintered by its claws, the sounds disguised by the storm, but the doors had remained steadfastly secure. It knew that its mate and cub had sensed its presence, faint scent-traces of fear and anger and hope leaking through the cracks of the unyielding doors before being whipped away by the wind. Enraged and frustrated, it had circled the house several times looking for another way in and found none. From within the kitchen, it could hear the emotion in the sounds that the Two-Legs made. It could sense the fear and the anger, serving to further enrage it.

It raised its head to the lower rim of the window and shrank back when another black-furred face reflected back at it. It knew what this was; had experienced the unnatural nature of glass before. Something to be seen through, like water when it drank from a stream and could see its own face. But invisible and dangerous; wit-

ness the jagged scar on its hind leg when it had once tried to enter the lair of a hated Two-Legs last summer, spurred on by the smell of cooking food. There was no entry here.

Snarling, it circled the house once more, hugging the ground and blacker than night.

There were still no openings, no means of entrance.

Enraged beyond control, it flew back through the night to a place where it could vent its anger. The storm wind seemed to carry it through the air as it cleared a broken fence, landed and rebounded with incredible grace—and threw itself at the remaining henhouse.

The flimsy wall, already weakened by the storm wind, instantly shattered. The roof slithered aside and the fowl within squawked and chattered in terror as it savaged and ripped, feathers and flesh shredding and flying in the wind. The taste of blood, even this thin and miserable blood, goaded it into frenzy. The small and terrified life, which disintegrated between its jaws and its claws, fired its own blood and slaked its ferocity.

In seconds, everything living was destroyed.

Standing stiff and erect in the ruins of the henhouse, chest heaving with exertion and the taste of blood in its mouth—it turned to look back through the night at the farmhouse. It knew from experience that the Two-Legs would not stay in there for long. Soon there would be a way in.

When that moment came, there would be richer blood to taste.

THIRTY-FOUR

"Shouldn't have told me to shut up," sulked Crip, looking back at the closed bedroom door.

"No, he shouldn't," Cath said, catching Drew's eye. He was leaning against a chair and by the look on his face, ready to do something drastic at any second.

"Wasn't for me, they couldn't have done it. Any of it."

"Done what, Crip?" said Cath carefully, moving to sit on the edge of the bed and still anxiously looking at Drew.

"The robbery."

"There's money in the suitcases?"

"You don't know nothing," Crip said. He leaned against the wall, attention still fixed on the closed door. "There's more than money in them suitcases. There's drugs and stuff."

"Three suitcases, Crip," said Cath. "So that means there should be one for you. Three of you, and three suitcases. One each."

"Yeah . . ." Crip pushed himself from the wall,

walked in a circle head down; then stopped again to stare at the door. *"Yeah!"*

"Like you say, they couldn't have done it without you."

Drew moved around the chair, sat down carefully—aware that Cath was trying something.

"That's right," continued Crip. "They need me. 'Cause I'm not scared to hurt people if I have to. I don't do it for no reason. But Pasco and Tully, they know they just gotta ask me to hurt somebody and I hurt them. That's what I do."

"So they shouldn't cut you out like that," Drew said, catching on. "Send you away. That's not right."

"They think I'm stupid. You think I'm stupid?"

"No," said Cath and Drew together.

"I know stuff. I know what was happening with that Kapler . . . what's his name?"

"Dietersen," Cath said. "Kapler Dietersen."

"Yeah. Him. See—he was buying drugs from this guy. Cash for the drugs. Tully, he got to know. Got them contacts, see? Got brains. He found where that Dieter—what's his name again?"

"Dietersen," Cath said.

"Yeah—he got to know where he lived. Got to know when that guy was coming with them drugs. So—we turn up. We off the guy and the Deeter-thing guy. And we get the money and the drugs. Tully knows this guy with a boat? So we do the job, we gotta drive to the coast and meet the guy with the boat. That's not far from here, right? I like the coast. My gramma used to take me to the coast. So the boat guy's gonna take us across to some-place with a funny name like Scandy—something . . ."

"Scandinavia?" Drew said.

"That's him. Anyway, we got the stuff but know we gotta get out of the country 'cause we gonna off some people. Definitely that guy you just said with the funny name 'cause Pasco says him and Tully got shafted by him on some other deal that they had. Anyway, we do the zero on him and the drugs guy and I got to off three or four others, I forget how many. . . ."

Cath felt nausea rise, felt sweat trickling down her back. The bedroom window was rattling in its frame as if the glass might implode at any moment. When she looked back at Drew, he was gripping the chair rest with both hands so that his knuckles seemed to gleam white. His face was set.

"They shouldn't be sending me up here like that. I know what they're talking about. Know what they're gonna do. They think I'm just fucking *stupid*. But I know."

"You're right," Drew said, trying to disguise the effort in his voice. "They're not treating you properly."

"Telling me to shut up all the time like I don't know nothing. I know something. I know when I can say stuff and when I shouldn't say stuff. It's like me telling you all this stuff now. It doesn't matter, does it? I know what they're talking about down there, know what's gotta be done. See, I can tell you this stuff 'cause it doesn't matter your knowing. 'Cause Pasco and Tully are deciding you both gotta be offed."

"Offed?" Cath said, with cold terror.

"Yeah. You know—killed. Well, it makes sense, don't it? Pasco gone and showed you the funny-name guy's hand, and you knew who it was and stuff. So they're probably deciding *how* you're gonna be offed. But look, you're a nice lady. So I'm not gonna let Pasco do to you what he's done those other times. I didn't say anything when he made me watch it them times. But I didn't like it. What he said before about having a party? I wouldn't have joined in. No, when you're offed, I'm gonna do it. And I promise I'll do it really quick."

"You're very kind," said Drew, his white mask of a face still set and cold.

Crip smiled widely, and meant it. "You're a nice fella, too. You and her—you listen and you're kind."

"You going to do me quick as well?"

"Anything you want!" beamed Crip, nodding his head.

"They still there?" Drew asked.

"What?"

"Pasco and Tully. I can't hear them."

"They'll be talking quiet so I can't hear I bet." The smile was gone from Crip's face again, the sulkiness returning.

"Maybe they're not there anymore, Crip."

"What?"

"Maybe they sent you up here so they could get you out of the way."

Crip stared at Drew's face intently, his baby-face frown creasing the skin of his brow.

"They keep you up here with us—and they sneak away with those cases—and leave you behind to take all the blame."

"You think they'd do that to me?"

"They sent you upstairs, didn't they? Told you to shut up."

Crip nodded his head, moved back to the door and placed his ear against the panel to listen.

"I can't hear anything."

"They're gone, Crip! They've taken those suitcases and they've left you behind."

Crip made a sound then, deep down inside. It was a

keening, moaning, sobbing sound of a child in distress. He stood back, shaking his head in denial—and then wrenched the door open so that it banged hard against the inner wall. He blundered out onto the landing.

"Don't you leave me! *Don't you dare leave me!*"

Drew leapt from his chair and slammed the door shut. Cath heard the snick of a lock, and then Drew swept up the chair he had been sitting on and jammed it under the door handle.

"What do we do?" Cath hissed.

"The window!" Drew grabbed her arm as they rushed to the bedroom window. "We've got to get out of here *now!* There's a drainpipe and a twenty-foot drop, but we've got to risk it."

Beyond the bedroom door, Crip was still bellowing—but now there were other raised voices as Drew slipped the catch on the window and yanked it up.

The window jammed when it had been raised no more than nine inches.

"Shit!"

The storm gusted into the bedroom.

Now there were sounds of heavy footsteps from the landing beyond as Drew struggled with the bottom frame of the window. Cath lunged forward, shoulder-to-shoulder with Drew, gripped the frame too, and heaved upwards with all of her strength. The window juddered up halfway and the wind was tearing at their clothes. Behind them, the bedroom door handle began to rattle furiously.

"Go!" shouted Drew above the storm. "You go first! Just get down there and away as fast as you can."

Cath squeezed through the frame, could see nothing but wild and raging darkness. But her terror had overridden any fear she had of heights as she straddled the windowsill, now groping to the side and finding the pitted metal of the drainpipe. She seized it with both hands; her lower body swung downwards and outwards from the sill. She cried out into the storm when her hip slammed into the wall. Her fingernails raked flakes of paint from the corroded drainpipe as her bodyweight dragged her down. Drew lunged out to grab her forearm until she had steadied. Legs kicking, Cath began to lower herself, hand over hand.

Drew looked back to the bedroom door, the lock and jammed chair shaking under the onslaught from the other side. It had to be Pasco and Crip. Tully would not be able to move, must still be downstairs. But who had the gun?

Drew slid sideways into the window frame, was squeezing himself through and reaching for the drainpipe when there was an animal bellow of rage from the other side of the door. He snapped his head back to look.

Just as an entire upper door panel splintered and cracked. On the second blow, the panel flew into the room; followed by a meaty fist and forearm. Drew had a fleeting glimpse of Crip's wild and bestial face— glittering eyes fixing on him—and then he swung out into the storm, gripping the drainpipe with both hands. The clamps fixing the drainpipe to the to the wall screeched, the pipe juddered and came away from the wall under their combined weight—and now Drew was dropping fast, one foot on each side of the pipe as it was dragged from its supports. Rust and corroded iron sliced his palms as he descended hand over hand.

Below, he saw Cath hit the ground, tumble aside on

all fours. The drainpipe cracked and screeched, the upper half now completely away from the wall—and Drew kicked and twisted wildly in the air, flailing to keep from falling directly on top of her. The drainpipe snapped at its halfway point, pitching Drew aside and away from her.

When he hit the ground on his side, the pipe shivering away into the darkness, the breath was slammed from his body. His brow and temple throbbed anew with sick pain where Pasco had kicked him. Cath was beside him now, pulling at his arm. On his knees, still winded, he heard the juddering crash and splintering of the bedroom door and of the chair being dragged aside.

Two heads were suddenly silhouetted in the window. One of those heads vanished quickly again.

Pasco—seeing them—and now dashing downstairs. Drew dragged himself to his feet, using Cath's arm and shoulder.

"Are you all right?" she shouted above the storm.

"Come on . . ."

Half staggering, half running away from the farmhouse, they sought the protection of the darkness and the storm. They would make it. Just a few yards more down the drive at the front and they would hit the main road and the hills and fields beyond, the darkness enclosing them. Then they would just keep on going through the night, putting as much distance between them and their unwelcome visitors as possible. The darkness would hide them.

And then twin beams of light stabbed out of the darkness directly in front of them, throwing their gigantic shadows behind them all the way back to the farmhouse. There was a screech of brakes being applied, a skidding crunch of gravel. Drew and Cath froze in shock, clinging together as the car that had roared into the main driveway came to a lurching halt on its suspension not ten feet from where they stood.

Police! Cath and Drew had the same instant thought. *They've come after them. We're safe!*

The car door flew open, snatched by the wind and making the vehicle rock on its suspension again. A familiar figure clambered out into the gale, hair flying.

"Oh no . . . oh no . . ." Cath moaned, as she moved to the car, placed a hand on the hood and shaded her eyes with the other to stare through the windshield at the small figure in the passenger seat. She began to pray then as she moved. "Please God . . . please God . . ."

But God, it seemed, was not to be pleased.

"Mum!" cried Rynne, kicking open the door and clambering out as Cath ran to her. "All the lights went out and you didn't come back and we were frightened and Faye said we should come to you and . . ."

"Oh no! Get back in the car, darling! Get back in the *car!*"

"Drew!" Faye shouted above the sound of the wind. "We were so worried. The telephones aren't working and we were worried that you . . ."

Drew seized Faye by the arm and dragged her back to the car.

"Faye, get in the car! *Now!*"

He saw her bewildered look of shock; saw Cath struggling to shove Rynne back into the vehicle, held the door as he pushed Faye ahead.

The night exploded with a shattering roar.

A fist-sized hole punched through the center of the windshield, the surrounding glass crazing into a mosaic of wild fractures; like broken ice on a frozen pool.

Silhouetted by the headlights, a terrible and familiar figure strode casually towards them—gun held out in front of him.

"Oh *Christ* . . ." moaned Drew, as Cath pulled Rynne close to her and watched as he approached.

"Oh my God . . ." Faye's voice was filled with horror. "My God . . . what's happening, Drew? What in God's name is *happening?*"

"More guests for the party," Pasco said, coming to a halt. His eyes and teeth shone in the headlights when he grinned. There was no humor in those glass-shard eyes. He stood to the side, and beckoned toward the farmhouse with the gun.

With cold horror, Drew took Faye's arm—exchanging a long look with Cath over the roof of the car.

They walked past Pasco toward the farmhouse. When they had passed, he moved to the car—switched off the engine, pocketed the car keys, but kept them in the headlights as they walked.

Ahead of them, Crip was standing in the front doorway.

Waiting.

When he stepped aside to let them enter, Pasco switched off the headlights that had floodlit the front of the building.

Gun swinging in one hand at his side, he followed.

THIRTY-FIVE

More of the hated Two-Legs!

The thin taste of the squawking small-life was gone now, but the fury it had temporarily assuaged had begun to swell within it again. Leaving the ruins of the demolished henhouse, it had prowled again; circling the house, watching and waiting. Warily, it kept a regular watch on the Round-Leg Beasts that served to carry the Two-Legs. They were dead now, as they always were when there was no Two-Legs to bring them to life. In disdain, it urinated on the Round-Legs of both beasts.

Suddenly, there was noise from the Two-Legs' lair—on the other side.

With grumbling fury shuddering its ribcage, the She Cat flew around the side of the house.

There was movement on one wall of the lair. Two figures clambered from a hole high up.

At last—there were two to kill.

And a possible way into the lair.

It slouched low, hugging the ground and watching; now moving its haunches from side to side in prepara-

tion, digging its hind claws into the soil, ready to launch itself forward in a killing run.

The first Two-Legs clambered and fell to the ground— a female, and in fear, by the pungent scent that barely registered before being snatched away in the storm wind. Moreover, it was the fleeting scent of an intruder that it remembered from its own lair; when it had discovered that its partner and cub were gone. It shuffled; ready to make its run as the second figure—a male— began its descent. This was a male Two-Legs the She Cat recognized, not only from its fleeting scent that had also been present in its lair, but from the way the figure moved. This was the male Two-Legs it had tracked back to the house—the male it had nearly taken earlier before the others had come.

A screeching shriek came from the lair—and a long thin something swung out away from the wall in its direction, the male Two-Legs clinging to it and kicking out its legs wildly. This was a bizarre form of attack that the She Cat had never seen before, could not understand the physicality of it, and was full of threat. The She Cat sprang backwards instinctively on its haunches, forepaws batting and swiping at the night air. The long, screeching thing—like a thin and living tree but not a tree—fell shivering to the ground as the Two-Legs came down through the air to complete the bizarre attack. It shrank back further at the Two-Legs' impact on the ground, alarmed. Fear temporarily overcame its urge to attack and protect. When it swung aside in the darkness and looked back, it first saw movement in the hole high up in the stone-lair wall, sensed anger there—then whirled to see that the male and the female were running from the stone lair into the night away from it.

A trace odor of fear was swept into its face and nostrils by the storm wind.

Enraged again, aware that there was entry to the stone lair on high, but that the long screeching tree that was not a tree might attack again if it tried to climb the wall, the She Cat took after the two hated Two-Legs that had first taken its cub and partner.

It would run them down and kill them both.

Maybe the other Two-Legs would come out when the death screams reached their ears.

Maybe they'd leave that entrance at the front of the stone lair open.

All these instinctive, inchoate but surging and powerful thoughts and emotions consumed the She Cat as she flew at the two figures through the night. The storm wind filled her gaping jaws, flooded her lungs and her belly, made her blood sing—as the fear scent came fast and strong and—

Light!

Two giant eyes in the night.

A screeching roar.

The She Cat reacted instinctively, swerving aside and streaking blacker than night behind a battered trough to the side of the drive.

Cries.

Excited jabbering sounds that only Two-Legs could make.

Close to the ground, she saw that it was another of the moving-not-living things on round legs. For the second time, one of these unnatural creatures that carried the Two-Legs and brought bright sun to the night had defied and stopped its stalking run.

But the wild night was still full of fear.

It sensed movement up at the stone lair.

The She Cat bent and curled its massive black and sinuous body against the far side of the trough, craned its powerfully muscled neck to look back and saw—

A Two-Legs—holding up a forepaw.

The night exploded.

The She Cat hunkered even closer to the trough, re-sisting the urge to flee. When it shifted forward, it could see that the Round-Leg Beast had disgorged even more of the Two-Legs. They were walking back to the stone lair in the bright sun stare of its eyes. Scent fragments—the stink of fear—whirled in the wind currents around them. The She Cat craned its head again around the edge of the trough. The Two-Legs who had made the night explode was still standing beside the Round-Leg Beast. It watched him lean inside and do the thing—whatever that thing was—that made the Round-Leg Beast die, the bright sun stare instantly gone. It watched him begin walking after them, and saw that the en-trance to the stone lair was open—and that the hated Two-Legs were re-entering. Was this the opportunity it had been waiting for? Could this last Two-Legs still make the night explode and bring death to it?

Slowly, low to the ground and sliding around the trough, it looked from the stone lair to the Two-Legs— from the lair—to the Two-Legs. It looked back once more to make sure that the Round-Leg Beast was still dead and not about to roar into life again. But there was no Two-Legs near to bring it to life again.

The Two-Legs were entering the lair.

The last Two-Legs could not see or hear it in the storm.

Bunching its powerful muscles so that they rippled under its thick black fur, it centered on the last Two-Legs—shifted and centered its gravity—dug its rear leg claws into the soft earth, and readied itself.

And then the Two-Legs turned, at the same time that the wind gusted and brought a brief sharp tang of scent to the She Cat. There was no taste of fear in that fleeting scent, no hesitation and no doubt. There was something else, something unnatural that the She Cat had never encountered before. It knew from its secret observation of these hated Two-Legs that they could not see in darkness. But something in the aggressive and confident stance of this Two-Legs halted her charge. Could THIS one see in the dark? Could it see her where she crouched—even now?

The Two-Legs raised the forepaw that had made the thunder.

Then it backed off into the stone lair, the entrance was suddenly sealed—and the She Cat's chance was gone yet again.

Growling, fangs gleaming in the darkness, it slid first to the trough—and from there through long grass to a fence, where it fixed its sight on the only chance left.

The hole near the top of the stone lair, from which the male and the female and the screeching tree that was not a tree—and which lay silent and dead in the grass—had come.

It was still open.

THIRTY-SIX

"What's the matter, Pasco?" asked the child-man, anxious to show his concern.

Pasco had closed the door, and was still staring at it with a troubled expression on his face. He weighed the gun, tossing it from hand to hand as he pondered.

"I thought . . . for a second out there . . . I thought . . ."

"You still mad at me?" Crip asked anxiously.

Pasco paused, still troubled—and then seemed to focus again and discard whatever was on his mind. "Yes, I'm still mad at you. Get the hell in there."

"See?" Crip turned, stomping like a bear-sized child into the living room where the others were standing together and waiting. He thrust his face into Drew's face, arms stiff at his side, fists clenched. "You messed my head! You got me into trouble with my friends! You got Pasco angry with me! And—you!" Crip bellowed at Cath, making Rynne cry out in alarm and cling even more tightly to her mother. "You pretend to be nice but you're not! You messed my head too. I should . . .

should . . . mess your *face!*" Crip raised his fist to Cath, stepping forward.

Straight-backed, face stern—Faye stepped between them.

"Young man! Behave yourself this *instant!*"

Crip froze, the glittering anger in his eyes seeming to grow dull.

"I'm sure you're a kind man and don't like frightening children. But you're being loud and you're frightening the girl. Please desist!"

Crip stepped back—just as Pasco elbowed him aside and glared at her.

"Everyone sit down," he said tightly. "And shut up."

Crip was still standing, apparently dumbfounded and with his jaw sagging as Cath and Rynne moved to the second sofa. Still straight backed, Faye sat next to them—at attention, as if expecting to be invited not to stay. Crip seemed unable to take his eyes off her, as if she were some puzzle to which he could not find the answer. Drew moved back to the chair he had previously occupied, wearily sitting and turning his attention to Tully; still in the same position on the first sofa. His face was ghastly, eyes glittering from a mask of pain.

"You think you're pretty bloody clever, don't you?" said Pasco—and Drew looked across to see that he was talking to him. "Trying to get away like that."

"I thought you'd made your minds up about something—and it wasn't in our best interests to stay around."

"You a mind reader as well?"

"Don't have to be with you."

"You've got a clever mouth."

"Look!" Cath straightened, the sound of her angry

voice making Rynne bury her head against her mother's chest. "It's not too late. You can still get out of here. We won't say anything. All right—we know who Kapler Dietersen is—*was*. . . . " Cath became aware of Faye stiffening. "But he—well—he isn't anything to us."

"Oh yeah?" said Pasco sarcastically.

"I mean—you just can't . . ." *Kill all of us.* Cath bit down on the words before they came out.

"I'm sorry, Cath," Faye said. "We shouldn't have come, but the lights went out and the storm, and you'd been gone for so long. I'm so sorry."

Pasco made a grotesque and sarcastic sound of sympathy, then tossed Faye's car keys to Tully.

"Hey, Tully. You could start a garage business—you got so many of these."

"Give me the gun, Pasco," Tully said through gritted teeth.

"So what we going to do now?" said Pasco, ignoring him. "Hey, I know. Let's send them all upstairs again, to different rooms this time. Then we'll have them jumping through every fucking window in the house."

Tully held out his hand. "The gun, Pasco."

Pasco weighed it in his hand. "We've got to *do* something."

"The *gun!*"

Pasco stuck it in the front of his belt, and then stood with his hands on his hips staring at Tully.

"No."

"You running things now?"

"With you sitting there bleeding to death? Yes."

"What's 'desist' mean?" Crip asked.

"What?" Pasco snapped.

"It means when you stop doing something," said Faye. Her voice was somehow ridiculously calm.

"Oh," Crip said.

"Crip, shut up—and come here."

Dutifully, the child-man did as he was told, head still down in deference.

"You want to be out of trouble with me?"

"Yes."

"Then get the girl."

"The girl?"

"The girl!"

"Which one?"

"The little one, you moron. The little girl."

Cath hugged Rynne even closer, Faye moving closer to them. Drew gripped the armrests of the chair, ready to rise—as Crip slowly turned, then took a step toward the sofa.

"You won't touch her!" Cath hissed.

Crip stopped, uncertain. He looked back at Pasco. "What for?"

"Do you want me to stay angry with you?"

"No."

"They tricked you, didn't they? Made you look stupid?"

"Yeah, but . . ."

"So get the girl."

"Pasco." Tully leaned forward, tugging on the belt around his leg and groaning. "What the hell are you doing?"

Pasco pulled the gun out of his belt again with a flourish. "Crip, you hold the little girl down here. The 'Nothing' lady over there is going upstairs with me."

"No, she's not," Drew said, rising.

"Yes, she is," said Pasco, swinging the gun toward him. "Because if she doesn't—Crip's going to hurt the little girl. Because that's what Crip does best. Right, Crip?"

Crip turned back to the sofa—just as Faye quickly stood and put herself in front of him again.

"Crip," Cath said, trying to keep her voice level. "You said you wouldn't let him—do things. Remember?"

"That was before you tricked me. Made me look stupid. Anyway—he's right. Hurting's what I do good." When he made to move again, Faye took another step forward so that they were face to face. Her eyes were hard and steady as she stared into Crip's piggy little eyes. He lowered his head bashfully, then said: "You better get out of the way, missus."

"No."

"I hurt a little old lady just like you earlier on tonight. I offed her. Tully wants me to—I'll hurt you really bad."

"I'm not a little old lady."

"Yes, you are," Crip said, head still down.

"Not like any little old lady you've met before, sonny."

"You!" snapped Pasco to Cath. "Over here. *Now!*"

Drew lunged—and Pasco had the gun barrel pointing at his face in a moment, only inches away.

The air was suddenly full of hateful and ferocious electricity.

"Pasco," Tully said. "You are one monumental idiot, with a head full of shit for brains. You're not going to do anything—and you're going to give me that gun."

"You're going to *shut up, Tully!*"

"No, I'm not. I'm going to tell you the reason why you're going to give me the gun."

"Too many clever mouths, too many people not doing what they're told. Maybe if I put a bullet in the lover-boy, eh? What then 'Nothing' lady? Do anything then, wouldn't you if I . . ."

"The guy with the boat. The guy who's waiting for

us? Know why he wouldn't leave? Know why he'll be waiting this storm out?"

Pasco kept his eyes on Drew, but his attention was focused on Tully.

"Because he's my brother."

Pasco took a step back, lowering the gun.

"Your brother?"

"That's right."

"You never said."

"No—because you don't need to know everything, Pasco. Too much information just seems to turn the shit in your head even shittier."

"So he's your brother. So what?"

"So if you fuck with me now on this, I guarantee you won't be getting on that North Sea boat."

"Maybe we don't need that boat. Maybe me and Crip can just . . ."

"Take those suitcases now, leave me here? Maybe try to sell the stuff somewhere else? Who do you know can get you the money I promised you for this job? Nobody, that's who. What contacts you got? None. So you can spend the rest of your life just selling it on street corners, a few quid here a few quid there—maybe until somebody rips you off, or the law catches up with you. My way and you'll be rich in a week. Everything you've ever wanted. Your way is no way at all. How about you, Crip? Who do you trust to make you lots of money?"

"I trust you, Tully. But I don't want Pasco mad at me."

"You're not mad at Crip anymore, are you, Pasco?"

"Tully . . ." Angered and frustrated, Pasco turned from Drew—glared at Tully—then walked in a circle, rubbing a hand furiously through his hair. "Tully, look . . . look . . . Come on, man. I need to *screw!*"

"Go somewhere and give yourself a hand job," Tully said calmly, holding out his hand. "Get it all out of your system. Calm yourself down. But first—give me the gun."

Pasco looked up in fury at Drew, then at the group on and around the sofa.

With a sound of anger and disgust, he slapped the gun into Tully's hand. Swiping up the tequila bottle from the floor, he wrenched off the top and drank long and deep.

And then the lights went out.

THIRTY-SEVEN

"We interrupt this program with a severe-weather warning. Gale-force winds and gusts of up seventy miles per hour—sixty knots—are already being experienced in the Northeast and are expected to worsen within the next few hours. The towns of Nicolham, Stamford and Osford have already suffered storm damage—and there are reports of damage, power disruption and failure to the villages and hamlets in the outlying areas. An emergency center has been established at Marsham, and Westerley residents are advised to stay in their homes, take necessary precautions and not to travel if it can be at all avoided. . . .

THIRTY-EIGHT

"Vic! The mooring rope's loose!"

Vic Tully choked on the vodka bottle, spraying alcohol down the front of his fisherman's jacket. Harry Caulder, well on the way to oblivion with his own bottle, had crashed through the front door of the concrete shithouse that served as base of operations for this pier—and had brought the storm in with him. He fought with the door, slammed it shut and blundered to the window as Vic tossed the bottle aside and staggered to join him.

Harry shaded his eyes to peer through the glass, but the reflection of the interior light bulb made it impossible to see anything properly in the storm blur beyond. Cursing, Vic swatted at the light switch and plunged the room into darkness. Now it was possible to see the foam turmoil of the sea beyond the pier, the gigantic black chasm of the sky; the half dozen moored and anchored boats rising and falling, slamming against the fortified pier stanchions—and the single forty-foot boat that had lost its stern mooring rope and was pitching in the foam, now rising on the swell and crashing hard against the pier with a sound like cracking thunder.

"*You* tied that boat up, you idiot!" Vic yelled, seizing Harry by his lapels and throwing him backwards across the room.

"I did, I *did!*" yelled Harry in return, arms pinwheeling as he regained his balance. "Tied it up tight, Vic! Fore, aft and anchored like always. Honest!" Vic's fists bunched up as he strode toward him.

"I told you what would happen if you screwed up, Harry."

"The storm's not my fault!" gibbered Harry, who had been on the receiving end of Vic's temper before and had no wish to repeat the experience. "Your brother not being here isn't my fault either. . . ."

Vic paused, muscles in his jaw working.

"Look, Vic, even if he was here, you wouldn't be going out in *that*. No way could you take the boat out in that."

"That boat smashes up—I'm gonna smash you up. You know that, don't you?"

"I'll fix it!" blubbered Harry. "Leave it to me—I'll fix it!"

Harry hastily hunted in the piles of tackle and debris up against the rear wall, found a coil of heavy-duty rope and hoisted it over his shoulder. When he grinned back at Vic, it was the expression of a frightened animal. In the next moment, the storm had erupted into the building again as Harry blundered back out into the night, heaving the heavy door shut behind him again. Vic watched the blur of his figure run staggering past the windows, watched him hanging on to the pier rail as he fought against the wind hand-over-hand to reach the boat.

Cursing, Vic strode to where he had dropped the vodka bottle. It was empty. He kicked it hard across the room, moved to the bunk cabinet and yanked out another. With the skill of a seasoned drinker, he held the bottle up high—head tipped back, and opened his gullet when he poured. A quarter of the contents went straight into his stomach before he drew breath again.

Everything had gone wrong tonight.

His brother had promised him big money for the trip—money that he badly needed. None of the long-range forecasts had suggested that a storm front was going to hit as badly as this one. There had been some warnings, but nothing that would have prevented them making the journey. The bastards! And his brother—the bastard. Where was he? The only luck he'd had that night was the fact that every other boat owner here had done the sensible thing—they'd tied up and headed for safety inland. So there was only Vic and Harry here tonight—and no one to ask awkward questions about Vic's brother and the two men with him. Except, of course—that his bastard brother and his pals hadn't shown up.

Vic made his way back to the window, rubbed at a pane—and stared out into the darkness. Harry had reached the forty-footer, was trying to lasso the stern rail with his rope—like he was some cowboy or something—but was missing every time as he staggered against the storm wind. The stern of the boat swung hard against the pier on a swell, and the impact in the boardwalk underfoot knocked Harry to his knees. Frantically, he threw one end of the rope up onto the aft rail—but the stern swung away from the pier again and the rope slithered off and into the water. Soaked, hair flying, Harry began hauling the rope back in again.

"You bloody *idiot!*" Vic yelled.

He drank again, slammed the bottle down so hard on the table that it cracked—and headed for the door.

The lash of the storm wind on his face blurred his vision. Salt spray soaked him as he clattered down the pier, hanging on to the rail. It was impossible to see where the sea ended and the ebony black sky began. As the storm raged in his face, Vic raged right back at it—blundering ahead toward the pathetic figure pitifully throwing the rope out to the boat, and pitifully missing every time. When Harry went down on his knees again, exhausted—Vic screamed obscenities at him, but his voice was swallowed by the storm. Vic reached him, saw him kneeling with his head sagging and with water pluming down across his head and running from his nose and chin. When he feebly groped with the rope again, Vic planted a foot on his shoulder and kicked him back. Harry flopped to his side, mouth working like a fish.

"Gimme that!"

Vic seized the rope, spooled it through huge fists until he had reached the improvised loop at the end of it and staggered forward—just as the stern came into the pier again. It smacked hard against the supports, but Vic's legs remained planted and firm in the impact. As the stern began to rise in the swell, and before it could swing out and away from the pier again, Vic threw the coiled rope—and the loop dropped neatly around a near-side rail end. Vic flipped and coiled the rope around a nearby capstan and prepared to brace his foot on it, hanging on to the rope. That rope would pull tight on the capstan, the boat would be tethered—and then Vic would pull more rope in around the capstan as it came back in on the swell again to the pier. Three more of those maneuvers and he would be able to tie it off hard to the pier, and the boat would be moored securely again.

But Harry, afraid of Vic's anger, blundered to Vic on all fours—trying to help by grabbing a loose coil of the rope—and Vic's foot came down, not on the capstan, but on Harry's scrawny legs. Vic fell forward, losing his grip on the rope and throwing out his hands to brace his fall as the boat came back into the pier again with a shivering crash. The rope slithered from the capstan, the impact throwing an off-balance Vic across Harry's body.

The boat swung out from the pier again and the rope looped Vic's waist and Harry's legs, dragging them over the side of the pier. Harry dropped clear of the rope and fell screaming, but grabbed Vic's ankle in the tumbling fall. Vic's left hand instinctively caught the edge of the pier, the rope still around his waist— and both men dangled and kicked in the foaming spray against the side of the pier.

The stern of the boat came rushing back in again.

When it surged out and away from the pier, the bloodied meat dropped into the water below.

The stains on the pier wall washed away almost instantly.

Forty minutes later, the stern of the forty-footer was ruptured.

Within the hour, it lay three-quarters submerged and rolling in angry water on the harbor bottom.

THIRTY-NINE

"Now what?"

Pasco slammed the tequila bottle down so hard on the side table that a plume of alcohol shot up from the spout in a wet spiral over his hands. Crip gave a hoarse cry—like a child suddenly locked in the dark, and Rynne clung so tight to Cath's neck that it hurt them both.

"It's the storm," Drew said tightly.

"The same thing happened where we were." Only Faye's voice appeared calm. "The lights went out there, too."

In the darkness it seemed that the storm raging outside had a new ferocity, the sounds of its rampage in the night now somehow amplified.

We're in a cage, thought Cath. *Oh God, we're in a cage.*

"You got a torch?" asked Tully.

"Second cabinet in the kitchen there," Drew replied. "Candles?"

"There are candles and a storm lamp in the cellar."

"Pasco. Get the torch."

"Let Crip get it."

"*Get* the torch!"

Pasco swung angrily out of his chair again, strode across the room to the kitchen and yanked open the first kitchen cabinet. He began to rummage, bottles and cartons falling from the shelves to the floor.

"The second cabinet," Drew said.

Pasco slammed the cabinet door so hard that it flew open again. More bottles and packages clattered to the kitchen shelf and floor. In the second cabinet, he found what he was looking for and switched it on. A spear of light stabbed through the darkness.

"Now what?" he snapped, flashing the beam from person to person.

"Get that fucking light out of my face," snapped Tully. "And now use your brain." He gestured at Drew with the gun. "Take him down. Get the candles and the lamp. Or do you want to sit in the dark?"

Pasco flashed the light over Drew, as if he wanted it to cause him physical pain.

"Come on then, move it!"

Shielding his eyes, Drew rose and made his way to the kitchen.

The cellar.

The Big Cat and its cub.

This time, they'd be discovered—and everything that had been running through his head since Crip's failure to see them in the cage would be resolved.

"Come on. Hurry up."

Pasco shoved him hard by the shoulder when Drew came level. Drew staggered in the doorway, looked down into the pitch darkness, then back at Pasco.

"What are you waiting for?" Pasco hit him hard on

the shoulder again. Drew gripped the doorframe and tried to keep his voice steady.

"The light? Or do you want me to break my neck on those stairs in the dark?"

"Stop fucking griping and just get down those stairs. I'll give you light."

Drew turned, and started down the stairs—blind in the dark.

Pasco stood at the top of the stairs, now shining the light around the cellar as Drew carefully descended. The beam lanced across the workbenches and table tops, the stained walls and the ceiling. He looked briefly at the storm doors, still locked and still rattling in the storm wind.

So that means they're still in here. They didn't escape outside. And if they're not in the cage, then they're hiding in the dark somewhere. I've got to say something. I've got to tell him—or that pissed-off male is going to come out from where it's hiding and tear me to pieces. . . .

"Afraid of the dark?" Pasco called, shining the light onto Drew as he reached the bottom of the stairs. His shadow loomed gigantically before him. Drew turned, shaded his eyes, and now he could see the edge of the cage nearest to the stairwell. He could barely see the bars, but only complete darkness in the cage itself.

"Look, there's something you should . . ."

And then Drew stopped.

The cage door was not open. It was still closed.

He could see the hasp and the iron bolt at the side of the cage.

The heavy-duty bolt had not been pulled open—it was still shot fully into place, and with the L-shaped end securely down and firm in its hasp.

Nothing had come out of that cage.

But all he could see beyond the faint outlines of the bars was utter darkness.

And there were no sounds from within.

My God. What is happening here?

"There's something I should what?"

"There's something you should know. I've got money. Lots of it. You take me with you tomorrow, and I'll take you to where it is. Draw it all out of the account. You can have it all. You just have to leave the others here. Not hurt them."

"How very kind. Know how much that stuff in the suitcases is going to get us? A bloody sight more than a farmer's savings. You just go and get those candles and that lamp."

Drew turned, his gigantic shadow turning with him to dominate the cellar.

"Where are they?"

"The old chest of drawers. Over there, to the left."

"Off you go, then. Don't break a leg in the dark, lover boy. You'll end up like Tully. Two broken legs. Two pains in the arse."

Drew walked on ahead.

How can they still be in there if Crip didn't see them?

His words to Cath: "There's something—I don't know what—but there was something going on. Some kind of camouflage effect that I just couldn't work out. I couldn't see it properly, Cath!"

Drew reached the chest of drawers, picked up the storm lantern and shook it. The lantern was almost full of paraffin. He held it up into the air, then stooped to open one of the drawers.

"Lover boy?"

Drew froze.

"There better not be anything else in that drawer other than candles."

"Like what?"

"Like a knife or an axe—maybe even a shotgun. Something you might use when you want rabbit pie?"

"Only candles."

"You better be sure."

"With the others up there—and Tully with a gun?"

"Go on then."

Drew pulled out the drawer. When he stood and turned so that Pasco could shine the light on him again, he held up his hands in the air; lantern in one, candles in the other.

"Bang," said Drew.

"Very funny. Now get back here."

Drew walked forward, flinching at the light in his face—now holding up a forearm across his eyes as he moved; and squinting ahead as he drew nearer to the cage. Only blackness behind the bars, hiding whatever was still in there. And there was the bolt, firmly in its hasp.

Drew reached the bottom of the stairs.

Tully continued to shine the light straight into his eyes.

Drew put a first foot on the bottom stair, and froze as—

Something growled from the darkness of the cage. It was a low and guttural grumbling—a sound he knew only too well.

And then, from above and beyond the house came a rumbling growl of thunder. The landslide shudder of noise drowned the sound from within the cage, now exploding into a full detonation that made the walls of the cellar shiver.

"Jesus *Christ!*" exclaimed Pasco, flinching at the sound so that his torch beam swung all over the cellar. "What kind of bloody storm *is* this?"

Drew glanced back at the cage, and saw nothing.

"Come up!" snapped Pasco.

As the detonation of thunder dissolved into the distance like a disappearing wave of sound, Drew ascended.

There was no further sound from the cage.

At the top of the stairs, Pasco shoved him ahead into the living room and slammed the door. Drew staggered to a halt, clutching the lamp and candles.

"You hear that thunder, Tully?" Pasco asked.

"I'm not deaf," replied Tully in the darkness.

"This is some wild kind of storm," Pasco continued. "Your brother better come good on this boat, Tully. I've put up with a whole boatload of shit from you tonight as it is."

"Shut your mouth."

Drew winced inwardly. Too much had been said by these men, too much information given away and now too freely to bode well for what lay in store. He looked at the other three on the sofa. Faye was still sitting stiff backed and watching, Rynne still clutching tight to Cath, whose face was spectral and white in the darkness. He knew that Cath was thinking the same thing.

"Bring that lamp and those candles here," Tully said.

Drew brought them to him, standing to watch as Tully painfully rummaged in his pocket. Each movement was causing him intense pain. Eventually, he held something up to Drew in the darkness. Drew took it from him—a box of matches. Drew stuffed the candles under his armpit, rested the lamp on the sofa armrest and fumbled to open the box. He began to strike the matches—one after the other.

"What's the matter with you?" Tully snapped. "Can't you light a bloody match?"

"That's just it," Drew said, striking again. "The matches are bloody."

"What the hell are you talking about?"

"These matches are all wet. They're soaked in your blood."

"Shit. You got matches?"

"There are matches in . . ."

Thunder crashed again, directly overhead—filling the living room with the sound of its detonation. Cutlery and crockery cracked and rattled in the kitchen, the walls of the room shivering under the impact. The storm wind seemed to shriek in reply, and in the next moment there was a splintering *crack* and the shattering crumble of masonry and wood falling apart. The kitchen window shattered as a tree branch burst into the house, glass splintering and flying—wind gusting though the broken panes. The storm howled into the living room.

"Get that window blocked!" Tully yelled.

Drew dropped the candles onto the sofa next to Tully and ran to the kitchen. Snatching at the branch protruding through the broken window he snapped off twigs, leaves and smaller branches as the wind gusted in his face. Pasco was suddenly next to him, cursing and elbowing as he yanked foliage aside and threw it behind him into the kitchen.

"What's happened out there?" yelled Tully.

"Looks like a tree down," Drew yelled back through the storm wind.

The protruding branches and twigs were clear of the

window. Jumping up, Drew seized the sturdy window blind and yanked it down across the window frame, fastening it at the sill. The wind died away, but the blind rattled and clattered furiously.

"Check the cars, Pasco," Tully said through clenched teeth, wracked with new and hideous pain.

"What?"

"Check the cars are *okay*. You do want to get away from here in the morning, don't you? If that was a tree coming down, I want to make sure the cars aren't damaged."

Pasco started for the front door.

"And you—what the hell *is* your name, anyway?"

"Drew Hall."

"Hall—find some matches that aren't wet."

"In the cupboard here."

"Get them then."

Drew went to get them as the front door opened and closed, returning to Tully. He retrieved the lantern from the sofa, lit it and handed it to him.

"Put it on that table there. Next to me. Get those candles lit."

Drew did as he was told, lit a candle and took it to Faye. She exchanged a look as Drew returned to the sofa and took more candles. When the door banged open again and Pasco re-entered, the candle blew out.

"Pasco! For God's sake!"

"Will you keep your hair on? I'm doing what you told me, aren't I? Never good enough for you, Tully."

"The cars?"

"They're okay."

"Do they need to be under cover somewhere, out of the storm?"

"They're sheltered out there in that forecourt as

good as anywhere. Nothing gonna blow down on 'em where they are."

"What about that fucking tree through the kitchen window."

"Got blew out from the side. Nothing else there."

Drew began lighting candles again, placing them on doors, shelves and cabinets. Pasco sprawled back in his chair, lifted the tequila bottle and emptied it. He watched Drew lighting and placing the candles, and then began clapping.

"Lovely job. Now it's just like fucking fairyland. Isn't it, Crip?"

"Yeah," snorted Crip. "Like fairyland."

"Find me something else to drink."

Crip rose and headed for the kitchen.

"You a proper farmer then?" asked Tully, when Drew had finished. Shadows guttered everywhere in the living room, making it look like some kind of bizarre underwater grotto. Orange light shone from the lantern on the table next to Tully, making his face look like a carnival mask. The window blind rattled fiercely. Downstairs in the cellar, the storm doors juddered and rattled in response.

"Don't know what that means," Drew said.

"You must know things. About animals."

"Some things."

"You ever fixed an animal? When it's been injured, I mean?"

"You mean like—a broken leg, maybe?"

When Tully smiled, it looked ghastly in the lamplight. "You've got a quick mind."

"I don't fix broken legs. I send for a vet."

"Vets are in short supply tonight. I bet you could give it a try, though. Bet you've seen it done."

"I've seen it done. But why should I even try?"

In response, Tully simply raised the gun.

"You're going to kill us anyway," Drew said.

"Not necessarily."

"You guarantee to let us go, if I try to fix your leg?"

"I guarantee you won't come out of this alive—any of you—if you don't."

Cath sat forward, prizing Rynne from around her neck.

"I'll do it," she said.

Tully and Pasco exchanged looks.

"I'm a nurse," Cath said. "I can help."

Pasco laughed; a short bark of derision. "You're no nurse. You're a 'nothing', remember?"

"I can help," repeated Cath, aware now that Drew, Faye and Rynne were all staring at her. She prayed that no one would say anything.

"You didn't say anything in the car," Pasco said. "Why didn't you say you were a nurse in the car?"

"Whose idea was the tourniquet? Who knew where the hospitals and emergency clinics were?"

Tully loosened the belt again and groaned. "You've been sitting there, watching me bleed all night—and you're giving me fucking aspirin for *this!* What kind of nurse is that, then?"

"Why should I help you when you've been terrorizing us? And for your information, I'm not a fully qualified nurse. I'm an auxiliary assistant, and I'm training to be a nurse. But I'm the nearest thing to a proper nurse you're going to find tonight."

"She's telling the truth," Faye lied. Her voice was as straight and steady as ever.

"So what can you do?" asked Tully.

"Make a splint," continued Cath. "Straighten your leg.

Strap it up—bandage it. Can't say it'll be pleasant for you. But you have to promise not to hurt us."

"What you going to use for splints?" asked Tully.

"I need something hard and straight. . . ."

"Well, I can help you out there, darling," Pasco said, grabbing his crotch. "No problem."

"Maybe two straight pieces of wood or metal," continued Cath, ignoring him. "Drew, do you have any . . . ?"

"You mean like *this?*" Pasco stood up, wavering—swept up the side table next to his chair and dashed it to the floor. Rynne squealed, and Faye pulled her close as Pasco trampled on the upturned table, yanking off first one leg and the other. He held them up like trophies. He seemed a great deal less steady on his feet than previously.

"Yes," Cath said in a voice that was both flat and disgusted, never taking her eyes off Tully, who continued to study her intently through the haze of his pain. "Like that. Drew?"

"Yes?"

"We need some linen or some rope. Something to bind them together once his leg is straight. Unless Mr. Pasco wants to pull down some curtains as well?"

"*Mister* Pasco? Now see, Tully—that's all a man needs. A little respect." Pasco slumped back in his chair. "You found anything else to drink yet, Crip?"

"Got lemonade here," Crip called, rummaging through cabinets.

"I said something to *drink* you idiot!"

Crip turned back. When he spoke this time, there was no subservience in his voice. "I'm glad you're not mad at me anymore, Pasco. But my feelings is still hurting 'bout being made to look like an *idiot*. I'm not gonna hear that stuff no more from anybody."

This time, when Pasco laughed, it was forced. "I'm sorry, Crip. I didn't mean nothing. You know that. Me and you is pals. Always have been, always will be. It's this storm and stuff. Hurting my head, you know? Now, you find me some booze and it'll make me feel much better."

"Yeah," Crip said, lightening. "My head hurts as well. You think it's the wind and the thunder and stuff?"

"That's exactly what it is, Crip. Tell you what—you find a bottle of something, and me and you'll share it. Make our heads better, eh? Where's the rest of the booze, farmer man?"

"You've drunk it all."

"Bollocks! Keep looking Crip, there's bound to be something in there. . . ."

"Pasco," Tully said.

"Yeah?"

"Shut the fuck up. You too, Crip."

"Shutted," said Crip, returning to his search.

"There are more towels there," Drew said. When Cath looked back to Drew, she saw the hardness in his eyes, saw the recognition that she had something in mind and was waiting for some kind of development. "In the kitchen drawer. You could use them to make splints."

"What about your *bra*, Nothing Nurse lady!" Pasco laughed, loud and braying. "You could use *that!*"

Tully squirmed round to look at him. "You been taking some of that stuff we got?"

Pasco spread his arms wide, a big grin on his face. "Who me? I'm just like Crip. I do whatever you tell me to do like a good boy."

"Crip," Tully said, still looking at Pasco. "Find the towels."

Crip moaned, clattering amidst the shelves and cabinets. "Too many things to do—you keep asking me too many things—"

"Which drawer?"

"Beside him now, on the left," Drew said. He and Cath still held each other's eyes. Mouth tight, Cath nodded imperceptibly.

"The drawer on your left, Crip. Calm down."

Crip pulled open the drawer so hard that it slid out of the unit and fell to the floor. He kicked it in frustration, took out a handful of towels and blundered to the sofa, tossing them at Cath before returning to the kitchen in his hunt for a bottle. "There's nothing here, Pasco. I can't find nothing here."

"Keep looking." Pasco grinned. "You're doing a great job."

"So do it," Tully said to Cath.

Cath stood, looking back to where Faye was holding Rynne. Her daughter was shivering with fear, but Faye remained straight backed and still. With the towels in both hands, she knelt down in front of Tully.

"Oh man," laughed Pasco. "The things I could find for you to do if you were kneeling in front of me."

Cath looked at Tully's shattered leg, left and right. The guttering shadows in the lamp and candlelight seemed to make the black-red wound there come alive. She touched the torn fabric of his jeans, and Tully hissed in pain.

"Violence is shocking," she had told the Welsh journalist, the words somehow coming back to her. "It is horrible. And I've tried to show that. I suppose if anything I've tried to deglamourize it."

"What are you waiting for?" he hissed again.

"This is no good," Cath said. "I've got to straighten

your leg to get the splints on. You'll have to lie length-ways on the sofa."

"Makes sense," giggled Pasco.

"So help me God," Tully said through clenched teeth. "You've been sneaking something down you when I wasn't looking. That's not just the booze talking."

"Not a good patient, is he nurse?"

"Help turn me round."

Pasco stood up from his chair, teetered and sat back again heavily. "Just gimme a minute."

"Shit!" Tully turned to Drew. "You—come over here and turn me around like she says."

Drew rose and moved to the sofa. Tully raised the gun and pointed it at him.

"I'm expecting you to be gentle and not do anything stupid. Give me your arm." Drew stood behind the sofa and held out his arm. Tully grabbed his forearm, hiked himself sideways, with the gun held up and never less than six inches from Drew's face. Tully's face contorted, and Cath could hear his teeth grinding as he hiked himself sideways again, now bracing his good foot on the bottom armrest of the sofa and shoving hard to straighten himself. His shattered leg trailed horribly below the knee along the side of the sofa as he moved, the foot bumping and dragging on the carpet.

"Shiiiitttttt . . ."

"There's something specific about human violence," she had said. *"Something squalid and horrible that sets our species completely apart. Animals will kill for food, or to protect themselves or their young. Humans are the only animals that will kill or maim for the sake of it."*

Tully's face was running with sweat. The place where he had been sitting, and the mass of towels he had first used, was drenched in sticky blood.

"Stand the fuck away!" snapped Tully to Drew.

Drew stood back as Tully swung the gun across to where Cath knelt. This time, the barrel of the gun touched her forehead.

"Lift that leg and put it on the sofa."

"I'll do it!" Drew started to move.

"Stay *put!* The nurse here'll do it."

"Look," Cath said. "This is going to hurt—and I don't want you to squeeze that trigger by mistake."

"Yeah," said Pasco. "She's right. Gimme the gun, Tully."

"You must be joking," Tully said. And then, to Cath: "Just do it."

"Christ, you be careful with that damned gun!" Drew gripped the edge of the sofa.

Cath reached down.

"I guess you could say that I'm appalled and fascinated by what people have called the 'culture of violence.' I like to think that, as a decent human being who abhors violence, I could never bring myself to actually harm another human being."

Using both hands, and with the gun barrel still touching her forehead, Cath gently took Tully's lower leg—one hand on the calf, the other by the foot. When she lifted it, a sibilant hiss came from Tully's mouth through gritted teeth—like escaping steam. There seemed to be hardly anything connecting his lower leg to the knee as she placed it on the sofa next to his other leg. Tully's head twisted, and the gun came away from Cath's head as she fell back and away. The gun thumped on the carpet, but Tully was still holding it.

Drew and Pasco's eyes locked.

Suddenly, it seemed that Pasco was no longer drunk or high on drugs. His eyes glittered as he lunged from the seat and Drew came around the bottom of the sofa.

The gun came up from the floor, Tully pointing it upside down and backwards at Pasco's stomach. Tully turned his head back to stare at Drew, who froze. When Pasco sat back, Tully righted the gun and pointed it—almost lazily—at Drew.

"I'm going to give you the benefit of the doubt," he said in a voice strangled with pain. "That you weren't going to do something stupid like I warned you about. Pasco? Anything left in that tequila bottle?"

"Nope. That's why I got Crip looking."

"Shit. Come on then, nurse. Do your stuff."

"Okay, I'm going to place these splints on either side of your leg. But Drew's going to have to help me. Unless you want your friend over there to lend a hand?"

"Get on with it."

"Drew, come round here. I want you to hold these splints against the side of his leg. I'm going to slide these towels underneath and around, then tie them tight. But first I have to straighten his leg."

Cath laid the broken table legs on each side of Tully's ruined leg and then, as Drew came around the end of the sofa and she brushed past him, she fixed him with as hard a stare as possible and hoped that he understood.

Drew knelt down by Tully, leaning over to hold the splints—and feeling the gun barrel come up against his temple. Pasco laughed again, wheezing and spluttering.

"Hey, this is good! The farmer's turn now."

Drew looked back at Cath as she stood at the bottom of the sofa.

"Hey," Crip said from the kitchen. "I found a bottle. Lick—lick—something . . ."

"Liqueur," Drew said.

Cath gently took Tully's foot in her hands.

"This will hurt," she said calmly.

"I could never bring myself to harm another human being . . ."

"Do it," said Tully. "And get it over with."

"Animals kill to protect themselves . . ."

Cath looked to where Rynne was being comforted by Faye—and thought she saw an almost imperceptible nod from the older woman.

"Or to protect their young."

Cath yanked Tully's leg back as hard and as savagely as she could. Sinew and cartilage *ripped* with a sound of wet cloth.

Tully screamed, high pitched and shrill as Drew grabbed for the gun, seizing his fist in both hands as Tully's finger squeezed the trigger in a reflex of hideous agony—and a second bullet shattered crockery over the fireplace.

"Faye!" yelled Cath. "Get Rynne out of here *now!*"

Faye was instantly on her feet, swinging Rynne from her lap as they headed for the front door.

Pasco frozen and wide-eyed by the suddenness and the shrieking, broke from his stupor and lunged at Drew—just as Cath seized his hair from behind and yanked his head back.

Crip headed straight for Faye, bellowing—arms outstretched.

"Mum!" called Rynne, dragging back on Faye's hand. Faye pulled her around, swept an ornament from the table as Crip came around the sofa and smashed it hard across the bridge of his nose before those meaty hands could fasten on her. Crip made a glottal sound and went down on his knees, blood spurting between the fingers clasped to his face.

"Mum!"

"Come *on*, Rynne!" Faye dragged her, now scooping the girl up as she ran for the door. Behind her, Pasco twisted and punched Cath hard on the side of her head, but she clung to his hair as he twisted—and they both fell awkwardly to the carpet, legs thrashing as Cath hung on. Tully, still yelling hoarsely, snapped his head back—and butted Drew on the chin. Drew lost his grip, and Tully yanked his gun hand free. Crip was on his feet again; face bloody, shaking his head.

Please God, thought Faye desperately. *Please God that bastard didn't lock the door when he came back.*

Cath saw Tully's hand raising the gun as Pasco lashed at her. She saw Drew groping ineffectually to grab for that gun hand as Tully punched him hard in the face with the other fist—saw the gun aim straight at Faye's fleeing back.

"Noooooo!"

Pasco punched her hard under the ribs, knocking the breath from her body, just as Faye wrenched the door open and let in the storm. The candles were instantly extinguished; the remaining orange lamplight—protected in its glass bowl—making shadows rear and lunge in the room.

A thunderclap filled the living room—a flash of lightning.

But it was not the storm.

The bullet entered under Faye's right shoulder, slamming her against the door lintel. Cath saw blood and fabric explode from her silhouetted body. She never let go of Rynne as she rebounded from the doorframe, and then dragged her out into the savage night.

Cath had no breath to scream, could give no voice to

the horror inside. Feebly, she clawed at Pasco's leg. Pasco kicked her hand out of the way, took her by the hair and punched—turning to yank a dazed Drew from the sofa and hurling him to the ground next to her.

"Crip!" Tully screamed, his voice fueled by agony and rage. "Pasco! Get after them! Bring them back!"

Crip was out of the door first, hand to his broken nose—straining to see where they had gone. But there was only darkness, and the sounds of their flight were masked by the sounds of the storm.

"Get after them!" screamed Tully. *"Bring them back!"*

Crip vanished into the darkness as Pasco blundered to the doorway, wind tearing at his body.

Tully pulled himself up on the sofa, yelling in pain into the storm wind that filled the living room, now raising the gun again and pointing it at Drew, as he began to rise, hair flying in the wind. Cath couldn't move, couldn't see straight. She groped dazedly, wanted to beg him not to do it.

"You—are—just—so—fucking—*DEAD!*" Tully shouted each word with hate and pain.

Cath tried to scream, but nothing would come.

Drew tried to twist aside but, still dazed, fell to his knees in a half turn as—

Tully pulled the trigger.

Thunder and lightning exploded in the room again.

Drew was smashed backwards onto the floor. He lay still.

Cath curled tight into a fetal ball, hugging her grief, her soul screaming silently.

Tully turned the gun on her.

"Don't!" called Pasco from the doorway. "Not yet. Let me have her first."

FORTY

"We can't leave Mum behind," Rynne sobbed as they staggered in the darkness, the wind snatching and tugging at them.

Faye felt strange. Someone had hit her hard in the back, and she couldn't find proper breath somehow. But she knew that they had to keep going, and they had to get as far away from the house as possible.

"Get help . . ." she gasped, dragging Rynne on through the night. "We're not—leaving her behind. We're going to . . ."

"Why are those men so cruel? Why are they so horrible to us?"

Cath shook her head, urging Rynne on and knowing that they would be coming after them. But now her grip on Rynne's hand was failing. She could feel the strength somehow leaking out of her body, and there was a roaring in her ears that she knew had nothing to do with the storm.

She saw the vague outline of a fence up ahead, and knew that the main roadway lay up ahead. If they reached that road, they just had to follow it all the way into the village. But she had to rest, just for a moment, just so she could get her breath back. She coughed, held her hand to her mouth. When it filled with liquid, she knew then that something was very terribly wrong.

"He was hurting Mum, Faye! That man was hurting her. . . ."

From behind them came the sound of a car engine being turned on, and in the next moment twin headlights stabbed through the dark to their left.

"Get down, darling!" Faye pushed Rynne ahead to the fence, the effort making her fall to her knees. Rynne staggered, turned and came back—now grabbing Faye's arm and pulling her on. There was pain in her back now, beneath her shoulder blade—and it was becoming much, much worse with every beat of her heart. Her mouth filled with blood again and when she spat, some of it spilled on her front.

"Faye! You're *bleeding*. . . . "

The headlights stabbed across the farmyard forecourt as the car screeched and jerked in circles, from side to side—trying to find them. Faye reached the fence and the long grass there, pulling Rynne down beside her. The headlights skimmed the gravel not six feet from where they were, now lancing out across the outbuildings and the barn and the valley side as the car circled and turned again. Something was happening to Faye's eyes as she looked at the headlights. Was the wind blurring her vision?

"Rynne, darling."

"We can't leave them there! We can't!"

"I want you to follow that road. Can you see?" When Faye pointed behind them, she could barely lift her hand. "You keep on going until you find a house with

lights. Then you—tell them what's happened and. . . ."
Faye's hand fell to her side.

"I'm frightened, Faye."

"I'll try and lead them away. I'll go that way—in the opposite direction from you and . . ."

"You're not going anywhere," Crip said from the darkness.

They heard his boots crunching on the gravel before they saw him.

"Run, Rynne! Run!"

Crip's bulky silhouette lunged out of the darkness, seizing Rynne's wrist as she rose. Faye struggled to rise, but could not; slumping back against the fence and with the roaring that was not the storm rising to fill her ears and her eyes as if she were sliding underwater. She watched Rynne struggling and kicking in Crip's grasp. He was holding her away from him in one hand with ease, her legs kicking and free hand raking and clawing at where he held her. Crip grinned as he watched. Turning away, so that Rynne swung with him, he held up his other arm—waved and yelled.

"Over here, Pasco! I got 'em over here!"

His voice would not carry in the storm.

Still waving, he looked back to where Faye lay.

"You hurt my face."

"I'm sorry."

"Too late for sorry."

Still waving, Crip was suddenly outlined when the headlights from the still-circling car fell on him. When he lowered Rynne to the ground, she sprang back; fastening her teeth on the hand that held her. Crip yelled, but kept his grip—slapping her hard across the head and making her hair fly. Faye tried to rise, but fell back against the fence.

"No biting!" Crip snapped.

Faye thought she heard a car door slam above the roaring, and knew that Pasco was coming and oh God—what was she going to do?

"Tell you something else," said Crip, walking slowly back to where she lay.

"What?" Faye heard her voice, slow and dragging—but did not recognize it.

"You're dying, you are."

"Young man. If you hurt that little girl, you'll go to hell."

"Not gonna hurt her," Crip said, pushing his head down toward her; jaw jutting like a schoolyard bully. "Gonna let Pasco do the hurting. He likes girls."

Beyond him, Faye was vaguely aware of another silhouette approaching—backlit by the headlights.

Oh God, she thought. *Let this be a dream.*

The roaring in her ears enveloped Faye, seemed to fill everything in and around her; seemed to be shaking the very fence that she was leaning back against. She saw the expression on Crip's face change. The intimidating expression began to dissolve; Crip's outthrust jaw sagging as his mouth opened. He was so close Faye could see there was fear in his eyes, sparking in the car headlights. Why was he suddenly so afraid of her? He let go of Rynne, and she rushed back to cling to Faye, wrapping her arms around her—but Faye could not feel her at all, could only mouth again: *If you hurt that little girl, you'll go to hell.* And now she could see that Crip was not looking at her, was not afraid of her at all. He was looking at something above and behind her; at something that filled him with terror, as he took one step back—and the rumbling roaring sound that shook the fence seemed to burst like a clap of thunder.

"Run," Faye said directly into Rynne's ear. "You must run, my darling."

"No biting. . . ." Crip said, in a little-boy voice filled with awe and terror.

And the massive black shape behind Faye and Rynne cleared the fence in one single, sleek-black bound—the storm in its throat and hell's fury in its glittering opal eyes.

FORTY-ONE

Pasco's vision was a wonderful kaleidoscope of night color. He was still in control and enjoying it. Even the struggle with the bitch hadn't spoiled his mood. In fact, things had turned out well, after all, and he was enjoying himself. He could see that Crip had hold of the girl, and by the way that he was bending forward—he must be talking to the woman, lying somewhere in that long grass close to the fence. But that was on the edge of the headlight beam, and he couldn't see her at all. Pasco had seen that bullet hit and if the old cow was still alive, it wouldn't be for long. Now, he felt really good. Tully had changed his mind, and Pasco was looking forward to what he was going to do when he got the old bitch and the little bastard back to the farmhouse. He hoped that the woman would live long enough to enjoy a floorshow.

He had been wondering about Tully. He'd never held back like this before, had always been content to let him do what he wanted—and the whole business tonight had been pissing him off big time. It had to be the pain. That must be it. Hell, that was one fucked-up leg all right. The Nothing lady had made her play, and now she was going to suffer for it.

"That Nothing lady wasn't no nurse. Hell, Tully—she was just pulling your leg!"

Pasco laughed out loud as he walked. Trust Tully to know that he'd been sneaking some of the suitcase heaven down. Now he would have to talk him into taking some himself. He'd need it for that leg—something to take the pain away.

Pasco saw Crip let go of the girl—saw her jump away from him into the long grass, could barely see her now on the edge of the beam. Was there movement there now in the darkness? The old lady? Crip was straightening up and standing back. Now another step back—

Something was wrong.

Crip was scared.

He was scared in a way that Pasco had never seen before. Alarmed, straining to see what he had focused his attention on in the darkness beyond the headlight beams, Pasco halted and was about to ask what the hell was the matter with him when—

Something gleaming black and roaring and huge flew over the fence, taking Crip in a powerful and enfolding embrace. Crip screamed, the high-keening scream of a terrified child. Pasco flinched back as the impact of that leaping night-black shape flung Crip back across the headlight beams to the darkness on the other side. Everything was too fast; the night colors were confusing to his eyes—but Pasco's good mood turned instantly to something else when he thought he saw a devil's face and teeth chomping at Crip's head. Now he could only see Crip's legs thrashing on the ground in the light while something that was hidden in the darkness hissed and screeched and roared as it ripped and slashed at Crip's upper torso. Crip's high-pitched screams reached a new height of terror and agony, and then—as something *crunched* in the darkness—Pasco heard those screams become a fading liquid gurgle.

Now there was only the sound of something rumbling in contentment, and the sounds of feeding.

Crip's legs slithered out of the headlights and into the darkness.

Pasco backed off, turned and ran back toward the farmhouse.

The girl was somehow ahead of him, silhouetted as she ran—and calling for her mother.

Pasco was soon behind her, now seizing her arm and dragging her as he hurtled back. He was filled with terror and could feel the presence of something awful on his back. And as he ran, he could not get the drug-fueled thought out of his mind.

Christ, the old woman turned into something—she TURNED INTO SOMETHING!"

FORTY-TWO

The She Cat had continued to circle the place of stones, looking for another way in—but always returned to the same place. The hole in the wall, high up—the place where the male and female Two-Legs and the screeching, attacking tree had come. It paused on every circling at the storm doors, to smell and to listen. But the wind was too strong for any trace scent now, and there was no sound from its mate and cub. Only once had it heard movement, but that was the sound of the hated and imprisoning Two-Legs—serving only to further its rage. When they had left, it had waited for some call, some sign. But there was nothing, and so the She Cat had continued to circle the house, returning to that same place—the high opening—time and again. It remained open, unlike the entrance at the front of the stone lair that the Two-Legs continually opened and closed, but always before it could make a confident killing run. There was no other vantage point near to that high opening that the Big Cat could use, no tree or ledge that it could use as a rebound to reach it. Many times it had crouched low, opal eyes fixed on the opening above; ready to make a run and leap at the wall, imagining its claws raking and finding purchase somewhere on that blank wall, tasting how it would reach that ledge and gain entry to the stone lair. But the wind constantly threatened to affect its balance even as it crouched, hissing and hugging the ground, making it uncertain.

And then when it was prowling the external boundary fence, listening to the sounds of terrified livestock, the entrance at the front had opened again. It had tensed, paused—ready to make its run again. But now there were figures running directly toward it. Two female Two-Legs, running not away from it—but at it. It crouched low behind the fence, feeling confusion and fear at this erratic behavior as they came. But it would not flee, because it had been thwarted and frustrated for too long. Now another Two-Legs—male—was running after them. One of the Round-Leg Beasts was suddenly alive again, roaring and running with its sun-eyes blazing through the night, searching for it. Could it be that the whole pride of Two-Legs had emerged to hunt it down? The female Two-Legs reached the place where it hid, and now the high wind brought the scent of terror from them—and the smell of blood! But still they would not even react to its presence, although they must surely see where it lay. The male Two-Legs joined them, with its brief wind-snatched smell of anger and hostility and blood. The Round-Leg Beast was now still and waiting, eyes staring as the light that was brighter than the sun fell on them. Another Two-Legs was coming.

Jabbering. The hateful sounds that came out of the Two-Legs' mouths.

Fear.

Anger.

And blood—the sweet and arousing smell and taste of the kill.

Still the Two-Legs ignored her as they jabbered.

None of the behavior made any sense to the She Cat. These were unnatural creatures with unknowable desires and hungers. The jabbering, the unnatural behavior, the frustrations, the proximity of her imprisoned mate and cub, the scent of fear and blood—all suddenly coming together now in rage and the need to act.

The She Cat made its move, uncoiling with incredible strength in a killing leap. It saw the animal expression of terror on the male Two-Legs' face, a sure sign of success. That look of terror and the smell of new blood, all overcoming the possibility that the approaching Two-Legs was even now drawing close with the possibility of thunder in its forepaw.

All that mattered was the successful kill.

FORTY-THREE

Pasco threw Rynne ahead of him through the front door, turned and slammed it against the night and the wind and the terror of what hid in it. When he blundered into the living room, the girl had already run to her mother, still recovering on the carpet and still trying to get her breath. Tully jerked up from the sofa, face beaded with sweat that glinted in the darkness as if he had just awoken.

"Where's Crip? Where's the woman?"

"Where's Faye?" Cath gasped into Rynne's ear.

"She's dead, Mummy." Rynne's body was wracked with sobs. "I think she's dead. . . ."

"Oh noooooo . . ."

"Fuh—fuh—fuh—"

"Oh God, oh God—not Faye . . ."

Rynne pulled away, fighting to control her sobbing, eyes glittering with tears and holding her mother's face in both hands, desperately trying to communicate with her.

"Fuh—Ferocitor, Mummy! There's a Ferocitor out there. . . ."

Pasco looked back at the door, walked in a circle in the middle of the room—and then stared back at the door again, shaking his head.

"That's not right, Tully. That's not *right,* man. . . ."

"What the hell is it? Where the hell is Crip?"

"He's *dead!* Crip is *dead,* man! He's all tore the fuck up and something is *eating* him out there. . . ."

Rynne crushed her mouth to Cath's ear, and hissed: "The Ferocitor got him, Mum! It *got* him!"

"Those fucking drugs! If you don't calm down, you're going to end up on the floor next to him." Tully waved at Drew's body, lying motionless at the foot of the sofa. Rynne saw him for the first time, and began to wail. Cath pulled her daughter's face to her breast, holding her tight as sobbing wracked both their bodies. "You shut that kid up!"

Pasco kept walking in circles, head in his hands as if trying to work out a desperate puzzle. There was too much night color in here, too much happening inside his head. Either something was bursting out of his head, or something was trying to burst in. It had to stop before his brain exploded.

"Pasco!"

"She changed, Tully. You shot her and she ran out there and when Crip got to her—*she changed.*"

"Changed into *what?*"

Pasco stopped, staring hard at Tully now, as if seeing him for the first time.

"The devil. She changed into the devil, and she just tore Crip to pieces."

Tully made a sound of disgust, pulled himself around

again—yelling at the agony in his leg—and aimed the gun at the two figures kneeling on the carpet.

"What are you doing?" Pasco asked in alarm.

"What the hell do you think? Probably what we should have done when we first got here."

Pasco quickly stood between them.

"No! Don't you see? It'll happen again."

"Pasco—I swear to God, you get out of the way or I'm going to put one in your drug-wrecked head."

"No, no, no! You don't get it. You shot her. Her outside. And she *turned*—into that thing. You shoot these two—her and the kid—and they're gonna turn. I swear, Tully. They'll turn, and they'll rip us up like Crip."

"What about him?" Tully lowered the gun in disgust, the effort of holding it off balance causing strain and burning agony in his leg. He gestured back to where Drew lay. "You see *him* turning into anything?"

"Don't you get it? He's a *man!* That cunt out there— she was a woman. *Female,* man! So are these. You put a bullet in them and they'll turn."

"Bloody *hell!* All right Pasco . . . I won't shoot them. I won't use a bullet in case they turn."

Pasco began to nod vigorously.

"So why don't we do it a *different* way?" Tully continued. "Why don't you kill them with a knife, or with your hands? Like Crip could do."

"Yeah . . ." Pasco said, the good sense of what Tully was saying registering immediately. "Yeah, that'll do it."

"So do it, then."

"God no." Cath had found her voice again, breath returned. "Please God no, not my daughter."

"But you made me a promise, Tully."

"What?"

"You said I could fuck her first."

"Just so long as they both end up dead."

"No!" Cath struggled to rise, Rynne still clinging to her. Pasco was laughing now, as if all his problems had been solved. He strode quickly across the room, still nodding vigorously—seized Cath by the hair and dragged her to the foot of the stairs. Rynne detached from her mother and flew at him. He backhanded her, and Rynne somersaulted backwards to the carpet. Cath gouged and kicked out, tried to get her heel between his legs. Pasco punched her hard, dazing her again—and began dragging her roughly up the stairs step by step, as if he were hauling a heavy sack.

Rynne struggled to her feet and came back at him.

Tully watched her, thought about the gun—but decided to leave it all to Pasco as fresh waves of burning hell washed through his mutilated leg.

Pasco swatted Rynne back down the stairs, hauling Cath onward and upward.

"Let's do bedroom things in the bedroom, sweetheart."

He laughed as Rynne came back up the stairs again after them.

FORTY-FOUR

The She Cat finished taking what it needed, dragged the remains behind the fence and into a gully. It would not gorge tonight. For if it gorged, it would instinctively want to sleep, and the call of its mate and cub was in its blood and too strong to be ignored. It returned to the other side of the fence and the high grass whipping in the wind, watched to see if there was any movement from the female Two-Legs slumped there. When there was none, it stood boldly astride the body, smelled the cooling blood and licked the face with its coarse tongue. It considered dragging this dead one into the gully to join the remains of the other, then looked back through the darkness to the place of stones. The Round-Leg Beast was silent, its eyes still piercing the darkness. But there was no Two-Legs near or inside, and the She Cat knew this meant the Beast was dead again, and its sun-glare vision was sightless.

It bounded away from the dead female Two-Legs toward the stone lair, paused briefly by the Beast so that it could urinate once more on its side, then moved swiftly on through the night. The Big Cat circled the stone lair again, then paused at the storm doors. It called, but there was no answer. Angrily, it circled again—and came to rest at the foot of the high wall and the high opening. It was still open.

The She Cat backed off, wind ruffling its black fur.

It looked up again. There was movement. Curtains billowed out in the wind. But there was no living threat there. The Big Cat judged the distance again. Still not enough. It knew instinctively what a fall from the height of that opening ledge would do to it.

It backed off even more, looked back once to where the dead Two-Legs lay in the darkness and coughed out its disgust and anger. Two-Legs' meat was not good meat.

Then it centered, hunkered down with muscles rippling on its shoulders and back, its ears flat back on its head—and charged at the wall.

FORTY-FIVE

Pasco was enjoying every moment now that Tully had found a way to make sense of things. The night colors in his head had changed again, would change even more for the better once he got this bitch into the bedroom and he could combine the loving and the hurting. Some part of him felt that he should be irritated by the whining little bastard who kept trying to make him let go of her mother—but hell, this was good fun; swatting her away with his free hand while he dragged the bitch by the hair with the other.

They reached the top of the stairs, and Pasco began to sing as he dragged her to the bedroom door. It was a song he had just made up from the waves of night color inside him. No tune, no lyrics. But deeply fulfilling. The little bastard was clinging to his arm now, biting and trying to pull him down. But this was somehow part of the song too, as was the moment when he swung out his arm and smashed her against the wall. The way that she fell away from his arm was beautiful—like she was an essential part of the song that was also not a song.

The Nothing No-Nurse lady was struggling again, coming out of her daze as Pasco dragged her to the bedroom door. She'd told a lie when she said she knew something about medicine—and that was a bad thing, deserving of punishment.

"Going to give you a taste of my medicine," Pasco grinned as he opened the bedroom door.

And then screamed—when he saw the devil at the window.

The She Cat scrabbled at the windowsill; front claws finding purchase in splintering wood, hind claws raking the outside wall as it hauled itself into the room. Its great black head snapped up at the sound of Pasco's scream—jaws widening, eyes gleaming in the darkness as it hissed its rage right back at him.

Pasco let go of Cath, seized the door handle with both hands and slammed it shut—just as the Big Cat slid completely from the window frame and into the room. No sooner had he done so than the door panel crashed under an impact from the other side. Pasco shrieked, leaping back; now standing frozen at the sounds of hell emanating from the other side—a roaring and spitting animal sound of wild hatred. The door shuddered and crashed again as the thing on the other side launched an attack on it. Pasco flew forward, slamming both hands against the door as if he could keep the thing inside the room.

"Tully! It's the devil! Help me, Tully! The devil's getting in!"

Cath grabbed Rynne's hand. Together they staggered and stumbled back to the stairs as Pasco continued to scream at the sounds of ferocity from the other side of the door.

"Tully! *It's trying to get into my HEAD!*"

Cath struggled to keep a focus in this blur where shock and terror had fractured reality irrevocably.

The Big Cat is dead in the cellar, not alive in the bedroom, not trying to break in, and Faye is dead (oh God) and Drew is dead (oh God) and every time we try to escape from this hell we're brought back to hell and this must be it, this must be the Circles of Hell, we're in the Circles of Hell and . . .

Cath shook herself violently, Rynne clinging tight, and looked down to see—

On the sofa below, Tully was fumbling in his sodden pockets for something, twisting his head and yelling: "Pasco! What the *hell* are you *doing?*" If they kept close to the wall, might he not see them until they'd reached the bottom of the stairs? Cath started down, both arms around Rynne, could now see what it was that Tully was pulling out of his pockets. They were bullets, and he was struggling to reload the gun.

Pasco was screaming horribly, as if competing with the frenzied animal sounds from behind the door, and now Cath could also see that Tully was reacting in fear because he too must be hearing those impossible Big Cat sounds and must know that there was more going on here than the confusion and drug-addled storm in Pasco's head. Tully tried to twist around on the sofa again as Cath and Rynne continued their slow descent.

Cath looked to the front door.

If they could reach the bottom of the stairs without Tully seeing them, might they make it across the room?

Thunder crashed overhead, shaking the walls, and Cath saw again in her mind's eye the thunderclap and flash of lightning that had filled the living room earlier. Once more, she saw the bullet exploding Faye's shoulder as she ran for that door with Rynne. And this *must* surely be the Circles of Hell, because now it was all going to happen again. This time, she would be running with Rynne—and this time *she* would be the one to be shot, and then Rynne and then—

Stop it!

They had reached the bottom of the stairs.

Pasco was no longer screaming.

But the ferocious assault on the door continued, as if the storm had come alive and wanted to devour them all.

Tully was turning the other way now, craning his head away from them and looking to the top of the stairs where they had once been.

"Pasco! Where are you?"

Cath kept her back flattened to the wall as she moved with Rynne, feeling the girl's trembling, and praying that Tully would keep his head turned away.

But this was hell, after all.

Tully twisted back—and saw them.

"No," Cath said. "You don't have to."

"Oh yes," replied Tully through gritted teeth. "I do."

Cath frantically looked toward the front door again—saw Faye reeling as the bullet slammed into her—then back to Tully.

He was raising the gun.

And Cath knew that when they ran, it would be in the dragging slow run of nightmare, giving Tully all the time he needed to sight on their backs before they reached that door. She could feel no strength in her limbs as she watched that gun barrel slowly come up.

Upstairs, the sounds of animal fury were unabated.

But now Cath could hear the sounds of splintering wood.

"Please don't shoot my little girl," she heard herself say hopelessly.

Tully grinned as the gun centered on them.

Cath pulled Rynne even closer, pushed her face close to her breast—and squeezed her eyes shut.

She flinched at the crash of noise.

But this was not the crash of a gunshot, and now there were cries of rage and pain. Cath opened her eyes again.

Drew was on the other side of the sofa, as he heaved it over with his shoulder. The sofa flipped, Tully sprawling beneath as it came down across his back.

"*Drew!* Please God, don't let this be hell! Don't let this be . . ."

Tully began to scream in agony beneath the sofa, the upper part of his body still free and with the gun still in his hand.

"*This way!*" Drew yelled, and Cath saw the bloody stain covering half his face; the carved and bleeding furrow across his scalp like a hair parting made by a butcher.

Face agonized, Tully was swinging the gun around and looking for them as suddenly, without conscious effort and with strength renewed, Cath ran with Rynne—not toward the front door and its clear sight line for Tully—but to where Drew was even now frantically beckoning as he pulled away from the sofa.

The cellar door in the kitchen.

"*Run!*" yelled Drew again.

Tully fired twice, one of the bullets ricocheting with a scream around the living room.

Stooping low, Cath shoved Rynne on ahead through

298

the cellar doorway, felt Drew's arm around her waist and fought the hysterical urge to weep uncontrollably as he in turn pushed her through the doorway. She looked back as Drew followed, slamming the door shut behind them—just in time to see Pasco stumbling down the stairs like a drunk.

Cath heard Tully yell: *"Get those bastards! Get them!"* Then Pasco: *"The Devil! The Devil's coming. . . ."*

"GET THEM!"

Cath groped for Rynne in the pitch darkness, grabbed her arm and started blind down the stairs.

"The storm doors!" Drew hissed, leaning his full weight against the door. "Get out through the storm doors! I'll hold this one—there's no damned lock on it!"

And then Drew cried out as the door crashed inwards and he sprawled down the stone stairs. Pasco stood silhouetted in the doorframe, swayed for a second and then started down after them.

"Go!" Drew yelled, and lunged up to seize Pasco around the legs. Pasco began yelling again, a torrent of obscenities and distorted biblical quotes, pummeling and clubbing Drew's back with both fists locked together. Drew clung tight under the onslaught. Cath dragged Rynne across the cellar, shoved her quickly under a workbench and then—rising again—seized the first thing she could lay her hands on from that workbench. As Pasco lost his balance and both men fell entangled and thrashing to the bottom of the stairs, Cath ran at them—the thing in her hand rattling as she swung it. When it connected with Pasco's back and he grunted in pain, she realized what she'd grabbed. It was a length of heavy-duty chain, spare links for the cage hoist. Pasco yelled, tried to pull back from Drew—who still hung on to him—as Cath yanked the chain back for a second swing. But Pasco stamped hard on Drew, breaking his grip, and backhanded Cath at the same time as the chain rattled around the forearm he threw up to protect his head. The blow knocked Cath to her knees. She raked in the darkness for him, wanting her fingernails to find his eyes— heard a grunt of pain from Drew as Pasco kicked out again—and felt the chain whip around her neck as Pasco seized it and used it against her. Sitting astride her and still jabbering like a maniac, Pasco tightened the chain with one fist and began tearing at her clothes with the other hand.

Rynne flew at him, remembering how her mother had grabbed his hair.

Bellowing, Pasco grabbed her with his free hand as she landed on his shoulders and tugged her hard, the impetus flinging the child away to collide with the bars of the cage at the foot of the stairs. Cath raked her fingernails down Pasco's face. He bellowed again and used both hands to tighten the chain around her throat. Stunned, Rynne sat up with her back to the bars of the cage; saw Drew struggling to rise, heard the sounds of her mother being strangled.

And felt something rough and moist on her hand.

Rynne looked down to where her hand was braced behind her on the floor next to the cage.

A cat was licking her hand through the bars.

A beautiful, black cat with a flash of white on its brow.

In that moment, Rynne saw the cat in the schoolyard—the one that had scratched Bianca because the grownups were being so mean about her mother. She had been wrong to call it a bad cat. It was a good cat. She saw the Ferocitor, leaping over the fence to kill one of the Bad Men for what they'd done to Faye. She saw Drew, the Big Cat man, who wanted to be friends. And when she looked back at the cage, she saw the bolt in its hasp, keeping the cage door closed. Rynne looked down at the cub again—just as the huge black head of another Ferocitor emerged from the darkness in the cage above it; pushing up to the bars, fixing her with its gleaming opal eyes and with what seemed, to Rynne, to be a plea.

Lights were sparking behind Cath's eyes.

Pasco's enraged face was only an inch above hers, spittle dripping as he continued to mouth obscenities while he twisted the chain tight. Her hands fell away from his lacerated face. He let go with one hand and began fumbling at his trouser zip.

Something screeched near the foot of the stairs.

Pasco looked up.

Rynne was standing now, stepping aside as the cage door swung wide open to judder on its hinge.

Pasco looked stupidly at the bars of the cage door, did not know what this was or what it meant.

"Are you frightened of the devil?" Rynne said, re-membering what had happened upstairs.

And Pasco screamed when the face behind the bed-room door emerged from the darkness of that cage, yellow fangs bared and opal eyes gleaming. That face reacted to the scream, as it had been secretly reacting throughout the night to the sounds of violence and fury and hate from the Two-Legs in this stone lair since its capture and awakening. All its pent-up fury and rage was released now—and the only thing it could see in the cellar was the screaming and fearful face of a hated Two-Legs. A face that smelled of fresh blood.

The Big Cat flew at Pasco, the impact snatching him from Cath's body and back across the cellar. Pasco shrieked as the cat furiously shook his body from side to side, jaws clamped on his shoulder but seeking his throat. Pasco kicked out with both legs and the jaws came away with cloth and flesh between the fangs. Blood sprayed the air, the smell and taste enraging the Big Cat to more ferocious assault. The jaws snapped back, closing on the hand that Pasco threw up to ward it off; first shearing away his fingers, the second savage bite severing his hand at the wrist. Still shrieking, he twisted around on his front to face Rynne—a terrified plea in his eyes—as the Big Cat came down on his back and buried its jaws in the back of his neck.

Cath was struggling to rise, discarding the chain, as Rynne ran to her and pulled her back to the foot of the stairs. They both crouched there fearfully as Pasco's scream was abruptly choked off.

The Big Cat's jaws had closed, shearing through the back of his neck until the fangs met in his windpipe. Pasco's arms and legs spasmed as blood sprayed around him. Gnawing, the Big Cat planted a foreclaw across his face from behind, worked its claws into the right side of his head from chin to ear—and then peeled Pasco's face off in one swift movement, discarding the bloody mask snagged in its claws before returning to work on his body from behind.

"Oh *God* . . ." moaned Cath.

Pasco's body ceased to shudder when the dull *snap* of his broken neck resonated in the cellar. The Big Cat finished with Pasco, gave one look of disdain at Drew, where he still struggled to rise, and padded back across the cellar toward Cath, licking its lips. Rynne pulled Cath back with her, shrinking back farther to the foot of the stairs.

"Please . . . not hell . . ." Rynne heard her mother's

whispered plea as the Big Cat came. "Please . . . not hell . . ."

Inches from them, opal eyes fixing them with a hypnotic stare, the smell of the creature's musk suddenly overpowering when there seemed to have been no smell at all before—the Big Cat sniffed first Cath, then Rynne. It grumbled deep down in its chest cavity. It was a sound of immense inner power that seemed to be an echo of the thunder grumbling in the skies. And then the Big Cat's head turned. Smoothly that head slid into the darkness of the cage, massive neck and shoulder muscles working beneath sleek black fur. It grunted—grunted again—and there was a low mewling sound in answer. When it re-emerged from the cage, the cub was hanging gently between its jaws.

Cath gasped.

It looked at Cath and Rynne again.

And then leaped effortlessly over them onto the stone stairs above.

It ascended.

Cath and Rynne scrambled across the cellar floor to Drew, trying to avoid the sight of Pasco's mangled body, and helped him to rise. When Cath looked back, the Big Cat was paused at the top of the stairs.

"The cub . . . ?" The words were out of her mouth before she knew she was going to utter them.

"I don't know," Drew said. "Come on, quick!"

Kill him, Cath projected at the incredible sight at the top of the stairs, and felt no compassion for the man who had killed her best friend, had meant to kill her lover and who would have killed her daughter. She looked back at Pasco as Drew struggled with the bolts on the double doors. *Kill him!*

FORTY-SIX

"Pasco . . ."

Tully clawed at the carpet before him with one hand, trying to haul himself out from under the sofa and refusing to relinquish the gun in his other hand. The sounds of ripping at the bedroom door upstairs continued, and he had heard the sounds from the cellar—the crashing, the struggling and then the terrible screaming. He had shouted out with savage encouragement, hoping that those sounds were evidence of what Pasco did best. But that screaming had sounded somehow like Pasco's voice, and now—apart from the raging of the storm and the splintering upstairs—he could not be sure that there were any more sounds coming from down below.

"Pasco!"

Tully dragged himself again. The fire in his leg had moved up to consume his entire body. It was as if his shattered leg had ceased to exist, and the agony there had traveled in his bloodstream to the rest of him. It was in his head, behind his eyes and God how he hoped that Pasco had given that bitch what she deserved for what she had done to him.

The sounds of that splintering onslaught to the bedroom door upstairs were now somehow different. The howling and the roaring that made no sense but had so terrified Pasco, and now terrified Tully in turn, were gone. Now there was only the sound of the onslaught on the door, but Tully could hear a new cracking and tearing—as if whatever was trying to break through had finally torn out panels and splintering wood was falling to the floor.

"Who's up there?" Tully yelled. "You stay the fuck away from me. I've got a gun!"

Tully squirmed and rolled, screaming again when the ridge of the upturned sofa jolted the thigh of his shattered leg. Now he was on his back and able to use his elbows. Bracing one of them down hard, he sat up and used the heel of his gun hand to raise the edge of the sofa. Yelling again, he dragged his ruined leg out from underneath. Tully flopped back, gasping for breath, soaked in sweat and with that hideous pain raging in him. Then he repeated the move, this time pulling out his good leg. When he flopped back and twisted, head on the carpet, he saw that there was something standing in the kitchen, in the doorway leading down to the cellar.

"Pasco?"

But there was something about the shape and size of this figure that was wrong. This wasn't Pasco, and it wasn't one of the others. This was the wrong shape, too black, too *wrong*.

Tully twisted again, raising himself once more on his elbows—and stared at what was observing him from that doorway.

When the splintering sound stopped—and something *whacked* to the carpeted floor upstairs, the impossible black thing in the doorway turned its head from him and looked to the stairs. Tully saw that the thing hanging from its mouth, which surely must be dead but was somehow alive, was staring at him with the same hellish green eyes. He moaned then, and knew that Pasco had been right all along.

This was the devil.

The thing made a sound then—a loud grunting, muffled by the smaller hellish version in its mouth. From somewhere upstairs, there was an answering sound like an inhuman cough. Something padded on the carpet up there, heading for the stairs. Tully heard the thing in the kitchen make another noise, and he snapped his head back.

It was not there.

This wasn't possible.

It could not have moved in the second it had taken him to look up to the stairs and back again—and there was nowhere for it to hide.

There was another cough from above.

Frantically, Tully snatched another glance—but saw nothing.

When he looked back again, the devil was where it had been before. In the same position, unmoved.

Now you see it, said a crazed sing-song voice in Tully's head. *Now you don't.*

The thing in the doorway turned its opal gaze back to Tully, and although it was impossible—he could feel the savagely expectant and awful *smile* in those eyes.

"*Noooooo!*"

Tully swung the gun up and fired.

The bullet caught the Big Cat in the left eye, exploding in a spray from behind. The cub fell from its jaws and was gone, as the male cat reared up on its hind legs—impossibly huge and slashing at the air with its forelegs. It fell back, writhing and clawing, collided with the kitchen table and scattered everything from it on the floor. The Big Cat leapt again, straight up into the air and landed on the kitchen drainer, scattering crockery. It raked wildly at the window blinds, shaking its head in agony. The blinds disintegrated in its claws, tearing away from the window so that the storm blasted in through the shattered panes. The animal spun away, twisting and contorting in the air, and landing not two feet from where Tully lay, slashing at the air.

Tully shot it in its flank, the impact punching it away from him. It skidded and sprawled back into the kitchen, made a sound like nothing Tully had heard before and tried to rise. Leaning on one elbow again and yelling at the top of his lungs—Tully shot it in the underbelly. The Big Cat rolled on its back, legs quivering.

Something roared with insane rage at the top of the stairs.

Tully twisted back, screaming—as the Devil Cat seemed to rematerialize on those stairs. It launched itself through the air, directly at him.

Tully fired again, the shot going wild, exploding a framed picture on the wall. The devil hit the overturned sofa, rebounded to the wall as if it could somehow fly—huge and black and deadly—as Tully twisted again. It landed in the kitchen, scattering chairs. Now Tully could see that there were *two* of these things, not one. The second was standing astride the still form of the first; now nuzzling the head of the dead one, which flopped lifelessly from side to side. Tully struggled to get a sight line on this second hellish creature, and froze—when it raised its own head high and gave vent to an inhuman sound that shuddered the broken crockery and kitchen shelves. It was a sound of rage and fury, but above all—anguish. The power of that sound terrified and immobilized Tully.

"Go away," he heard himself whisper. *"Go away!"*

The Big Cat twisted its head from its fallen mate to look back at Tully.

"GO AWAY!"

In answer, it seemed, to Tully's shout—it was gone.

Tully frantically backed off on his elbows, breath sobbing in his throat.

"You're still there!" Tully's voice was a high-pitched whine. "I can't see you—but I know you're *still there!"*

Tully fired at the place where the second devil had been.

And suddenly, at the sound of that shattering detonation—the devil was in midair, flying at him—monstrous and huge and blacker than the blackest night.

Tully fired again.

The Big Cat passed over him, landed on the stairs—twisted again and leapt once more to the overturned sofa. Screaming, Tully dragged himself back and fired again—the shot shattering the storm lantern on the table next to it. The lantern exploded in orange flame, liquid fire splashing against the wall, over the sofa—and onto the Big Cat's back. Gigantic fire-shadows filled the room as the creature bellowed in pain and fury. It leapt for the kitchen again as Tully fired again and missed, the black fur of its shoulders alight and making a blazing trail of fire and smoke as the creature flew through the air, landed next to its dead mate and then—in one powerful rebound—dived straight at the broken kitchen window. The frame and the remaining glass shattered on impact, exploding out into the storm as the Big Cat vanished through the window— instantly absorbed by the night.

FORTY-SEVEN

The bolts on the storm doors would not loosen as Drew frantically yanked at them. They had opened and closed easily before, but now it was as if something had been clawing at the wood from the other side and had actually gouged out chunks and bent the metal of the hasps on the inside.

"God *damn* it!"

From upstairs came the sounds of hell.

Gunshots, roaring—and Tully screaming.

Drew staggered away from the storm doors to a workbench, searching for something to prize the doors open; now flinging open drawers in his desperate search.

Upstairs, something bellowed with such a terribly inhuman cry of anguish that Rynne cried out loud. Cath froze, Drew paused—and then remembered the hammer in one of the drawers. He wrenched the drawer open, found it and lunged back. Heedless of what the sound might attract from above, he pounded two-handed at the fastenings.

More crashing and growling reached them from the living room.

More gunshots.

The flare of orange flame from the doorway above.

"What in God's name is *happening?*" gasped Cath—and Rynne cried out again when there was an explosion of glass from the kitchen.

"Die!" yelled Cath up the stairs to Tully. "Just *die!*"

Senses swimming from the multiple beatings and the wound in his head, Drew gave the fastening another two-handed blow with the hammer; putting what little strength he had behind it. The fastening shattered. In the next moment, he and Cath flung open the doors to admit the storm.

This time, the icy blast of air felt good.

They clambered out into the night, staggering in the wind blast.

"*Pasco!*" Tully's voice drifted to them from behind.

Ahead of them was Faye's car—still facing away from the farmhouse with its headlights stabbing out into the storm. Cath knew that somewhere out there lying in the darkness was Faye's body, and a terrible sense of desolation threatened to engulf her. But was this their chance to escape?

"The car!" she shouted to Drew, already moving.

"No good," replied Drew. "Tully's got all the car keys. This one, yours—and the Land Rover."

Drew looked around in the wild and raging night, then grabbed them both—pulling them with him. "This way!" He shoved them ahead, up the rough track that led to the valley side where they had first encountered the Big Cat; snatching glances back to see if Tully might stagger out after them. With any luck, the shattered leg would keep him there, or slow him down if he came.

"Where?" gasped Cath.

"The valley side. Just as far away from here as possible. I know places we can hide and shelter."

The front door of the farmhouse crashed somewhere behind them.

"Mum!" yelled Rynne. "The bad man's coming."

"Run!" Cath yelled.

All three, holding each other, staggered away up the rough track and into the night.

FORTY-EIGHT

"Doing things to my head, doing things to my head, doing things . . ."

Tully kept the mantra going in his head in a desperate protective device as he finally managed to drag himself to his one good leg against the side of the overturned sofa. The flames on that sofa and on the table and wall behind it had been snuffed out by the rain and wind blasting in through the kitchen window. But the swirling smoke made him gag as he stuffed the gun in his jacket, grabbed a chair and used it as a clumsy walking stick to blunder across the littered carpet to the kitchen and the cellar door.

"Doing things to my head . . . to my head . . ."

His veins felt filled with liquid fire, the kneecap of his shattered leg as if it had been dipped in molten lead; but there was no feeling beneath that kneecap, as if there were nothing there at all. When his lower leg flopped and twisted as he moved, it was as if it didn't belong to him anymore. He used the chair like a walker, reaching the kitchen and the cellar door—and there was the black devil lying stiff and silent on the floor. It hadn't disappeared, like it had done earlier. There was no sign of the smaller version it had been carrying in its mouth. But that was okay, because now he understood what had been going on. Somehow, the drugs that had screwed Pasco's head had also gotten into his system. He didn't know how, but somehow Pasco had slipped the same stuff to him—maybe when he was trying to get the gun away so that he could get into the bitch's pants. Tully had been fading in and out of consciousness, so there was a chance that Pasco had been able to do *something*. There could be no other explanation for the thing lying on the carpet, the way it had appeared and disappeared, and then the other thing that had come at him. They were hallucinations that had turned both him and Pasco crazy. If there were any way he could get up those stairs, he'd find that the bedroom door hadn't been torn down—that it was still intact. Tully hung on to those thoughts. He could still see that thing on the floor because the crap was still in his system. He had to fight against it.

"Doing things to my head, that's all. Doing things . . ."

Something clattered down below in the cellar. It sounded like doors banging open. Wind gusted up the stairs to join the wind blasting through the kitchen window.

"Pasco!"

There was no answer, and he knew now that Pasco—like Crip—had fucked up badly and let the others get away. Tully grabbed the chair, looked down again at the devil thing—and knew that it just wasn't there.

"My head—doing things to my head—it isn't there—and I'll be okay soon."

Using the chair again, he turned from it and hopped back to the center of the room where the three suitcases waited. Angrily crashing the chair down, staggering on his one leg, Tully leaned down and gripped one of the suitcase handles. He looked up to the front door and willed himself to make it. Hefting the suitcase back up and resting it on the chair, he took deep breaths and felt the oxygen filling his lungs and seeming to fan the surging in his veins like a bellows to a furnace. He yelled at that fire-agony, willing that pain to help him as he jerked up the chair and again threw it forward like a walker in front of him. The chair slapped down hard, the suitcase wobbled and he quickly grabbed the handle to stop it falling off the chair, teetering on his leg. Something rolled around the chair leg. The flashlight. He'd need that. Stooping, crying out—he grabbed it up and stuffed it in his belt.

Sweat pouring from his face he repeated the maneuver with the chair and the suitcase.

He would make it. If he concentrated he would make it.

"Doing things to my head . . . my head . . ."

Whump!

Vic, you and the boat better still be there. Don't you let me down, you bastard!

Whump!

Pasco said you were all tore up, Crip. But are you tore up? Those things aren't there, and Pasco's head was fucked. Either Pasco offed you or you've run away. God help you if you've run away, Crip. The old woman is as good as offed, but if you've done a runner and the law gets you and you let your baby blabbermouth go, I'll . . .

Whump!

Pasco and Kapler Dietersen's hand. I told you not to do anything! I told you!

Whump!

All that stuff the farmer and the bitch know about—and the kid—

Whump!

They've got away. Pasco let them get away, and when they get to the police they're going to put everything together, and all of that will point to you, Tully.

Whump!

The blood all over that sofa! They'll trace the DNA!

Whump!

They've got your DNA dozens of times, Tully. But you're the luckiest bastard alive, because you've never been caught and they've never pinned your name to the label. How lucky is that?

Whump!

Yeah, but the farmer, the bitch and the kid know your name, Tully, for Christ's sake! The only way you're getting out of this one is to make sure they can't tell anyone.

Whump!

They're long gone. . . . They must be long gone. . . . Oh Christ . . .

Tully had reached the door. He hopped around the chair, his clothes soaked in sweat and looked quickly back into the farmhouse to where the two other suitcases stood side by side. One would have to do. He could never manage them. There was enough in this one. The plan had been to split with the other two, and although Crip wasn't a problem—he hadn't had a chance to work out how he was going to screw Pasco out of his share. One way or the other, Pasco was always going to have to be offed. But from the sounds in the cellar, it looked as if Tully had been saved the trouble. With luck, the blame for whatever had happened here could be laid on Pasco. After all, the two suitcases were there, weren't they? Anyone else involved would surely have taken them.

Tully flung open the door. The wind seemed to freeze the sweat-sodden clothes on his body. He shoved the chair ahead of him. It tipped and the suitcase fell to the gravel outside.

There was a walking stick next to the door, the kind a good old farmer might use when he was out there doing what fucking farmers did. Tully seized it, and limped to lean on the doorframe. He saw the other car that the old lady and kid must have arrived in, headlights still blazing; strained to see through the swirling in his eyeballs if anyone was in there. With luck, it would be the farmer and the females—trying to get away and realizing they didn't have the keys.

"Shit!"

The car was empty.

Tully staggered out into the storm, leg dangling in the wind—the foot turning at impossible angles. He looked right to left—and saw movement on the dirt track leading away from the farmhouse. He staggered, kneeling heavily on the suitcase with his good leg; now dragging the torch out of his belt and shining it up there.

"Yes, yes, *yes!*"

There they were, staggering against the wind; sticking together like a happy family and not scattering the way they should if they didn't want to get caught. Tully braced himself on the walking stick, lunged up and grabbed the suitcase—filled with a new energy born of utter desperation but logic skewed by the agony raging in his body. He fell before he reached the car, but would not allow the molten pain in his knee or the swirling chaos in his head to prevent him from what he had to do. He yanked the driver's door open, levered himself up with the walking stick and fell in sideways onto the seat. He jammed the walking stick in next to him and began to haul the suitcase in over his body, clumsily fumbling and shoving until it had wedged in the foot well of the passenger seat.

Breath sobbing, Tully pulled the door closed against the storm and fell forward against the steering wheel.

The horn blatted, loud and long—bringing him to his senses.

Tully sat back and let loose a string of curses when he saw that the car did not have automatic transmission.

Behind him, the happy family was getting away.

Tully found a set of blood-soaked keys, tried them in the ignition and threw them on the floor when they wouldn't work. The first key in the second set turned the engine over straight away. Head swimming, Tully seized the walking stick and jammed it onto the clutch pedal. The engine roared as he wrenched at the gear stick.

The gun felt heavy inside his jacket.

FORTY-NINE

The car horn blatted from below.

"Tully!" Drew snapped, staggering to his knees.

Cath grabbed him and hauled him up. The furrow in Drew's scalp had begun to bleed copiously, as if he had just this moment been wounded. She threw her arm around his shoulder and hauled.

"Look!"

Cath followed Rynne's pointing finger back down to the farmhouse.

Faye's car was turning clumsily in a circle, jerking and jouncing on its suspension as if the person driving it were drunk. Headlights swung in the storm, flashing over the outhouses and ruined fences.

"Leave us alone!" Cath yelled back at the car, with the same savage anger she had projected in the cellar. That anger had not been enough to kill him as she'd wished back there. Maybe it would be enough to just send him away now.

It was not.

The car came to a halt, facing up the dirt track—and fixing them in its headlights.

"Leave us ALONE!"

The car came on, trundling up after them, headlights drunkenly swooping from the ground to the sky as it shuddered in and out of the ruts in the dirt track.

"The barn," Drew gasped.

Cath looked wildly from side to side at the lack of any shelter or cover they could use, then up the track to the barn and its wrecked half-door. How could *that* help them? The only choice was for them to split up.

"Drew! Take Rynne—run off over there. I'll make Tully follow me. When he comes after me, you take Rynne and find somewhere to hide."

"Mum, no!" shouted Rynne, clinging to her arm.

Drew shook his head furiously, blood beading and flying from his chin in the wind. "No . . . no . . . the barn. The *barn!*"

There was a flat *slap* of sound, and something whistled in the air.

Cath looked back at the approaching car.

Tully was leaning drunkenly out of the window, trying to level the gun as the car jounced and rattled up the slope.

"The barn!" Drew yelled again.

They ran to the ramshackle building, its fractured planking shaking and banging in the furious wind.

FIFTY

They've got to die, said the suitcase.

"I know that, I know that."

Me and you. That's all that matters now.

"Yes, Mother."

Pasco and Crip were standing on either side of the track waving, as Tully kept the walking stick jammed on the clutch pedal and the car trundled on in first gear. The headlight beams were Tully's eyes and the happy family was scrambling on up ahead like rabbits. Leaning through the window, Tully snapped another shot off at them.

Take your time, the suitcase said. *Aim better. You know you can shoot better than that.*

"Yeah," said Tully. "Vic taught me good."

Thanks, Vic said from the backseat.

"Don't mention it," said Tully.

FIFTY-ONE

They staggered into the barn, wind shrieking through the gaps in the planking, straw flying around them. It was as if the building and everything in it had come alive—except the huge dead bulk of the combine harvester. The car headlights made shadows leap and rear as Cath looked frantically around for the reason Drew had insisted they run here.

Drew broke away, staggered to a pile of junk lying at the side of the combine harvester and grabbed something from it.

A hand scythe.

Stumbling back to the entrance, he raised it high as the headlights fell on him—and another gunshot tore a chunk out of the planking next to his head. Cath ran to him as he flung the scythe at the car, now less than thirty feet away and heading straight for the barn. Cath saw Tully's wild and white face as the scythe spun through the air. Drew had been aiming for the windshield, but the scythe missed—slicing the wing mirror off and into the night.

The car came straight at them.

Cath ducked back, seized the first thing she laid her hands on and hurled it with both hands. The rotted chunk of wood rattled across the hood and over the roof, but the car did not stop and came on, headlights blinding.

"Cath . . ." Drew flung up his hands, as if he could somehow physically stop the car, his silhouette gigantic in the headlights.

Cath scooped Rynne up in her arms and ran back into the barn as—

The car plowed straight into the barn entrance, shattering the remaining half door and bringing debris down on its roof from above. Cath heard the car engine roaring, wood shattering and cracking; felt the barn itself seem to shift and sway as they fell against the back wall. Cath twisted to look back, expecting to see the car bearing down on top of them as the engine roared and roared.

The car was jammed solidly in the barn entrance.

The passenger side was flat against the barn wall; planks that had fallen on its roof were also wedged tight down that side. On the driver's side, the shattered half door had also tangled and wedged the vehicle tight. Dust and straw flurried, and as Cath stared hard she could see Tully's outline, still in the driver's seat and now unsuccessfully trying to shove that door open against the shattered tangle.

There was no sign of Drew.

Oh Christ, was he *under* the car?

Cath struggled to keep a swell of nausea down, born from fear and shock. Frantically, she looked for another way out and could see none. Tully was shrieking in the car at his inability to open the driver's door, banging it over and over against the wood. He twisted out through the window and fired another shot wildly into the barn, punching a ragged hole in the roof. When he jerked back inside and faced front again, Cath pulled Rynne down low so that he could not see them. His face did not look human. Had he gone insane? The car engine began to rev furiously as Tully tried to drive on ahead into the barn; now throwing the gears into reverse and trying to back out. The car moved back only slightly, enough for more planking to fall down at each side, tangling the vehicle's bodywork even further. The rear wheels screeched as they spun, kicking up clouds of soil and straw.

A shadow darted past the front of the car as Tully had his head turned back. Something clanked and clattered as it passed.

Cath's heart leaped.

"Drew!"

Tully twisted back again. Had he heard her voice? Cath kept low and tried to see where the shadow had gone. Somewhere to the side of the harvester? The car engine kept revving, and Tully was screaming in insane rage again as Cath pulled Rynne along the back wall of the barn—toward the deeper shadow of the harvester and to where she thought she had seen Drew.

"*Drew!*" This time she shouted loud, hoping that Tully's mad raging would mask her voice and not given away their meager hiding place.

"Here!" hissed a voice from the darkness.

Cath and Rynne scrambled on hands and knees through the darkness, around the rear end of the harvester, toward the sound of the voice.

"*I know you're there!*" Tully yelled. Another wild shot

screamed from the car. *"Me and Vic are going to kill you fucking DEAD!"*

By the wheel of the harvester, a familiar dark shape was struggling with what seemed to be a petrol can. The furious revving and roaring of the car was making the bulk of the harvester shake. Cath and Rynne scrambled to him.

"What are you doing?" Cath could see that Drew had wrenched the top off the can, was busying himself in the shadows in the far side of the harvester. The pungent smell of petrol filled the air.

"Keep him busy, Cath!"

"Maybe we can kick a hole in this wall? Get out this way."

"Too solid, too thick. Look, keep him busy somehow. I don't know if this'll work. The bastard thing has been sitting here rotting and idle and the tank's probably full of crap but if I can get this cleared I might be able to—oh shit!"

"Drew what are you doing?"

Drew grabbed for the can, petrol slopping as he lunged back into the darkness.

"Keep him busy, Cath!"

"Stay with Drew!" She told her daughter.

Cath pushed Rynne down and scrambled back around the rear of the harvester just as the car engine died. Looking around the back of a massive rear wheel, she could see Tully writhing in his seat as he twisted the ignition, trying to restart the car. He began pounding the steering wheel, screaming again. Cath realized as she watched that something really had snapped in Tully's mind. The car engine caught again, and he slammed it into reverse. This time, the vehicle was shuddering backwards, planks cracking and splintering at each side as the rear wheels found some purchase. If he managed to get that car out of the barn, then he could get that driver's door open—and despite his shattered leg, Cath knew that he'd be coming in after them. The barn walls were shaking, in danger of collapse.

"Tully! You couldn't hit a barn door, you bastard."

When he snapped his head round to face front, Cath stepped out from behind the wheel. She flung the handful of earth and pebbles she had scooped from the floor—the only thing she could find. They exploded in harmless powder across the windshield, but Tully was enraged enough to lunge sideways through the window as Cath jumped back behind the harvester. She heard a *click*—and a curse. Could it be that Tully's gun was empty? She looked back again, saw Tully furiously fumbling at his jacket pockets—and somehow carrying on an angry conversation with an invisible passenger in the rear seat.

There was movement on the hidden side of the harvester, next to the barn wall. Cath glanced back and saw Drew climbing the side of the machine. A door was opening high up there—the door to the cab at the top of the vehicle. Drew's silhouette swung on the door and vanished into the cab. Cath looked away again, back to Tully—

He was waiting for her.

She yelled and snapped her head back as Tully fired his reloaded weapon. The bullet tore a thick shred from the rear tire.

The car began to shudder more furiously as Tully threw the gears into reverse yet again. Cath ducked low, looking from below and beneath to see that Tully was reversing again; now with more success as the vehicle bucked and screeched backwards through splintering wood. This time the car was going to make it out of the barn, and its roaring and buckling progress seemed to be shaking the harvester from side to side on its giant wheels. But now she realized that something more was happening here. Something else was happening to the harvester. It was making its own screeching and grinding sounds, joining in with the car as it squeezed out and away, side panels buckling. Now, it was coughing and roaring as it shook, and Cath backed off in alarm. Something barked and coughed beside Cath's face and she reeled back gagging as thick clouds of foul, choking dust blasted into her face and filled the barn.

"Mum!"

She staggered back to see Rynne beckoning to her between the far side of the harvester and the barn wall. Choking, Cath realized that the combine harvester had suddenly come alive; that the thick and roiling dust had spewed from its exhaust. She blundered through the smoke to her daughter, who pulled her to where Drew had climbed. The cabin door was still open and flapping as the harvester roared and smoke gushed in the barn. Cath pushed her on ahead, climbed with her as the gigantic bulk of the machine swayed and rattled. When Rynne reached the cab, Cath shoved her ahead and climbed up behind.

Drew was in the driving seat, furiously struggling with the controls. When he saw them clambering in, it looked as if he might yell that they should stay back—but when he saw the look in Cath's eye, he held his words—and then yanked the steering wheel hard over.

The harvester juddered and lurched.

Below and to the right, the car screeched and buckled.

Cath held tight to the seat with one hand, keeping Rynne steadied with the other. She knew what Drew intended—to squash the murderous bastard in his car. Drew tugged again, this time looking directly into her eyes. The harvester jerked again. Below, something splintered and cracked. Drew looked out of the side window from on high.

The car screeched slowly backwards out of the barn, planking and debris tumbling and splitting on all sides. The fender snagged on the grille at the front of the harvester and was torn off. Drew saw Tully furiously struggling with the wheel, tires screeching and burning rubber drifting up around its chassis. He spun the wheel hard the other way—and in the next moment Tully had got the damned thing out, the car slewing aside as it pulled away from the barn.

Grimly, Drew put his foot down.

The harvester shuddered and lurched forward, tearing out supports on the nearside wall. Cath and Rynne yelled together when timbers and joists hit the cabin roof, denting it down toward them before sliding off to the side with a ragged crash.

The car slewed to one side again, straightened— and began to reverse down the dirt track away from the barn. The chassis and suspension were wrecked, the car moving only as fast as gravity on this incline would allow.

The harvester roared out into the storm.

Behind it, the barn began a slow collapse in clouds of splintered wood, metal and straw—as Drew cranked the thresher, and the Beast turned to follow the battered car downhill.

FIFTY-TWO

Tully looked back to see that the barn had suddenly turned into a house made of metal, roaring and belching smoke and coming down the hill after him. There was a waterfall coming out of its front; a waterfall that tumbled, span and clattered hungrily.

You didn't kill them, said the suitcase.

"I'll kill them!" snapped Tully. "You'll see."

How you going to spend me unless you kill them?

"That's money talking," said Pasco, who had joined Vic in the back seat. *"Get it, Crip?"* Crip was sitting on the other side of Vic, and laughed in that familiar way.

"Good one," said Crip. *"Money talking."*

"Not money," said Vic. *"Drugs."*

"Will I grow a new leg, Vic?" Tully asked.

"Oh yes," replied Vic. *"But only if you kill them."*

Tully looked back.

Vic's eyesockets were empty, eaten by the fishes.

"What have you done to my brother?" Tully screamed.

But Pasco and Crip were gone.

Tully jerked around to look forward again.

The waterfall was almost upon him.

There were knives in there.

Screaming, he leaned out of the side window and fired directly into the threshing, clattering blades—the sound of the shot drowned by the slashing and squealing of metal as the blades stabbed and punctured the hood of the car. Now he realized at last that this wasn't a waterfall at all. This was the storm come alive with the jaws and the teeth of the devil cats from the nightmare in the farmhouse. But now there were hundreds of those teeth, chewing into and over the hood, rending the metal and devouring the engine. Those whirling, devouring fangs continued their relentless advance toward the windshield.

Tully shoved at the car door handle, but the door would not budge.

The frame was buckling even as he watched, wedging the door in its frame.

Tully began to haul himself through the window, firing into that clattering nightmare.

When the windshield imploded and the main frame of the car snapped, the impact jerked Tully back into his seat to face front.

Holding the gun out through the windshield aperture in front of him with both hands, face now blank, he kept pulling the trigger as the roaring, thrashing teeth and fangs chewed through the dashboard and steering wheel. When those flailing teeth took away his shattered leg below the knee he knew then that, just as the devil things in the farmhouse had been unreal, what was happening *now* was unreal. He felt no pain when that leg was taken, and that was nice.

The gun was empty.

Now Tully was on a roller coaster with his big brother, Vic. That was why everything was shaking and rattling—

Shake, rattle and roll, Vic used to sing.

Vic had promised him a new leg, and that was okay. It had been mean of Pasco and Crip to let the fishes take his eyes, but what the hell—he had his suitcase here and theirs were back at the farmhouse, if the devils would let them have them.

But then the gnashing, flailing teeth that weren't really *real* found the suitcase next to him. It blew apart as the not-real teeth tore it to shreds, and white powder exploded all around him.

"NO!" screamed Tully.

The white powder filled the air like a bizarre snowstorm, swirling and whipping away out into the night as if it had never existed. But Tully didn't want that white powder; he just wanted the money that it could bring. He grabbed for it wildly as it evaporated into the air, screaming.

"I just want the money! *I just want the money!*"

Then the teeth turned to jaws and knives—

They found his other leg and his groin.

And suddenly they were real.

Very, very real.

Cath willed Drew on, unable to look past the shattered windshield of the cab, just wanting to put an end to the nightmare—as the high, thin screaming voice came up from below; bringing with it all the horror and terror of what had happened so long ago on that New York street—with blood everywhere on that rain-washed sidewalk, and so much blood since.

Cath lunged forward, pounding her hands on the dash.

"You can't *have it!* Do you hear me? You can't have it—*so just go!*"

Cath clapped her hands over Rynne's ears when the screaming rose in insane agony above the sounds of the thresher and the storm. The harvester lurched again, the thresher rending and devouring, engine roaring.

"Just GO!"

When the engine stalled—the thresher now jammed with wrecked metal and upholstery—the screaming had stopped.

Drew slumped forward across the wheel, his head down.

When both he and Cath began to weep, Rynne put a hand on each head.

As the harvester rocked on its suspension in the storm wind, it felt like another caressing hand.

FIFTY-THREE

Drew and Cath walked back to the farmhouse as the sun rose above the valley. Rynne watched them from the open doorway.

Behind them, Faye had been covered with a sheet from the back of the Land Rover—and they had stood holding each other for a long time as Cath gave vent to her grief.

The storm had gone, and the farmhouse looked as if a bomb had hit it; with its shattered windows and cracked brickwork. Splintered fences, uprooted bushes and trees, and the remains of disintegrated outbuildings and henhouses littered the farm and dirt track. The feed shed had lost its tied-down roof completely, which had disappeared somewhere into the valley. Most of the livestock had survived, but there was not a single hen in sight. The wreckage of the kitchen blind flapped loose over a glittering pile of broken glass, as if it were beckoning to them.

They did not look back to where the combine harvester stood silently with its half-digested prey, scattered metal and engine parts all around it.

Rynne turned—as if hearing something—and ran back into the house.

"I wish I'd never found them," Drew said as they walked.

Cath knew what he meant.

"If I could, I'd take that dead one in there—take it out somewhere in the valley, and bury it. Never let anyone see it."

Cath pulled him close. "Get rid of the evidence?"

"In more ways than one."

"The police will have their hands full with this one."

"Now we're going to have people all over the place looking for them."

"Not if we can help it."

"I like the sound of that word—*we*."

Rynne was suddenly in the doorway, just as they were about to enter.

"Mum!"

"Oh my *God* . . . "

Cath and Drew froze.

"Look what I've found."

Rynne was holding a bundle in her hands. Something that she had wrapped in a rug taken from the kitchen floor. Something with sleek black fur and two flashes of white over its eyes.

"Oh my God," echoed Drew. "The cub."

"Be careful, darling." Cath reached out, remembering the slashed boot and jeans and what this small creature was capable of doing. She pulled her hand back again when it hissed a warning.

"It was hiding next to the dead one. I wrapped it up and it didn't even scratch me because it's a lucky cat."

"Give it to me, Rynne," Drew said gently. "Very carefully . . ."

Something behind them growled.

It was a rumbling, guttural sound of contained power that was only too familiar.

The cub hissed a reply as Cath and Drew turned.

The She Cat was standing not twenty feet from them.

Sleek and black and powerful. The fur on its shoulder had been burned. It opened its jaws to growl again, a steam of breath rising in the chill and bright morning air, the sun seeming to spark in those savage but wonderful opal eyes.

Rynne stepped forward between Cath and Drew—Cath quickly putting a restraining hand on her daughter's shoulder. The cub hissed at the movement, and the She Cat stepped forward with another rumbling growl, so deep and resonant it seemed to be coming from underground.

"Don't move," said Drew, and flinched when Rynne took another step forward.

Slowly, she bent down—placed the bundle on the ground and unwrapped the rug.

The cub pulled free and ran to its mother.

The She Cat held the Two-Legs in its gaze as the cub twisted and curled around its mother's forelegs.

There was *power* in the early morning air.

Real and vibrant power.

The She Cat bent its head, took the cub gently in its jaws and looked back at them again.

It made a sound then, deep in its throat—like a cough.

Then the Big Cat was gone—streaking up the dirt

track toward the valley side like a living shadow, jet black, beautiful and with incredible fluidity and grace.

It paused briefly before the wreck of the harvester and the car.

And then streaked away from it, heading for the long grass.

Soon it was gone.

"I'm not going to let anyone find you," Drew said, when it had disappeared.

"Neither am I," said Cath.

Woman, man and child walked back into the farmhouse.

THE WYRM
STEPHEN LAWS

Something hideous is about to happen to the small town of Shillingham. Why does a madman shoot at the workers tearing down the old gallows at the crossroads? Why are the children drawn to play in its shadow, as if by a silent command? What is the eerie, thickening fog that surrounds the village, cutting off the inhabitants from the outside world?

Beneath the ground, something stirs. As the workers continue working and the bulldozers roll on, a dark and unimaginable evil, imprisoned beneath the gallows for centuries, slowly awakes. It is alive. It is powerful and cunning. And it wants revenge.

STEPHEN LAWS

FEAR ME

Gideon loves women…to death. He seduces them, uses them horribly, then discards them, drained of their very lives. Until the day three women disobey him and dare to fight back, to seek revenge, leaving him in a pool of blood. Releasing them at last from his depravity.

The women don't know that Gideon can't be killed that easily. They don't know what he really is. He has returned to seek vengeance of his own, and their mere deaths will no longer be enough to satisfy him. He will make them pay dearly for crossing him. But first he will destroy everyone they love.

A
DROP
OF
SCARLET
JEMIAH JEFFERSON

Ariane Dempsey is a dedicated scientist specializing in blood diseases. None of her colleagues suspect that she is also a vampire. Lately, her research has taken a very personal turn—she is trying to find a drug that will help her lover, John, whose mind has been unstable since Ariane first made him a vampire.

But the drug she develops has unforeseen effects and word spreads instantly through the vampire community. Vampires from all over the globe descend upon the city. They will pay anything for the drug—or they will kill for it. Ariane will soon learn that, even to those of their own kind, nothing is more dangerous than a desperate vampire.

TIM WAGGONER

DARKNESS WAKES

In the small town of Ptolemy, darkness is a living thing. Its home is in the shadows of a bizarre club named Penumbra, where it is worshipped by followers who need the pleasure it gives them. They live for it. And they kill for it.

When Aaron was first introduced to Penumbra, he thought it was just a secret club where members could indulge their kinkier fantasies. As he learned the club's true purpose, he began to change in subtle, horrible ways. Now it's time for Aaron to prepare his first human sacrifice. It's too late for him to back out now, but murder is the least of Penumbra's sins. The true terror is still to come, when…

DARKNESS WAKES